LYONS LEVELED THE BIG REVOLVER

Tracking the figure partly concealed by the boxes, Lyons pulled the trigger and put two of his remaining shots into the moving target. The Magnum slugs powered through the flimsy timber, filling the air with dusty splinters, then cored through the guy's chest, toppling him in a flurry of arms and legs before his bloodied form hit the concrete.

A strained silence followed the shots. The Able Team leader flipped out the Python's cylinder and ejected the loads. He slipped a fresh speed-loader out of his pocket and inserted it in the cylinder. With the revolver fully loaded again, he crouch-walked away.

He had seen two shooters still alive, so there had to be one more. Lyons accepted there might even be more who hadn't shown themselves yet.

Hell of a day, he thought. And it isn't over yet.

DON PENDLETON'S

STONY

AMERICA'S ULTRA-COVERT INTELLIGENCE AGENCY

MAN®

PULSE POINT

A GOLD EAGLE BOOK FROM
W❂RLDWIDE®

TORONTO • NEW YORK • LONDON
AMSTERDAM • PARIS • SYDNEY • HAMBURG
STOCKHOLM • ATHENS • TOKYO • MILAN
MADRID • WARSAW • BUDAPEST • AUCKLAND

Recycling programs
for this product may
not exist in your area.

First edition February 2014

ISBN-13: 978-0-373-80443-6

PULSE POINT

Special thanks and acknowledgment to
Mike Linaker for his contribution to this work.

Printed in U.S.A.

PULSE POINT

PROLOGUE

Hanson was waiting in their usual meeting place, sitting at a table outside the coffee shop on Immanuelkirchstrasse. He was nursing a cup of coffee, and when he saw Trainer, he beckoned the waiter and ordered more hot drinks, then waited as his contact joined him.

"This must be important," Trainer said, facing Hanson across the table.

"Your decision when I've told you."

They sat in silence until the fresh coffee had been delivered. Whenever they met, they went through the same ritual, no one committing until he was ready.

"*So?*" Trainer said.

"Two days ago Emanuel Absalom left the university, went home and was then seen leaving his apartment carrying a travel bag. He went directly to the rail station and met Pierpont. They took a train for Paris," Hanson said. "I had people waiting at the other end."

"*And?*"

"Absalom and Pierpont disembarked at Gare du Nord. They were met by a couple of minders. They took over for Pierpont and escorted Absalom to a waiting car that took them into the city. We picked up Pierpont and questioned him. The guy insisted all he'd done was deliver Absalom as requested. We couldn't do anything, because Pierpont hadn't broken any laws, and we have no legal jurisdiction over him. Trouble is, he was right. All the man had done was act as a guide to a man legally free to move where he wants."

Hanson lapsed into an uneasy silence, and Trainer watched him for a moment.

"Now you're going to tell me that your men lost them?"

Hanson had the grace to avert his eyes. "Paris is a big city. The minders must have known they would be watched. They led our local guys on a false trail, using a double for Absalom, until they lost them on the metro. This was a well-setup run."

Trainer took his time drinking his coffee, placing the empty cup on the table. He stared out across the busy thoroughfare.

"This is going to piss off Washington," he said. "Absalom has been on their shopping list for some time."

"So why didn't they make the man an offer themselves earlier?"

"I'm just a lowly grunt, same as you. The policy makers on the Hill work out these deals. If they'd wanted Absalom that bad, he would have already been in the USA."

"I raise my hand on this," Hanson said. "He was lost on my watch. If they want to bring me home and give me a janitor's job, okay. I could do with a change. Berlin was getting on my nerves. Same with Paris. Maybe that's why I lost my concentration."

"The way this has gone down, we'll both be pushing mops."

"What's your best guess where Absalom's gone?"

Trainer didn't hesitate. "I figure the North Koreans have bought him. Absalom is going to be working for them. You've read the internal reports. North Korea is going all out to perfect a pulse weapon, and our slippery friend Emanuel Absalom is one of the best when it comes to that kind of technology."

CHAPTER ONE

FOUR MONTHS LATER—COAST GUARD STATION, HONOLULU, HAWAII

Delroy Yates, U.S. Coast Guard Service, was crossing the strip, heading for the base main office when he glanced up, attracted by a brilliant flash of intense light over the rescue unit. As he saw the HH-65A helicopter falling out of the sky, he knew instantly there was something wrong. The 9,200-pound aircraft plunged in a dead drop and hit the concrete no more than five hundred yards from where he was standing. As the machine split apart, sending debris in all directions, Yates saw a body tossed from the shattered fuselage, hitting the ground and bouncing like a rag doll. And then flames showed around the ruptured fuel tank, as crackling electrical cabling ignited the leaking fumes. The fire spurted, falling back into the wreckage before the expanding flames blew out and up, sending a raging ball of fire into the air. One of the shattered main rotors scythed across the concrete like a deadly blade.

As Yates began to sprint toward the crewman who had been ejected from the wreck, the fire spread along the broken helicopter. Leaking fuel pooled over the concrete, bursting into flame. Yates ignored the possible risk to himself, as he closed in on the crewman. The man was moving sluggishly, one leg of his uniform pants alight. The heat was terrific. Black smoke was curling up from the blaze, filling the sky over the base.

Yates reached the injured crewman, dropped to one knee. He slapped at the flame on the man's pants and extinguished it, scorching the skin of his own hands. The man's face, bloody and badly scraped, turned in his direction. He tried to speak, but no sound came out.

That was what alerted Yates. There was no sound behind him. He should have been hearing the howl of sirens from the fire trucks and ambulances. He glanced over his shoulder. He could see uniformed figures running toward the wreck.

But not a vehicle was moving. He could see them parked. Not one had shifted. Yates couldn't understand.

The injured guy grabbed Yates's sleeve with a bleeding hand. He moved his torn lips again, and this time his words came out.

"…all went," he said. "We lost power. Everything. No electricity. We were dead in the air. Nothing worked… Nothing worked…"

Yates looked over his shoulder once more and saw figures rushing to help. Medics carrying their equipment. Uniformed firefighters.

But no fire trucks.

No ambulances.

Nothing.

All the base vehicles stood in position.

Yates glanced up at the tracking radar unit. The scanner was not revolving. It was still.

He felt the injured guy gripping his arm and remembered what the man had said.

…all went. We lost power. Everything. No electricity. We were dead in the air. Nothing worked… Nothing worked…

THE FULL EXTENT of the power failures was not realized until an hour later. It took that much time to establish that the loss of power covered the entire base. Everything was down that had an electrical power requirement. When circuits were checked, they had been fried—totally wiped out, from the power supply for communications to the simplest items. No radio. No television. Watches had stopped. Once this had been realized, the base commander sent out a number of personnel on bicycles with orders to locate the closest spot where the power was still on, to find a telephone and to call for help.

In his office, conscious of the silence around him, Henry Calvin swiveled his seat around and looked out the window. Fire crews were extinguishing the burning helicopter with hand equipment. Medical personnel stood around waiting for their chance to get inside and treat any of the crew who might still be alive.

The injured crew member, Danny Telfair, had been stretchered to the base medical center.

Calvin looked beyond the crash site to the line of helicopters and aircraft. He was grateful no more of them had been airborne at the time of the helicopter disaster. A tap at the door brought his second in command into the office.

"Without stating the obvious, Jim, what's our main problem?"

"You want the whole list?" Jim Peterson asked.

Calvin sighed. "Tell me."

"Basically we're dead in the water. No power. No communications. No aircraft. No motor vehicles. Somebody did a good job on us, sir." Peterson ran a lean brown hand through his dark hair. "This what I think it is? An EMP strike? If it was, there was no heavy detonation above us."

"Or the department hasn't been paying the power company." Calvin allowed a bitter smile to show. "Hell, Jim, it can't be anything else. There's no other explanation. The signs are plain to see. EMPs are usually created from a nuclear explosion." He paused, then added, "I did read some article on how there's talk of creating EMPs from nonnuke sources. Maybe that's what this was."

"We can't even check to see how widespread this is," Peterson said. "There have to be ships out at sea. If they got hit by this, they'll be floating around helpless."

Calvin nodded. "Jim, get our techs working. See if they can salvage anything. We need some kind of communication network up. All base personnel need to go though our supplies. Look for anything that might be useful. How is the kitchen coping?"

"The cooking facilities are supplied by gas, so food is no problem at the moment. Everything has to be prepared by hand. No electrical equipment working."

"Tell the staff to cook up what they can from the freezers, before it thaws. At least we can keep the base from starving."

"I've given orders for a search for oil-fueled lamps. We'll need those when it gets dark. And I put a detail on seeing what they can do about repairing any battery lamps. It's a long shot, but worth looking into.

"This is no accident, sir. Someone deliberately targeted us. The questions are who, *why,* and what comes next?"

CHAPTER TWO

PACIFIC OCEAN

The small wooden coastal freighter sank after some kind of powerful discharge that ripped a large hole in the top deck and below the waterline. There was an unconfirmed report that the shipboard explosion happened some minutes after launching a small object from the aft deck of the ship. Whatever was launched headed in toward the Hawaiian coastline, and there was a detonation over land at a height of just less than a quarter mile. The reported blast was more of a powerful flash than an explosion.

The ship had been sailing beyond the Hawaiian limit, in international waters, and had not presented any kind of threat. It was a familiar sight in the area, so no one normally paid much attention to the scruffy vessel. The unexpected launch of the projectile had come as a complete surprise, and by the time a Coast Guard cutter reached the area, the vessel had sunk completely, leaving nothing but floating debris and a number of bodies.

There were no living survivors, and the later-recovered bodies showed evidence of high-intensity burns. They were flown immediately to a hospital on the main island where the bodies were isolated.

A Coast Guard investigation team was shortly in the area, with divers preparing to check out the sunken ship.

It was reported that the area affected by the power outage extended no more than a couple miles from the Coast Guard base. There were a small number of vehicle accidents when drivers unexpectedly lost control. Cell phones and landlines ceased to function. Domestic equipment that depended on electrical power, amounting to the majority of household devices, all quit, as well.

For the people inside the affected area, the dead zone, it was a frightening time. It was as if they had been cut off from the rest of the country. There was little they could do except wait for the arrival of functioning vehicles and rescue services from still-working areas.

If the incident had been designed to prove a point, it had worked.

CHAPTER THREE

THE WHITE HOUSE

Hal Brognola sat facing the President of the United States and waited for the Man to speak. The call from the President had been urgent, so Brognola had dropped everything and made it to the White House on the double. He had been escorted to the Oval Office and left alone with the Man. The President had poured coffee for them both, then sat down facing Brognola across his desk.

"I guess this is Stony Man urgent, sir?"

The President nodded. "I can see why they gave you the top job," he said. "Never miss a trick."

Brognola smiled.

The President tapped a blue folder on his desk.

"This was brought to my attention two hours ago. As soon as I read it, I had to bring you in because of possible threats to U.S. security in Hawaii and, by default, the rest of the country." The President passed over the file. "I don't know how familiar you are with EMP development, Hal, but it looks like we've just had a taster on how serious it can be.

"As well as data on the Hawaii incident, there is also input from a South Korean agent working inside NK about their pulse weapon development. Not the first time we've had concerns. This undercover agent has his own source working inside the research establishment in North Korea.

Last report he received said the North Koreans were about
to launch a test of their equipment.

"It's too much of a coincidence that Hawaii comes under
attack following that report. And we are aware that Hawaii could be a prime target of unfriendly powers in the
area because of our involvement in the Pacific. We have
too much invested in the region to allow complacency to
hold us back."

The President reclined in his chair and allowed Brognola
to read through the contents of the folder. He studied
Brognola's expression as the head of the Stony Man operation took in the information. The big Fed absorbed the
data, processing it in his mind, as the facts were integrated.
When he had finished, he closed the folder and placed it
back on the desk.

"You think I'm overreacting to disparate reports?" the
President asked.

"Taken individually, these *could* be separate," Brognola
said. "Then you look at the whole. Too close. And a connection. We know North Korea's ambitions. The anti-U.S.
stance. Tentative threats against our presence in the Pacific arena. Kim Jong Il kept the pot boiling right up to his
death, and Kim Jong Un hasn't made any attempt to ease
the situation. If NK is still determined to maintain its hostile attitude, we have to stay alert, sir."

"Hal, I'll never understand why North Korea is determined to keep rattling its sabers. Hell, I understand their
politics. Die-hard pro-Communist, maybe these days even
more than China. North Korea is on the edge. Lack of
food. A dispirited population. And they still keep throwing money they can barely afford at these overambitious
schemes. We offer to help, and all they do is slap our hand
away."

"Entrenched Communist attitudes," Brognola said.

"They see South Korea growing, but *their* country on its knees. And there's the U.S. presence, military and financial. North Korea has a long memory. They would love to have us leave South Korea and allow them the opportunity to take their second strike. They only have their close neighbor China in the background, sending financial aid and supplying special raw materials.

"The NK regime has an obsessive hostility toward America and seems determined to maintain the status quo. If they could come up with a scary new weapon, I think we all know how that would pan out." Brognola emptied his cup and gestured in the direction of the coffeepot.

"Help yourself," the President said. "The least I can do after bringing you in on Sunday."

"Family is used to me disappearing at a moment's notice."

That made the President smile. "Mine too."

One of the telephones on the desk rang. The President picked it up, listened, not interrupting, until he had the caller's full report, then made a brief acknowledgment before disconnecting. "That was Jack Pullman," he said.

"Crisis advisor Pullman?"

The President nodded. "That incident in Hawaii earlier this morning. It has been confirmed as an EMP attack. The blackout had a two-mile radius."

"Going to take some time to bring the base back online," Brognola said. He watched as the President sank back in his executive seat; there was no need to have it described to him that there was more.

"Pullman also verified the reports on the sunken freighter." The President tapped the blue folder. "A Coast Guard cutter located five bodies. All identified as Korean. They had suffered high-degree burns from an extremely high-powered electrical discharge. Pullman stressed the *ex-*

tremely high section of the report. Not the kind of discharge that would be generated by anything on a coastal freighter."

"If we postulate a theory based on the facts we have," Brognola said, "maybe we're looking at a test run that worked but then backfired on the launch source."

"My thoughts, as well. Hal, there was no report of any aerial detonation apart from a high-intensity flash overhead just before the base went black. So arguably we could be looking at a nonnuclear EMP device."

"That doesn't make me feel any less concerned. If someone is developing this weapon, and we are thinking North Korea, then there's a new game in town."

"We have the intel," the President said. "The South Korean covert agent I mentioned has been sending in reports of a research site up in North Korea. The South Koreans have been monitoring the situation. Their man has been reporting that pulse technology is what NK has been working on at this place. The South Korea agent's inside contact has been feeding him up-to-date information. Her last communication confirmed that North Korea was planning a test firing. Due to tight security, she wasn't told where the test would be carried out, but she was hoping to sabotage the firing."

"And Hawaii took the hit?"

"Everything points to that conclusion," the President said. "Hal, we need to track this to source and put it out of action. As small as this incident is, the target *was* the United States of America. That is not an option I will accept. I won't let another attack on U.S. soil go unpunished, Hal. Next time it could be here on the mainland. This is not to be allowed to happen.

"I am tired of appeasing these people and giving them the opportunity to strike at us, believing we're too damn scared to hit back.

"We have enough to initiate Stony Man missions. You send in your people. No half measures. If it has to be down and dirty, so be it. All it takes, Hal, as much as it damn well takes. Put Stony Man on a full footing. The whole facility. Find who is behind this and bring them down with extreme prejudice. Anything you need, call me direct, and you'll get it.

"One additional fact to consider, Hal. Dr. Emanuel Absalom. Greedy rogue physicist. Sources say he signed on to work at the North Korean site a few months ago."

Brognola took no longer than a few seconds to make his first requests.

"I'll need aircraft standing by to fly the teams to the prime destinations. Phoenix Force to South Korea. Able Team will head for Hawaii and look into the situation there."

"I'll have your rides ready to go by the time you get back to Stony Man."

Brognola headed for the door.

"Hal, anything you need on this. *Anything.* And wish the teams Godspeed and good luck from me."

CHAPTER FOUR

STONY MAN FARM

As soon as everyone was assembled in the War Room, Hal Brognola, head of the covert SOG, leaned both hands on the conference table and looked over his two specialist teams.

On his right was Able Team, led by Carl Lyons. The tough blond-haired former L.A. cop had a direct, no-nonsense attitude when it came to dealing with the bad guys. Rosario "the Politician" Blancanales and Hermann "Gadgets" Schwarz were his Able Team partners. Both were seasoned warriors who carried a multitude of skills between them.

Able Team was a trio of hotshots that had the ability to deal with any threat thrown in its direction. They operated for the most part within America's borders, though from time to time they had worked abroad. In a way they would have a foot in each camp on the upcoming mission. Their bailiwick this time around, though they had yet to be informed, would be Hawaii—overseas but still a part of the USA.

The other team, Phoenix Force, was a five-man unit led by the hard-nosed, unpredictable, but tactically brilliant, David McCarter. The former British SAS man had built a reputation as a reckless, direct-action commando who had no fear and who would tackle any situation he was presented with.

His promotion to Phoenix Force's top position had tempered his wildness to a degree; he still had the ability to go charging in, if a given situation called for it, but he carried his responsibility for his team seriously and would never, deliberately, place them in peril.

Gary Manning was a Canadian explosives expert and the team's sharpshooter. Rafael Encizo, a Cuban, was a fiery individual who feared very little. Calvin James, the black warrior with natural charm and varied talents, was a former Navy SEAL and was also the team medic. T. J. Hawkins, a Texan, was the youngest member of the team but was second to none when it came to laying down the hammer.

Not one of the Phoenix Force men would have hesitated if McCarter had given the order to walk through fire. Their unswerving loyalty was borne out of countless missions where absolute trust in each other had become the norm. It was the unspoken bond that grew between any fighting group.

It was the same kinship that had tied together combat soldiers from the shores of Iwo Jima to the bloody beaches of the Normandy landings, through to Vietnam and beyond. It still held soldiers together in Afghanistan or any hot spot that demanded a U.S. fighting force. As long as men fought together, and sometimes died together, it would continue to exist.

As Hal cast his eyes across the two groups, aware that he was about to launch them on yet another mission with no guarantees as to their survival, he felt, as he always did, that Able Team and Phoenix Force were the best. Without fanfare, or expectations of plaudits if they returned alive, these selfless men were ready to step up to Hell's front door and tackle the Devil himself.

On Brognola's left sat Barbara Price, an attractive woman who was Stony Man's mission controller. She had a file on the conference table that would hold all the mission briefings for both teams. In the short time since the President had issued his go for the mission, Price had compiled every piece of information available.

With single-handed efficiency she had organized transport to the relevant destinations and cleared any possible restrictions that might hamper the teams once they arrived. If it could be achieved, Price would make it happen.

She had the ability to coordinate complex arrangements and make them look simple. Unflappable, cool in any crisis, she sent the teams out across the globe and, once they were dispatched, would worry about them every step of the way, until they returned to the fold.

On the opposite side of the table sat Aaron Kurtzman. The Stony Man computer genius nursed a large mug of his infamous coffee, supposedly strong enough to scar stainless steel. Although his body was confined to a wheelchair—due to a spinal injury sustained during an attack on the Stony Man complex a number of years back—his upper body and especially his brain had not been damaged.

Kurtzman's mastery of the cyberworld enabled him to control and direct his own team of specialists. Their facility had the most cutting-edge computer systems in existence—though even that never satisfied Kurtzman, and he was constantly updating his equipment in order to stay ahead of the game.

If information was available somewhere, Kurtzman's team would find it. What they did was completely covert; Brognola understood how Kurtzman operated.

To complement the combat teams, Kurtzman would, if necessary, hack into any source he found and extract what he needed, and no one would be any the wiser. He broke every rule in the book big time, circumvented firewalls and snuck into code-protected files; if his unlawful raiding helped on a mission, Kurtzman would use his team without losing a moment of sleep.

As for Brognola, he turned a blind eye to Kurtzman's indiscretions. Too much could depend on the final outcome of a mission to worry about bending rules and treading on other agencies' toes. The bearded cyberguru, known affectionately as the Bear, was also highly protective of the Stony Man operatives. As far as Kurtzman was concerned, they were family, and he was dedicated to keeping them alive.

For today's meeting, Price had arranged a video conference with Erika Dukas, a languages expert the mission controller had known at the NSA. Her expertise in Korean was the primary reason for her attendance. Brognola glanced across at the wall screen. "You're up, Erika."

Dukas cleared her throat before she spoke. She was normally a confident young woman, sure of her abilities and skilled at her job.

McCarter had picked up on her momentary hesitation and caught her attention.

"No one's going to bite you, love," he said lightly. "Well, Carl might, if you tick him off, but we made him take his calm pill earlier, so you should be okay."

The irascible Briton's remark eased Dukas's tension. Even Lyons offered her a quick smile.

"Okay, I'll give you what I've learned so far," Dukas said. "Bear with me, because there's a lot more I need to do, before we learn exactly what this information offers. My early translations from Chosongul, the written phonetic Korean language, are a little shaky, this style is tough.

"Whoever gathered this information didn't lay it out in any order. I'm guessing the data was taken from different sources, so it's kind of haphazard, written by hand, most likely from computer displays. The copies Hal passed me were from the insider working at the research lab in North Korea."

"From what we were told," Price said, "the agent who gained this information was under a lot of pressure, taking chances to write down the data whenever the opportunity presented itself. And then getting her data to her outside contact who passed it along to his South Korean home base. They liaised with U.S. military intelligence."

"Important to this meeting," Dukas said, "are some key phrases I managed to isolate. Not too hard were references to NNEMP. Nonnuclear electromagnetic pulse weapons. There was a passage describing the requirements for the weapon. And we also have a name. There are a couple references to a Dr. Emanuel Absalom," Dukas added. "I looked him up, and it turns out he's a physics specialist from Europe. Worked in a German university before he vanished."

"His vanishing act was some four months ago," Price said. "He was on a watch list, but it appears he took off from his home in Berlin and evaded his watchers with help from the people transporting him out of the country. Since then no sign until his name appeared on Erika's documents. It now looks definite that he's involved in this NNEMP deal."

"What details do we have on him?" Blancanales asked. "Just for curiosity's sake."

Price flipped over a few pages in her file. "Absalom is in his late forties. No wife, no family. His background is in solid state physics. He was always a loner, according to those who knew him, something of a man with his own agenda. Clever guy but quirky. No particular political leanings.

"Always looking for the next challenge and doesn't care where it comes from. He'll go for whoever offers him the best financial backing." Price paused before adding, "A mercenary scientist. Absalom is reputed to like women and gambling and takes on these assignments to earn the money to attract them."

"Sounds like a reasonable kind of bloke."

The comment had come from David McCarter. Heads turned, and the Briton grinned at the response. It took a few seconds before they all realized he had simply made the comment to see their reaction.

"Constructive input is always welcome," Price said. "Thank you, David."

McCarter leaned forward, face calm again. "I'm guessing this Absalom specializes in the kind of physics that would be of use to anyone wanting to develop advanced NNEMP weapons."

Price nodded. "The man would be eminently capable of working in that field."

"That's all we need in the mix," Hawkins said. "A mad scientist to build the machines."

"Erika and I had our heads together earlier and pulled some background to this NNEMP," Price said, returning to the main subject, with a nod to Erika.

"NNEMP needs a low-induction discharge," Dukas explained. "A chemical explosion as the primary energy source." She grinned. "It's all very complicated."

"Involves the explosion and a capacitor," Price added. "Either a single-loop antenna, or a flux compression generator. All brought together to produce the electromagnetic pulse."

"Hey, hold on there," McCarter said. "Are you being bloody serious here? Only time I ever heard the words flux and capacitor was in the movie *Back to the Future*. I hope you aren't going to tell me there's an Emmett Brown lurking in the wings."

"No, you're safe, David," Price said, a faint grin on her face. "No time travel involved here."

"Glad to hear that," McCarter muttered.

"You have to admit, though," Schwarz said, "that NNEMP does smack of making time stand still when it shorts out all electrical gizmos."

"*See,*" McCarter agreed, somewhat mollified.

"Okay, guys," Brognola cut in. "What else do you have, ladies?"

"NNEMP doesn't have the power or range that a nuclear blast produces," Price said. "It's extremely limited."

"But even a limited discharge could have chaotic results," Kurtzman added. "Consider it dispersed over a city. Power supplies shut down. Think of the effect on hospitals. Transport coming to a stop. No electricity. We depend on that for almost everything. Computers fried, and they control a lot of the power infrastructure. You don't need a large-radius arc to create one hell of a mess. And what could happen if one of these discharges took place over a military base?"

"Intel informs us the North Koreans are hot on developing this kind of system," Brognola said. "And South Korea is desperate to halt the research, which is why they needed to find out where the development base is. They have a lot to be worried about. Apart from U.S. targets, South Korea would also be in the target frame. North Korea would turn cartwheels if it could fry South Korea's power grid and weapons."

"If this gizmo is perfected, we'll *all* have a lot to be worried about," Manning said.

"Which is where you guys come in," Brognola said. "Phoenix, you're heading for South Korea. Liaise with the contact who has the background on the North's NNEMP development. If you can locate where this development is being carried out, shut it down. If we can link North Korea and the Hawaiian strike, all the better. We need to come down hard on this. That order comes direct from the President."

McCarter grimaced. "I guess Able Team gets the choice assignment, then. Sun, warm water and grass skirts."

"Hell of an assignment," Blancanales said. "But someone has to do it."

"Shouldn't we have flipped a coin?" James asked. "Isn't that what democracy is all about?"

"No," Brognola said. "It's about me being the boss and deciding who goes where."

James grinned. "I knew you'd say that."

"Okay, guys," Price said. She pushed files across the conference table. "Mission data. All the names and locations we currently have. Your cells will be synced to Stony Man via the Zero orbiting platform. We now have a solid comm link with Zero, so keeping in touch should be constant."

"It's the *should* that worries me," Hawkins said.

"We've been working on the Zero connection over the last couple of months," Kurtzman said. "Akira has it finetuned, and every check he makes works well. Right now it's working 99 percent efficient. But Akira isn't happy with even that. He wants 100 percent."

The orbiting platform, Zero, launched by the U.S. Air Force, was one of America's latest defense facilities, and had both defensive and offensive weapons capabilities. Zero's uniqueness was how it functioned.

Stricken by terminal cancer, USAF Major Doug Buchanan had been offered the chance of survival by accepting the command of Zero. In a bold move Buchanan had been the first man to take on the challenge of letting himself become a symbiotic guinea pig. The bio-couch attached to him kept his cancer at bay and allowed him to control Zero.

He rode the orbiting platform, providing his Earthly

command post with information, the eyes and ears of Zero scanning for problems and also providing state-of-the-art communications for selected recipients. Stony Man had been granted accessibility to Zero via a request from the President, who kept their covert status through a secure connection monitored by Kurtzman.

The excellent connection Zero provided allowed some of the best and most secure cell channels in existence. Using his own program, created in-house, Kurtzman was able to block any intrusions that might have compromised Stony Man's anonymity.

"Phones are being organized now," Kurtzman said. "Fitted with new extended-life power cells. Just remember to keep them charged, if you can get to a power source. Phones are good, but not if you don't keep them charged…"

"Kissinger has your ordnance ready," Price advised. "Just remember that, if you go in North Korea, it's doubtful you'll be able to pick up anything you've forgotten."

"Sounds as if you've covered all the bases," Encizo said. "Do we get any spending money? Vouchers?"

Price smiled. "The way this is shaping up, I don't think you'll have much time for shopping. But there will be cash money, if you need to oil the wheels."

"Ah, the universal lubricant," James said. "Never underestimate the power of a roll of Uncle Sam's sweeteners."

Brognola slid a photograph across to McCarter. "That's Kayo Pak, your contact from South Korean intelligence. He's a good man from what we've learned and has established himself inside North Korea. He will be there to meet you when you arrive."

A second photo was handed to Lyons. "Oscar Kalikani, a Honolulu cop. Works on the Hawaii Task Force. Has an excellent record and he's up to speed on the Hawaii incident. Tough officer. Stands no nonsense from anyone."

"Remind you of someone we know?" Blancanales asked his partner.

Schwarz nodded. "Yeah. He's sitting on your right."

"Do I really have to take this pair with me?" Lyons asked. He looked at Price. "Don't you have any trained chimps I could have?"

Price jerked a thumb to indicate Blancanales and Schwarz. "Oh, you got 'em. Last pair we had in stock."

"And they work for peanuts," McCarter said, straight-faced.

"Aaron has had the team trawling the internet, picking up any pieces of intel from every agency they can dig into," Price said. "Adding this to the information the President passed to Hal, we've gained a degree of background that gives an emerging scenario."

"Latest intel from the North Korean insider tells us the physicist, Emanuel Absalom, has been positively placed in North Korea for the past few months and as the top gun at this research site. Development has reached the stage where the North Korean team has built their first working proto-type. And it was used on the Hawaii strike."

"How credible is this information?" Schwarz asked.

"It comes from the female member of Absalom's group working alongside him. She gained her information and passed it to her contact in North Korea, Kayo Pak."

"Sounds like a brave guy," Hawkins said.

"Well, he's your point man in North Korea."

"And the lady?" McCarter asked.

"Li Kam. A fully qualified physicist."

Price slid another photo from her folder and pushed it across the table for everyone to see. The image was of a young Korean woman. In her late twenties, she was confi-dent looking and attractive.

"Kayo Pak messaged to his home base that Li only found

out Hawaii was the target area a short time before the actual launch. Apparently Absalom kept that from his team. But Li managed to get hold of the data." Price paused, glancing across at Brognola. He caught her eye and nodded for her to continue.

"By the time Li found out where the test was going to occur, the NNEMP device had already been readied for the trial. But knowing about the test beforehand, she did what she could to sabotage it by inserting a code into the onboard computer, the idea being that it would cause the NNEMP burst to malfunction and stop the operation."

"She took one hell of a risk," James said. "The North Koreans don't take kindly to anyone turning against them."

Price said, "Pak had recruited her months ago, and she has been feeding him as much as she can. She was the one who advised about Absalom heading up the research. According to her, Absalom brought everything together. She jumped at the chance to work against the North Korean regime.

"Her issues go deep. She lost her family to treatment they received from the North Koreans. Pak saw her potential, because she worked in the same field as Absalom and had been offered a chance to work in the same research program because of her knowledge. It was an opportunity that couldn't be passed over by Pak.

"He offered to get her out of North Korea, if she could help him get data on the work being done."

"Pretty risky for the girl," Hawkins said. "The North Koreans are paranoid when it comes to security."

"Apparently it was Li Kam who suggested the idea," Brognola said. "She wanted to convince Pak how well into the research the North Koreans are. He took what she sent him and had it pushed along for our people to analyze."

"You want us to do something for this woman?" McCarter asked, already half guessing the answer.

Brognola nodded. "The President wants her out of North Korea. He made it clear we would welcome her in the U.S. Her hands-on work in the practical field of NNEMP, and especially at the North Korean research facility, would give our people a boost, maybe allow us to push further ahead with our own development."

"Onward and upward," McCarter muttered cynically.

"As long as potential enemies are determined to work on these weapons, we have to keep up," Kurtzman said.

"I'm in the picture," McCarter said. "Too bloody right I am. But wouldn't it be a sunny day if we all stopped trying so hard inventing things to kill each other?"

"David, it would be fine if that ever happened," Price said. "Until that day we just have to try and keep the balance."

"I'll keep that in mind, love," McCarter said, smiling. "And don't worry, I wasn't going all melancholy. That was me being wistful and contemplative. I'm still really the gung-ho bugger I've always been."

"Glad to hear that," James said.

"I want you guys off and running," Brognola said, indicating Phoenix Force. "This Hawaiian strike means the North Koreans have their weapon at a critical stage. We need to neutralize it, before they can move forward. Sorry to hand you a loaded deck, but there's no way we can let another strike get under way. Go in, meet Pak and put the research unit out of action. Next time the Koreans make an attempt, there could be a bigger result. The President is determined to kill this, before it becomes a fully realized threat."

McCarter pushed to his feet and the rest of Phoenix Force followed.

Okay, let's gear up and move," he said.

"Good luck, guys," Lyons said.

"We'll think of you enjoying the Hawaiian sunshine," James said as he followed his team out of the War Room.

"Something tells me any heat we get won't be from lounging on the beach," Blancanales said.

Lyons nodded at Price. "Update *us* on this trip to paradise," he said.

Somehow he didn't imagine Able Team would be enjoying a stress-free vacation when they eventually touched down on the Pacific state.

CHAPTER FIVE

HAWAII

Xian Chi settled himself in the comfortable leather chair and studied the people coming and going through the lobby of the hotel. He liked to watch people, to study them and imagine what they were thinking. It amused him. Men and women, all different races, a mix of colors and persuasions. All caught up in their own lives. Sad. Happy. Each wrapped in private thoughts. It made him feel content, knowing he was among them without their knowledge of his reasons to be here on the island. They went about their business, blissfully unaware he was here to bring discomfort to their very existence.

He caught sight of the man he was here to meet, as the North Korean stepped through the door and crossed the lobby to join him. As always, Soon Il Tak wore a sullen expression on his face. Even while playing his undercover role as a businessman, the North Korean remained passive. He saw the whole of life as a constant struggle, a battle against the enemy he was committed to destroying. Little amused him. Nothing broke through his rigid demeanor. Chi tried to imagine Tak bursting into laughter over some trivial matter. Xian Chi found that difficult and also found it sad. He was a committed Chinese Communist—a Chi-Com—himself, but that did not mean he had no moments of unconfined joy in his life. To the contrary Xian often found life utterly enjoyable.

Tak paused in front of him, his stocky body held stiff beneath the cheap dark suit he wore. He refused to dress down. Chi had yet to see the man in casual attire. Tak's arms hung rigidly at his sides as he stared at his Chinese counterpart.

"Sit down, Tak," Chi said. "You look like a bad tailor's dummy." Chi spoke in English as neither man had mastered the other's language. "Relax before someone thinks you have died standing up."

Tak lowered himself into one of the armchairs facing Chi. The expression on his face remained the same.

"You persist in trying to provoke me," Tak said. "*Why?*"

"I persist in attempting to make you see you need to drop that ridiculous pose. Look around, Tak. See how everyone behaves."

"I see the way they behave. They are stupid and coarse, believing they are superior beings who should own the world. The men are fat and dress like wayward children. The women walk around half dressed and cluck like chickens in a pen."

Chi smiled. "You have to admit it's a very comfortable pen," he said. He bounced in his seat. "And these are very comfortable chairs, too, don't you agree? And whatever you may think about the Americans, do not forget how successful they are. Their technology is brilliant. Their country is rich, and they have such incredible global influence. You may despise them but never forget how powerful they are."

A passing server, dressed in light-colored slacks and a colorful Hawaiian shirt, paused as Chi raised a hand.

"May we have coffee, please?" Chi asked. "For two."

The man nodded. "Certainly, sir."

"Very pleasant," Chi murmured as the man walked away.

"Can we get to the matter at hand?" Tak asked, irritation in his voice. "Drinking American coffee is not why I am here."

"Tak, you should try it. Much better than the terrible stuff I have to drink at home. Tell me, do they ever serve coffee in Pyongyang?"

For the first time since he had appeared, Tak's expression altered. He showed a definite frown, and Chi counted that as a small victory.

"In Pyongyang we concentrate on important matters," Tak snapped.

"Of course. Foolish of me, Tak. So what can I tell you?"

"I need to be able to report that the matter is being handled. That there will be no more setbacks."

"Why should there be? Our people are in place. We have backup. A secure base. Tak, I have been here in Hawaii long enough to have established contacts who will keep us informed and reinforced if needed. Have faith."

Their coffee arrived. Chi signed for it, poured a cup and pushed it across the low table.

"Try it," he said. "It won't be laced with poison. Tak, even you must take a drink sometime. A mere cup of American coffee will not identify you as plunging the depths of depravity."

He watched Tak pick up the cup and taste the coffee. Chi smiled a little, as Tak quickly drank the rest of it. When he replaced the cup on the table, Chi quickly refilled it for him.

Chi heard his cell ring in his pocket. He slipped it free and checked the caller ID, then answered it. The caller spoke in Mandarin. Chi replied. As he ended the call and placed the phone on the table, he felt Tak's intense stare.

"That was Kai Yeung," Chi said. "One of his team saw Kalikani meeting three Americans and escorting them to a hotel."

"You suspect a problem?"

"Oscar Kalikani is a special police officer. He is part of the Honolulu Task Force, permanently assigned to terrorist watch. So those three arrivals will be similar, here for a special reason. They have to be, so soon after the Coast Guard strike.

"You think they might be looking for us?"

"Not us personally. But the Americans are almost as paranoid as you North Koreans. They see problems everywhere. These men could be here in Hawaii for something that has nothing to do with our presence. Not an impossibility, but I doubt it."

"I am sure they are here because of suspicions over the event at the Coast Guard base."

"Yeung will check. He has contacts. If there is anything that should concern us, he will find out."

"Then what?"

"Then, my dear Tak, we will deal with it."

For Xian Chi his time in Hawaii might soon end. If it did, he would, of course, accept whatever his masters in Beijing ordered him to do. Here on the islands he was totally in charge of the Chinese presence. He ran the Hawaiian unit. He was overseer, paymaster, arbitrator, and his decisions were final.

He employed who he needed, dismissed those he thought had outlived their usefulness and retained the absolute right to terminate anyone who posed a threat. All those employed by Xian Chi understood these things. If they did not, or went against him, they would soon pay the price. He never wavered from his set rules. There were no exclusions. Chi demanded and got complete obedience. It was the way Beijing operated in regard to their people in the field, so Chi did the same.

His role here in Hawaii was double-edged. On the surface he was Beijing's overseer for the North Koreans. He had monitored Soon Il Tak and his people, as they had prepared and put into motion their trials of the NNEMP weapon. Beijing had helped finance the operation as well as providing local backup. While North Korea had little resource on the islands, China had ample. They had their own people, many who had been in place for some considerable time. They were neatly embedded in the culture, running businesses, and their physical presence did not stand out among the existing Asiatic population.

America had a powerful military presence in the area, both on land and especially at sea. The U.S. Navy used the Pacific as an expansive defense priority, and it gave them a great tactical advantage. That presence had always been a thorn in Beijing's side, and China looked at America's involvement in the area with envy. The need to develop some modern weapon that could be used to weaken the U.S.'s hold was paramount.

The emergence of a workable NNEMP device had everyone's interest. When North Korea's development appeared to be moving ahead, Beijing saw an opportunity to jump on the bandwagon. With its usual guile, Beijing gradually eased itself into Pyongyang's favor by responding to requests for financial assistance.

North Korea was after money to prolong its research. The country was not awash with cash. It was in financial trouble, which was not unusual; due to the lack of foresight by the ruling body, North Korea had little to bolster its economy. Lavish spending over the years on its frantic arms program, far in excess of what it made from North Korea's poor production base, meant the expensive development program was slowing down.

Beijing, always a supporter of the country, saw the opportunity and stepped up to the mark with ready finance.

There was opportunistic zeal behind the generous backing. With an eye on—but not ignoring—the future, China would allow North Korea the chance to work on and fine-tune the fledgling weapon.

Xian Chi was instructed to offer his services and had suggested the North Korean trial be carried out on Hawaiian soil. It was a practical experiment that would be employed away from North Korea itself, in case there were any problems, which had proved out when the ship launching the NNEMP was involved in a mysterious explosion within a short time following the discharge. The NNEMP effect had been successful in its principal intention, crippling a Coast Guard station and showing it was workable. However, the setback that took the launch vessel to the bottom of the Pacific was proving to be difficult to understand.

Chi had reported the incident to his masters in Beijing. They, in turn, ordered him to maintain his backup for the Koreans, while at the same time looking out for any opportunity to profit from the Korean error.

The North Korean research base was now frantically looking into why the mishap took place. Soon Il Tak had been ordered to recover the launch device from the sunken ship. However, the Americans had become involved, sending out their own marine investigators. For the moment all Tak and his Chinese backup could do was watch. If and when the Americans found the launch device and brought it to the surface, Tak would be ordered to take it from them and get it back to North Korea.

That would prove to be a difficult task.

Chi decided Tak would be up to it. The Korean would be in his element going up against the Americans. His social graces might not be too great, but in a situation involving striking out against the USA, he would be more than at ease.

Tak had a small group of his own countrymen under his control, and he could call on extra men through Chi's Hawaiian contacts. The Chinese themselves could call on a number of local contractors willing to provide what was needed.

"I need to make contact with Macklin," Tak said, pulling his cell from a pocket. "Arrange for him to put his people on standby."

Chi nodded. "I will see that Yeung determines where the salvaged unit is to be taken."

"Will he be able to do that?"

"Have faith," Chi said. "Yeung has lived here on the islands almost as long as I have. A good agent for us. He will find out where the Americans are taking the unit. After all he has his spy working within HPD, feeding us up-to-date information."

When Tak's call was answered, he spoke briefly. "I will join you shortly," was all he said.

"While you make your arrangements, I will monitor the local situation and keep you informed," Chi said. He reached down and indicated the leather attaché case on the floor beside his seat. "You were not going to forget this, were you?"

He pushed it across to Tak. The North Korean nodded and picked up the heavy case.

"On behalf of my government…" he began.

"No company dogma here, Tak, please," Chi said lightly. "We are oiling the wheels, as the Americans say. If it helps us to achieve our aims, it is worth every penny."

Tak stood, nodded briefly to Chi, as he turned and walked out of the hotel.

CHAPTER SIX

Soon Il Tak waited with growing impatience. He needed an update from his local contacts on the ground. Since the accident with the ship, it had been impossible to get close to the area. The local police had cordoned it off, and now that the American police had become involved, getting information had become even harder.

Dive teams had been brought in and were preparing to examine the sunken ship. Security had been stepped up, and there was an exclusion zone where the vessel had gone down. The divers had spent most of the day in the water, and as the afternoon wore on, it became clear they were going to be around for some time yet.

Tak understood the matter at hand required swift action, if he was going to retrieve the piece of hardware. Pyongyang had already made it clear they wanted retrieval. The equipment mounted on the ship held important information, and Tak's North Korean masters wanted it out of American hands.

His people were spread around the area, each of them attempting to gain information on the American operation.

Tak had already realized there was not going to be time for extensive planning. If the Americans got to the ship and realized the importance of the item mounted on the aft deck, they would want to remove it and transport it to a secure place. To regain possession of the equipment, Tak had to have his people ready and willing to move quickly.

He had only just reached his parked car outside the hotel, then placed the attaché case in the luggage space at the rear, when his cell vibrated in his pocket. He took the call. It was one of his own informers. Tak had used the Hawaiian called Mako as a go-between and had always been satisfied with the man's input. The man spoke quickly, without wasting time, informing Tak he had solid information concerning the matter at hand. They arranged to meet.

Twenty minutes later Tak confronted his informer in a local coffee shop. As always they took a table outside the establishment.

"This is going down heavy," Mako said. "Cops are all over it. I have to take it slow in case anyone catches on."

"Just tell me what you have learned so far."

"The incident at the Coast Guard base. My source tells me the place went black. No power. Everything shut down and a chopper was totaled."

"I already know about that," Tak said impatiently. "I'm really interested in the ship that sank off the coast."

Mako, a heavy-shouldered man with an unshaven face and eyes hidden behind dark glasses, nodded. "That seems to have everyone's interest. Talk been flying around HPD. Cops are arranging for transport to be at the docks when the divers bring up some gizmo off the ship."

"Where will it be taken?"

"My contact tells me there's a three-vehicle convoy being set up—two police cars and an HPD armored van to run this thing to an electronics company up-country from the city. It's some high-tech firm that specializes in experimental stuff."

Useful news, Tak thought. "Do they have any idea when this transport will take place?"

"Tomorrow morning is all I got. I'll keep my ears open. As soon as I know, you'll know, Mr. Tak." Mako slid a folded piece of paper across the table, and Tak closed his hand over it. "Details of the route and the address of the electronics company."

"Excellent work," Tak said. "Check your account in a couple of hours. I believe you will like what you see."

"Good doing business with you, Mr. Tak." Mako drained his coffee.

Tak watched the man go, smiling to himself.

So easy to buy these people, he decided. Americans were wholly seduced by material gain. It would be their downfall. He waved away the server, when the girl asked if he wanted anything. It was time to make his rendezvous with Macklin.

His cell rang as he returned to his car. It was one of his men at the dockside.

"There is activity on the docks. A diving platform has been towed out to where the ship went down. A number of divers are already in the water. There is a crane on the platform."

"Good. Keep watch. I need to know when the Americans recover the equipment. I have found out where it will be taken, if they do raise it. It appears nothing will be done until morning, so I will have time to organize our people for retrieval."

Tak ended the call and quickly called Chi.

"My man Mako has updated me on the situation. His HPD feed has given him details on the recovery operation. We now know when and where, so I am going to pass this to Macklin. Time will be short, but I am confident he will organize things. I would prefer it if we had the opportunity to make better arrangements."

"We cannot always have such opportunities," Chi said. "We must move with what we have. I have just received confirmation from my own police source that the data

Mako gave you is correct. We must proceed with what we have."

Tak speed-dialed another number and waited for it to ring out. The voice was instantly recognizable: deep, with a commanding presence.

"I'm on my way," Tak said.

"Been wondering when you were going to contact me."

"I may need your team in action quickly."

"That's how we operate. Just waiting for your call."

"In this case speed is of the essence. There will be little chance to do much preplanning. Can you handle it?"

"All I need are the details."

"This will be in the manner of a retrieval. Something belonging to my principals has fallen into the hands of the opposition. It is important we get it back. I can be with you within the hour. I had business to settle before I left the city."

"I'll look forward to seeing you."

Tak unlocked the Toyota SUV and quickly drove off, making his way out of the busy center where he picked up the main highway and headed north. His journey took him into the lush countryside, with the Pacific Ocean on his left. After driving a quarter hour, he was climbing into the hills, where houses were spaced out along the narrower roads in this area. This was unspoiled Hawaii. Away from noise and prying eyes. It suited Tak, and it also suited the man he was about to visit.

An unmarked turn-in drew him away from the road, down a driveway overhung by heavy ferns and palm trees. After a couple hundred yards the driveway opened onto a circular area and the single-story stone-and-timber house. The only signs of any human presence were the two high-end 4x4s parked nearby. Tak braked alongside the pair of vehicles and climbed out. He moved to the rear of his

Toyota and opened the tailgate. He drew out the leather attaché case Chi had given him and carried it with him, as he approached the front door. It opened before he reached it.

The man was tall and athletically built. He sported a head of straw-colored hair, cut short. He had the kind of rugged good looks that would have earned him nice money in Hollywood. He smiled when he recognized Tak.

"Always good to see you, Colonel Tak."

He invariably used Tak's military rank, even more than Tak did himself.

"Major Macklin, a pleasure."

"Been a long time since I held rank," William Macklin said. "I leave it lay nowadays."

He led the way inside, and Tak followed him through the house until they reached the main lounge area that backed onto the rear of the structure. Wide sliding glass doors opened onto the overgrown patio area.

Two other men lounged on couches, nodding at Tak's appearance.

"You know Borgnine and Spelman."

Tak nodded in the direction of the seated men. Neither spoke. Nor would they until it was important.

"Take a seat, Colonel," Macklin said. "Drink?"

"Anything as long as it is cold and wet."

Macklin crossed to the wet bar, opened a minirefrigerator and poured chilled fruit juice into a frosted glass. He knew Tak didn't like liquor. He added ice and brought it to his visitor. Taking his own drink, Macklin sat down and waited.

"As I already said, there is, unfortunately, a limited window of opportunity here. It will need your expertise in mounting a rapidly organized operation. Very rapid."

"Give me the details."

Tak told it exactly as it was, leaving nothing out. This would not be the first time he had used Macklin and his people. Macklin's team was professional, without any kind of loyalty except to themselves and the people they worked for. They worked for money, not country, and once on board, their professionalism was 100 percent. Tak knew they would not come cheap. Hence the solid weight of the attaché case he had brought with him. In anticipation of the acceptance of the operation, he had come prepared. The case held cash, U.S. dollars from the fund Chi had provided for such times as this.

No one spoke until Tak stopped talking and took a long drink from his glass. The cool liquid felt good as it slid down his dry throat.

Macklin stroked the taut flesh under his jaw as he absorbed Tak's briefing. He looked across at Borgnine and Spelman. Their faces were immobile.

"So going on what you've just laid out for us," Macklin said, "I'd guess we have around fifteen hours before things start to get mobile."

"Unless there are problems removing the equipment from the deck of the ship and getting it to the surface," Tak said.

He took a buff-colored envelope from his inside pocket and handed it to Macklin. It contained detailed descriptions and specifications of the equipment to be retrieved. Macklin opened the flap and took out the paperwork. He studied the sheets, then passed them across to his partners. Tak allowed them the time they needed.

"They should be able to fit this into a panel truck," Borgnine said.

"Eight hundred pounds," Spelman said. "We can handle that."

"Any problem with radioactivity?" Macklin asked.

"No," Tak said. "This is not a nuclear device at all."

"How damaged do you expect it to be?"

"There may well be fusion burns that went directly through the outer casing. That would have carried on down through the hull and opened up a hole that caused the ship to take on water and sink."

"But that wasn't expected?"

"Definitely not. The deliberate sabotage to the NNEMP projectile caused a massive surge that followed the flight path all the way back to the launching device. It had enough power to cause extensive damage."

"No shit," Borgnine said.

Spelman asked, "There isn't likely to be any of this *surge* still around, is there?" Spelman asked.

Like his partner, Borgnine, Spelman didn't say a lot, but when either of them had questions, they were on the button.

"No, no, no," Tak said. "The residual power generated would have burned out directly before it went through the boat's hull. It was not in the original design of the equipment. We believe someone had added new operating codes into the computer program."

"So you have a hostile element at the research facility?"

"It appears so."

"Out of curiosity," Macklin asked, "has this saboteur been identified and caught yet?"

Tak gave a rare smile. "The matter is being pursued, even as we speak. Not here on the islands. It is a separate matter, being handled by the people on site." He splayed his hands across the top of the attaché case resting across his knees. "So do you think you can recover the equipment?"

"Are you able to keep us up-to-date with the recovery schedule?"

"The situation is being monitored, and I have a source placed who will be able to inform me when the package is to be moved."

"Then I'd say we're in business, Colonel Tak."

Tak opened the attaché case and showed Macklin the stacked bundles of hundred-dollar bills. There was a secondary package in plastic that held more cash. Tak removed it and handed it to Macklin.

"For incidental expenses," he said. He showed the open case to Borgnine and Spelman, so they were able to see the main cash amount. "As on our previous deals, there will be an identical amount payable on the successful completion of the operation."

He closed the lid and handed the case to Macklin. Borgnine took the case and left the room.

Macklin weighed the plastic pack of money in his hands. "This should get us what we need. It can pay the guy who'll rent the vehicles we need."

"Will you be needing additional men?" Tak asked.

"Maybe. It's no problem. We'll keep them to the minimum. A couple of extra hands should do it. I can assemble a team in a few hours. Colonel, you keep me updated on the situation. As long as we know the when and the where, this should go easily."

"My current information is that the police will be handling the delivery. What if the military are involved?"

Macklin smiled. "I don't give a rat's ass who gets involved. They get in our way, we'll deal with them."

"I am sure you will."

Macklin saw Tak out to his car.

"I'll be in touch once we're done," Macklin said.

Tak drove to the road for his trip back to the city. He was not a man who took many things for granted, but now that Macklin was on board, he began to experience a feeling of satisfaction. If everything went as planned, the NNEMP equipment should soon be in his hands and on its way back to Pyongyang.

MACKLIN REACHED FOR a second cell he had on his desk. It was a burn phone, with only one number keyed in. He tapped the speed-dial function and waited as the number dialed out. It was answered on the third ring. Macklin recognized the voice instantly.

"He just left," Macklin said.

"Excellent. Do you foresee any major problems?"

"Not especially. Tak's informants seem reliable. I'm mobilizing my team now. We'll be ready to move once I get the go-ahead."

"Very well. As soon as you gain control of the item, call, and we can fix the exchange."

"Will do."

"Good hunting, Macklin."

XIAN CHI SAT back, a contented look on his face, as he considered the events about to take place. If everything progressed as he imagined it would, then his time in Hawaii would have an extremely satisfactory outcome for the Peoples Republic of China.

It was ironic, he thought, that North Korea, with its limited expertise, should manage to develop the NNEMP process ahead of China, only to have it sabotaged from within its own ranks. And then to snatch the *something* salvaged from the disaster right under NK's nose. That it would be China added further irony, because the Beijing regime had helped fund the North Korean development of the project.

Xian Chi, acting as paymaster and advisor to Soon Il Tak, had followed the program, and the unexpected setback had presented him with his opportunity to snatch the

NNEMP launch equipment away from Tak. It had been a unique chance—and one the Chinese could not ignore.

As soon as Tak had left the hotel for his meeting with Macklin, Chi had called his headquarters in Beijing. His brief but detailed update had brought an instant response from his commanders. He received his new orders and accepted them without question. If Beijing had decided it was time to up the stakes, Xian Chi was not going to query them.

He had learned early in his career that the logic of his Chinese superiors was unmovable. With the North Koreans having allowed a saboteur to infiltrate the NNEMP program, they had lost full control over the weapon. In Beijing's eyes the North Koreans were no longer capable of maintaining security, which meant the equipment resting on the seabed had to be taken off their hands.

Transporting the item overseas to the PRC would place it in the hands of the Chinese, and they would take it apart and learn every detail. The Chinese were masters at retrofitting anything. Their teams would be able to recreate the original, incorporate the knowledge into their own research and advance their own NNEMP. The North Korean failure would become China's success.

Chi saw and understood the logic. He would allow Tak the privilege of recovering the item, then take it off Macklin's hands.

Chi's final act in the matter would be the elimination of Tak. The man had served his purpose now. Removing him would enable Chi to close the book. Without Tak, the North Koreans would be left with no answers. Tak and his Korean team would not be able to voice any suspicions once they were dead.

Chi would have no regrets. Sacrificing Tak was necessary. In the great scheme of things, the Korean's life was insignificant. Added to that was the fact Tak was becoming a bore. The man had no style. His mantra was 100 percent that which was dictated by his North Korean masters. He would not veer from it by a fraction.

He lived and breathed what had been drilled into him by the overpowering masters in Pyongyang—or should that be *master?* Chi wondered. North Korea was ruled by one man, and the country followed his rule with blind obedience. That rigidity infused all thinking. Independent thought was frowned upon and punished severely.

Soon Il Tak was a true child of North Korea. All thought, all action, was for the state. Nothing else mattered. Nothing else was even allowed to filter through. And it was that blind obedience that stifled creativity. Tak would walk the decreed line and never once consider looking left or right.

While Xian Chi followed Chinese policy, he had no qualms when it came to free thought. His country today had moved on a distance from the staunchness of the old ways. China, while still following the well-trod paths of Communism, had emerged from the shadows to embrace, in part, the twenty-first century. It had increased global trade, had embraced technology and conducted business on a worldwide scale.

China looked with envious eyes on the rich pickings still out of its reach. It maintained a delicate balance with the West, and even America, though there was still an underlying desire to oust the USA from its encompassing involvement with the Pacific Rim. Behind the economic overtures, China wanted more influence in the Pacific. And to that end it looked for new and powerful means of upstaging America.

The NNEMP concept appealed to the Chinese military. If the weaponry could be fully developed and added to the ChiCom arsenal, it would prove a devastating weapon. It would be a means of hitting out at American targets without reducing them to radioactive wastelands, a clean way to cripple and still maintain the infrastructure.

What use would the Hawaiian islands be if there was nothing left but rubble and poisonous earth? Better to disable the American defense shield and then move in before any chance of restructuring took place. It was a far-reaching dream, yet one that Beijing was looking at.

Taking over the North Korea development was a small step but one worth risking a reaction. North Korea, if Chi's plan worked, would have no idea what had happened to its hardware. Their first reaction would be that the Americans had it.

If they admitted the *something* was theirs, by default they would also admit *they* had launched the strike against the USA. Such an admission would work against them. North Korea might be a hostile regime, but it was not a stupid one. Loss of face, especially when America was involved, would be less than welcome in Pyongyang.

As far as China was concerned, the matter would be quietly written off. Beijing would play the disappointed backer mourning the loss of financial assistance but staying a few steps back. It would quietly hide away the stolen equipment and allow its own scientific teams to work on it in anonymity. Any success would be kept strictly under wraps. There would be no fanfares. No flag waving. The perfected weapon would be entered into the Chinese arsenal, ready to be used in some future capacity.

A good result for China.

North Korea would have to lick its wounds and think again. Only this time there might not be financial assistance coming its way from Beijing. After the Hawaiian fiasco, North Korea would have little to make a fuss about regarding China's reluctance to bankroll them a second time.

Chi glanced at his watch and decided he was ready to eat. As he made his way to the hotel restaurant, he felt satisfied with the result he had achieved. He had the time to relax and also the inclination to enjoy a good meal. He smiled.

Wasn't that the American way?

Secure a good deal, then give oneself a reward.

CHAPTER SEVEN

The USAF C-17 Globemaster touched down midmorning at the U.S. Air Force Base at Osan, South Korea. The weather had changed during the final half hour of the flight, and heavy rain was streaming across the runway as the massive transport made its way across the concrete apron. Thick black clouds were banking up overhead, threatening more bad weather.

Gary Manning pulled his ball cap low as he stepped from the C-17's rear ramp, staring out across the base. Behind him McCarter stomped down the ramp and stood next to him.

"Bloody hell," the Briton muttered. "Just remind me, did we have a choice of missions this time round? If we did, somebody pulled a fast one on us."

Hawkins took a long look at the inhospitable scene. "Boss, we done got ourselves screwed," he drawled.

Encizo and James paused beside the others as they took in their South Korean welcome.

"Man, this is not what I signed up for," James said.

Behind Phoenix Force the packed cargo interior was being readied to off-load its freight, and one of the crew paused beside the Stony Man unit.

"You guys just chose the wrong day to drop in," he said.

Then he pointed at an Air Force Hummer rolling in toward the aircraft. "At least they sent someone to collect you."

"See, things are picking up already," Hawkins said.

The Hummer stopped short of the ramp and a slim uniformed figure climbed out from behind the wheel. He wore tan BDUs and highly polished boots.

"Major Cassidy?" McCarter said.

The man nodded. "Put your gear in the back, and I'll get you over to somewhere dry," Cassidy said.

He led the way to the rear of the Hummer and helped load Phoenix Force's gear. He slammed the door shut and moved to climb back inside the vehicle. The rest of Phoenix Force crowded into the rear, leaving McCarter to take the seat beside Cassidy.

"My orders are to give you what you want and not to ask too many questions," Cassidy said as he drove away from the aircraft. "In fact no questions at all."

"Don't hold that against us," McCarter said. "We get stuck with these bloody information blackouts wherever we go. Major, we're just doing our job. Its very nature forces us to keep closemouthed."

Cassidy smiled. A genuine expression. "Don't worry. I've worked clandestine ops myself, so I get the picture. Just sing out, if there's anything I can do." He paused, glancing across at McCarter. "That's a British accent you've got."

"We're a mixed-up crowd," McCarter said. "But it works for us."

The Hummer sped across the base, raising high sprays of water as it hit puddles. Through the rain McCarter could see the distant buildings of the base. Cassidy swung the Hummer to a smooth stop outside one of them. Phoenix Force climbed out, grabbed their gear from the rear and followed the major inside.

"We were asked by your people to provide the basics.

Not sure how long you'll be here, so we catered for all eventualities. Cots and bedding. Ablutions at the far end. With hot water. You have electricity. Power points. You can use the PX, if you need. Mess hall is down the line. Now this is an active base, so there's pretty well round-the-clock food available."

"All the comforts of home," Hawkins said, taking a wander around the facility.

"I could send over a TV, if you need one."

McCarter said, "I try to keep them away from television. Too many violent programs and excitement isn't good for them. The way things are moving, I doubt we'll be here long."

Cassidy stared at the Briton for a moment, before he realized it was McCarter's sense of humor breaking free.

"Something tells me that you guys will find plenty of excitement when you move on from here." He took a long look at each member of the group and made up his mind. He nodded his head in understanding. "You do realize the neighbors are not exactly the friendly kind," he said.

Cassidy had worked out for himself that this tight group of men had not come all the way to South Korea for any peaceful break. It wasn't the first time he had encountered their type. They were the guys who came without any official fanfare, stayed in the background, before they embarked on whatever mission was waiting for them, then disappeared quietly. There were occasions when they never showed their faces again, having carried out their business and moved on.

Covert operations.

Shadow warriors.

Black ops.

Need-to-know kept their operations in the dark. John Cassidy had lost his curiosity over these people long ago.

It did no good to make waves by trying to find out the reasons why. Even if he did learn their particular agendas, there was no profit. What they did was way above his pay grade, and there were some things it was better not to know. So Cassidy followed his orders. Provided what was asked for and left it at that.

"Couple of flasks over there filled with hot coffee," he said.

"Best thing I've heard all day," James said. "One thing this burg isn't is warm."

"You need anything else just call me on the wall phone over there. Hit number one and it goes straight through to my office."

"We should be getting a visitor," McCarter said.

"I was told. He'll be escorted here when he arrives."

"Thanks for your assistance," McCarter said. "Much appreciated."

When Cassidy had gone, the Phoenix Force warriors unpacked their gear and laid out their ordnance on one of the trestle tables that had been erected for their use.

James had opened one of the stainless-steel flasks and poured himself coffee.

"That is good," he said after tasting it. "Just how I like it. Now what is it? Yeah, reminds me of me. Hot and black."

"Sweet, as well?" Manning asked.

James grinned. "With what I have going for me, I don't need to be sweet, brother."

"I think he was talking about the coffee," McCarter said.

"You think?" James said innocently.

They checked out their weapons. Each man had a Beretta 92F handgun except McCarter. He adamantly refused to change from the Browning Hi-Power and carried one with him at all times. The 9 mm autopistol had served the Briton for many years, and he saw no reason to swap it for anything else; McCarter's skill with the pistol couldn't be faulted. He hit what he was aiming at ninety-nine times out of one hundred, so it was no contest. It fired the same bullets as the Beretta handguns the others used, so there was no disparity when it came to ammunition.

The same applied to the semiautomatic machine guns the team was using. Each man would carry an FN P90 SMG. The Belgian-made weapon fired 5.7 mm rounds and could deliver 900 rounds per minute from the top-mounted translucent magazine which held 50 rounds in parallel rows.

For extra silence the P90 could be fitted with a suppressor which allowed the use of special subsonic ammunition to further reduce sound. Screw-on suppressors were included in the backpacks Phoenix Force would be carrying.

Built from impact-resistant polymer, the P90 had an effective range of 200 meters. Its bullpup design allowed the weapon to maintain a compact size and add an ambidextrous capability, even to the shell casings being ejected from the underside of the SMG.

The compact P90 was easy to store and carry. A fire selector gave a safe position, semiautomatic and full-auto. With the selector in the full-auto position, the trigger allowed a two-stage pull function, where a slight pressure gave semiautofire, with the full pressure being applied for all-out auto.

Phoenix Force had used the P90 previously on clandestine missions, and where a restricted carry weight of equipment was needed, the weapon was ideal. A nylon strap could be used to sling the P90, easy to carry and bring quickly into operation.

Over their camou dress, they would wear a harness to accommodate the loaded magazines for their individual weapons. Pouches for extra magazines and a sheathed Tanto combat knife hung from each waist belt. They would also have lightweight comm sets to enable them to keep in touch, once they were dispersed on mission. McCarter also carried one of the sat phones so he could contact Stony Man, via the Zero connection, if the need arose. Lightweight backpacks would hold extra magazines, plus fragmentation and smoke grenades.

Calvin James, as the team medic, also had a field pack in his backpack.

As the resident demolitions operative, Gary Manning had a comprehensive selection of explosives in his pack, along with detonators and a couple remote units, if he needed them. Manning only had to choose the target, place the pack and activate the detonators. The burly Canadian had a sure touch with explosives, and pretty well anything he tackled would be efficiently wiped out.

The intention behind Phoenix Force's upcoming foray into North Korea was to locate the facility where the ongoing development of NNEMP weaponry was being carried out. A high-risk incursion into North Korean territory. If successful, they were aiming to destroy the development lab and any construction in progress, putting a stop to the work and an end to the research.

None of them had forgotten the second part of the mission: to locate and extract Li Kam, the young Korean woman who was putting herself on the line to provide information about the North Korean development of the NNEMP weapon.

The five men were aware of the difficulties ahead, but every mission they undertook for Stony Man was under the same rules. They handled the deals no one else could. And they undertook them with the clear proviso that, in the field, they were on their own. Phoenix Force, as with everything applied to Stony Man, officially did not exist.

Their nonexistence on any books allowed them complete freedom of operational decisions.

On the reverse side of the coin, they had no recourse to expect help, if they were compromised. Each Stony Man warrior understood the limitations of assistance he might expect if something went wrong. Hal Brognola and the team back at the Farm would do their utmost to help, but the anonymity of the setup often worked against them more than token assistance. The Stony Man operatives understood and accepted the criteria.

The safety of the Stony Man operation had to be maintained. Its success depended on it remaining a covert organization. Despite the strictures placed on them, the Stony Man teams never once considered stepping away from the responsibility that was placed in their hands. They accepted the way things were and worked on the premise that their lives were less important than the missions they were taking on. They understood the threats and the dangers placed in front of them, and stepped up to the mark each time.

Someone had to take on the madmen intent on inflicting suffering and mayhem on a beleaguered world. In truth the big wars were not always what solved global problems. Sometimes success came from a few men stepping up and putting out the small fires before they grew into raging infernos.

Phoenix Force, Able Team and even the man who had been the creative force behind them, Mack Bolan, were in for the long haul.

As they waited for their South Korean contact, the group took time to relax. Once the mission was underway, they might not get the chance. *Rest and eat when you can* was something they all ascribed to. In the field, distractions could occur at a moment's notice. Keeping their physical needs met was crucial to operational success, like the need to keep a vehicle well maintained and fueled up. Miss the signs and the vehicle could fail at a critical time.

No matter how dedicated, or motivated, the fittest men could not go on indefinitely. Pushing themselves to the limit had a point where even the toughest would begin to falter. Exhaustion would eventually be reached, and even extreme willpower would drain away.

The men of Phoenix Force were well aware of their limitations, and they would always admit to needing a recharge time. One man failing could have an effect on the others, even putting them at further risk. So staying in prime condition was more than simply important. It was vital, because none of them would want to be the one who put his teammates in jeopardy.

An hour later their contact arrived.

Tien Hiko was of average height, lean and carried himself with ease. He wore dark clothing, and there was nothing about him that suggested he was anything more than a local worker—which was how Hiko wanted to look. When he was shown into the hut, he nodded to his escort, dragged off the cloth cap he was wearing and faced Phoenix Force.

"I am Tien Hiko," he said in clear English.

McCarter made the round of introductions. Hiko studied the group, keen eyes scrutinizing them closely. He flicked his gaze over the weapons on the table, nodding to himself as he assessed the potential firepower gathered there.

"Do you think you have enough?" he asked lightly.

McCarter smiled. "I guess we'll find out, if things turn nasty."

"Going into North Korea, that is very possible and very likely."

"You been over the border?" Encizo asked.

"Yes. A couple of times. But not for as long as Kayo Pak. He has been in North Korea a long time. Perhaps too long. Under such pressure. Apart from the mission, North Korea is a sad place. Very sad."

James handed the Korean a mug of coffee, which Hiko took gratefully.

"Can you update us?" McCarter asked. "Don't want to hurry you, but we get the feeling things are kind of on the knife edge. We were briefed before we left. I just want to confirm we're talking the same language."

"Kayo Pak lives in a fishing village on the coast about five miles from the research center. He has a sound base there as a net repairman and fisherman, which allows him to move around. We built him a full background before he went in, and it's holding. He feeds us information about what goes on there.

"He's the guy you have to thank for the data we forwarded. In turn he's been receiving the data from his own person working at the base. Li Kam is a North Korean who trained as a specialist in pulse physics in Pyongyang. She works in Emanuel Absalom's department on the current project. Her knowledge on the NNEMP is second only to Absalom's."

"And she *can* be trusted?" Hawkins asked. His skepticism was not hidden.

Hiko nodded. "If you read her file, you'll understand she has no reason to love the North Korean regime." He tapped the folder.

"Is she in the clear?" McCarter asked. "I'm sure there must be one hell of an investigation going on following the Hawaiian incident."

Hiko nodded. "In her last contact with Pak, she said that Major Choi, the man in command of the project, has shut the place down. No one in or out of the compound any longer, except for the military. So she's inside. Choi is going to be checking into every aspect of the operation."

"And if she's caught?"

Hiko didn't need to respond. He simply opened the file and slid out a photograph. It showed an attractive young woman in her late twenties. It was the same image Phoenix Force had seen back at Stony Man during their briefing.

"We need to get her out of that place," Hiko said. "And if possible destroy the research lab. Li has confirmed that all the specifications for the project are kept there in a main computer bank. If the place is destroyed, the North Koreans lose everything they've built up. Years of it. And Kayo Pak needs to leave, as well. He's risked too much himself to stay behind now. He will relocate in South Korea and take up other duties."

"Can you contact him?"

"Yes."

"We'll go in and meet him," McCarter said. "He can guide us to the base."

"You cannot simply cross the border and walk to the base. It is at the top of North Korea, a long way from even the closest crossing. Bordering China and Russia. And also your faces would not fit."

McCarter dropped a hand on the Korean's shoulder.

"We won't be walking across country, old son. We discussed this during the flight. The U.S. Navy can ferry us up to where we can swim ashore and meet Pak right on his home ground."

"You make it sound so easy."

Encizo said, "It won't be easy. No question there, Hiko. These things never are. But one way or the other, we have to do it."

Hiko nodded. "Yes. Major Choi is a hard man. Extremely suspicious of everything. If he works out that Li Kam was responsible for creating the *accident,* he will have her arrested and taken away. If that happens, we may not be able to save her."

"Up to us to get to her first, then," Encizo said.

"How soon can we move out?" McCarter asked.

"Let me finish this coffee while you put your gear together, then we can go."

"Tell me more about Li Kam," McCarter said as he started to pack his equipment.

"Li Kam has been doing this for a couple years," Hiko explained. "Her parents died at the hands of the North Korean regime. They were just simple fisherfolk who ran up against a local corrupt administrator. When they refused to back down, the man had them arrested and sent to one of the camps for so-called reindoctrination.

"They survived for almost a year in the same camp but were separated. They saw each other every day through a barbed-wire fence. Kam's father died first. He just gave up. Refused to work so the guards beat him every time he defied them. In the end he died from his prolonged injuries. The day after he died, Kam's mother took her own life by tearing open her wrists on the barbed wire.

"Li Kam was later recruited by Kayo. Her computer skills and qualifications in physics already had her fast-tracked into the North Korean program, looking into pulse weapons, when she was noticed by agents searching for new talent. Believe me, Li is no fool when it comes to putting on a performance. She submitted a paper praising Emanuel Absalom's work.

"After Absalom had read her paper, even before he signed on with the North Koreans, he had asked for her to join the team. She was offered a position in the research department working on NNEMP weapons. We couldn't have done better if we'd chosen ourselves."

"And she's been able to feed you data?" McCarter asked.

"She's been our eyes and ears on the project for the last few months. Her qualifications as a system physicist have been invaluable. She has been able to interpret all the research being done. And she has kept a close watch on Absalom's work on a daily basis. Her only regret is the fact she was unable to prewarn us about the Hawaii test. Even she was not informed about it. She knew there was going to be a field trial, but the location was kept from everyone in the facility."

"Sounds as if there isn't much departmental trust in that place," Encizo said.

"You're not wrong there," Hiko said. "The North Korean military mind-set has a default that is fixed on paranoia. They exist on mistrust. They can't, won't, trust. In their eyes, there's a sinister plot around every corner. Which makes for an extremely suspicious atmosphere." Hiko paused. "This is where our deceptions have been blessed. To have Li actually inside the project was something we could not have planned better."

McCarter said, "How the hell have you managed that?"

Hiko smiled. "With care and a lot of luck, I guess." He took a moment to reflect. "Li's worst times come when Major Choi is prowling around. He oversees the research unit for the North Korean hierarchy. A real party man who watches and listens to everything, from what Li tells me. He allows no slack in the lab. Everything has to be according to the rules. He would see any deviation as deliberate. You break the rules with Choi, and *he'll* break you."

"Sounds like a barrel of laughs," Hawkins muttered. "Let's hope we don't run across him."

Hiko inclined his head. "If you do, you'll recognize him."

"Has there been much from Li Kam since the Hawaiian mishap?" Manning asked.

"She managed to get one brief message to Pak about how things have been tightened up, before the site was closed off. The unit is on edge. Choi is convinced the problem lies there."

"He believes they're at fault?" McCarter said.

"For what?" Hawkins asked. "An error? Sabotage?"

Hiko remained silent, and it was that nonanswer that made McCarter look at him closely.

"Bugger me," he said. "You know what happened. Don't keep us hanging, mate."

"Choi is right that the fault came from inside the unit."

"But he can't figure out what caused it?" James said.

Hiko shook his head. "He has no proof. Not yet at least. He had guaranteed no one in the unit would learn when and where the test took place. The only one in the unit who had prior knowledge was Absalom and, of course, Major Choi. So he had to be careful about accusing anyone."

Hawkins said, "Son of a bitch. If Choi finds out who worked the sabotage, it could end up being hard on her."

"Yes." Hiko went on, "Li knew a test was planned but not where or when. The only way she could attempt a breakdown was by planting a bug in the programmed system. One of her specialties is computer coding. She planted a worm in the program. It was supposed to destroy the outgoing missile before it reached the target.

"Unfortunately it worked the opposite way. The NNEMP reached its target because the worm acted too slowly. It reduced the NNEMP's effect to less than was expected. Even so, it still caused damage on the Coast Guard base and killed the members of the helicopter caught in the burst. But it also blew back into the launch platform on board the vessel. The explosion damaged the ship and caused it to sink." Hiko shrugged. "I don't have any regrets about the North Koreans who were killed. What they did was an act of war."

"And Li?" James asked.

"What do you think?" Hiko said. "I do not think she will have any regrets—apart from the fact her sabotage did not work exactly to plan. The North Koreans killed her family. She would see this as going partway to getting some kind of justice."

"So Choi hasn't been able to figure out how this happened?" McCarter said.

"Not yet. He doesn't have enough computer knowledge himself to be able to understand something like that. From what Li passed to Pak earlier, Absalom would be in the dark, too. He understands the NNEMP but has to depend on Li and the other techs to translate his theories into computer language.

"For Absalom, losing the ship meant they also lost the unit. He's going to be more concerned about that than the loss of life. Until they get their hands on that unit, they won't be able to work out what happened, unless one of the techs can figure it out and discover that someone altered the computer program."

"A tricky time for Li," Manning said. "If this Major Choi is as keen as you suggest, he'll be keeping the research team under close watch while he investigates."

"It's certain he won't be making things easy for them," Hiko said. "Choi will be under pressure from Pyongyang to find out what happened. His own career will be at risk, as well."

"And the North Koreans can't openly claim the wreck, because they'd be admitting they were involved," Encizo added.

"Yes," Hiko said. "They will be angry at the loss of valuable equipment but fearful that any recovery might point the finger at them, if there's anything left to identify. So their team in Hawaii is going to be uneasy."

"We need to update our people and have a watch put on the area," McCarter said.

He moved away and took out his sat phone to put in a call to Stony Man. When he made contact, he brought Brognola up-to-date with the situation.

"I'll pass the information along to Able Team," Brognola said. "They'll need to be aware the North Koreans may be mounting a damage limitation operation. Once the salvage team makes recovery, time is going to be on short supply for the Koreans."

"They'll be in a panic," McCarter said. "And that will make them even more dangerous."

"We need to ramp up your mission," Brognola pointed out. "If suspicion falls on Li Kam, she'll be taken down fast. You need to get into North Korea and extract her. And put that damn research facility out of action, as well."

"Okay," McCarter said. "Shall we do the weekly grocery shopping at the same time, boss?"

Brognola gave a gruff chuckle. "Sorry, was I being a little heavy-handed there?"

"The bruises won't show if I stay in the shadows."

"Just go carefully. I want you guys back in one piece. All of you." Brognola cleared his throat. "Stay safe."

McCarter ended the call, a slow smile edging his lips as he stowed away the sat phone.

"They're on it," he said as he rejoined the group. "Our team in Hawaii is about to get an update on the situation." He turned to Hiko. "And we need to make tracks for North Korea. Is the research site heavily defended?" McCarter asked, scanning the map.

"There is a small military unit stationed at the research facility," Hiko said. "Choi keeps the place low-key. The site is pretty isolated, so they don't get too many visitors. Locals stay well away. The last thing they want is to come within range of the guards' weapons. There are helicopters for ferrying people back and forth, and making air patrols.

"The research team lives on site. They only leave occasionally to make trips to the local village to buy fresh food and to take breaks from the lab. When they do, they are driven there by the soldiers and supervised. Li Kam passes her information to Kayo Pak when she goes to the village. But since the Hawaii problem, Major Choi has halted all outside activity for the research people. All other supplies and equipment are flown in."

Encizo tapped the map. "Not far from the coast. That could be a possible way in for us."

"There's a small natural harbor close by," Hiko explained. "It is where a security section is housed. Li said the area is watched over by a couple patrol boats stationed in the bay."

McCarter spent some time poring over the map and the coastline that bordered the harbor. "So we go for insertion from the water. Just like we discussed on the plane," he said.

Manning said, "Get the Navy to ferry us in as close as they can and let us off."

"You realize how cold that water will be this time of year?" Hawkins said. "Not that I don't like cold water. Preferably in a glass with ice cubes on a hot day."

"Man has a point," Encizo said.

"Bunch of old ladies," McCarter scoffed. "Hiko?"

"Not impossible," the Korean said. "You would need to allow time to get over the low temperature. Not much point having all those weapons if you're too cold to handle them."

"I bloody hate it when common sense prevails over reckless adventurism," McCarter said. "But I bow to your wisdom. So we'll go in a couple hours before dawn. Find ourselves a spot to get organized and thaw out the blue bits."

McCarter couldn't come up with any alternative scenarios. Coming in by land would have been more or less impossible given the distance from the North-South line. An air drop posed similar restrictions. Even a HALO jump would have left them open to being spotted by the North Koreans. The ocean incursion looked to be the most likely, and even that was not without its problems.

Apart from having Stony Man run some satellite scans over the research station, Phoenix Force would be going in with limited forward planning. It was not the most advisable way to make a strike. If this had been done the correct way, there would have been time spent on meticulous planning, with every avenue explored and every possibility covered.

Stony Man and the operatives who carried out the missions under its banner very seldom had that privilege. They were, as usual, given their orders and moved on them within a short time. Once in the field, they hit hard, and they hit fast, without having to refer back to their base whether a target was a go.

Nor did they need to wait for permission to pull the trigger; decisions were made on the spot, and the covert operatives were not beholden to anyone sitting hundreds, maybe thousands, of miles away. Split-second assessments were made by Phoenix Force and Able Team, because an enemy might have his own weapon up and ready to fire. Survival, the success or failure of a mission, came down to simple field decisions. McCarter understood these criteria, and he trusted his team to work along the same lines.

"You okay?"

McCarter glanced up from the map and looked across the table at Gary Manning. The broad-shouldered Canadian had a serious expression on his face.

"Fine," the Briton said.

"Really? You want to convince me? From here you look worried."

"This could be a tricky one," McCarter said. "We're going in with little, or no, intel on the target. Into a bad place. And…"

"And we've done this before. Many times," Manning said. "We all understand the setup." Manning lowered his voice. "No sweat, David. We're behind you. Don't worry about the rest of us. You lead the charge, and we'll follow." He paused, then said, "In this case it could be a hell of a distance behind." A grin followed his final words.

"There I was thinking I'm the crazy one on this team."

"Don't you believe it, mate."

CHAPTER EIGHT

Barbara Price, the mission controller, listened as McCarter outlined what Phoenix Force required and refrained from making any comments, until he had finished. She was used to the combat teams requesting the impossible, and even as McCarter was outlining his request, her agile mind was working on the logistics of the problem.

"I'll get back to you ASAP," she said.

"Sorry, love," McCarter's voice came over the sat phone. "I know it's a lot to ask."

Price chuckled. "No problem," she said. "Have I ever let you down before?"

"No. I'll wait for your call."

Price clicked off and leaned against her desk, staring across the room as she assimilated McCarter's request. She ran a hand through her hair, took a breath and picked up an internal phone. She pushed a button.

"Hal. Barb. We need to talk. Fast. And you have to get the President on standby."

"I DID SAY anything your people needed?" the President asked. "Remind me, Hal."

Brognola smiled at the President's grim humor. "Sir, I cannot tell a lie."

"Stay on your end, and I'll call you back. Let's see if I really do have the clout I like to imagine I have."

Brognola glanced across at Price as she entered his office.

"We still in a job?" she asked.

"I'll let you know when the Man phones back. He's about to start calling in some heavy favors on this one."

"I had a word with Aaron. He's opening a secure line through to Zero. He's asked for a satellite sweep of the North Korean location Hiko gave us."

One of Brognola's multiple desk phones rang. He picked up. It was Kurtzman.

"We have our feed from Zero," the cyberboss said. "We'll keep monitoring. How is it at your end?"

"On hold until I hear from the President," Brognola explained. "He'll be burning the wire right now trying to find a ride for David and company."

"Sounds just like a Phoenix request."

"Call you back, Aaron," Brognola said, as he cut Kurtzman off and picked up the ringing phone.

"Your people have their ride, Hal."

"Thank you, Mr. President."

"You need to make a call to Navy HQ in South Korea. A Commander Halbrecht is waiting for your call. He'll be your Navy liaison, deal with the logistics, and arrange for Phoenix Force to be picked up and taken to rendezvous with a submarine patrolling the area. Wish your team good luck from me, Hal." There was a brief pause. "Call if you need anything more."

"Thanks again, Mr. President."

CHAPTER NINE

The Virginia Class sub was 377 feet in length and had a displacement of 7,800 tons. The sub's power came from a nuclear reactor that converted seawater into superheated steam. The steam drove the turbines that powered the boat and also provided electrical power to the whole of the sub. The reactor had a conservative lifespan of around thirty years. The Virginia Class subs were the U.S. Navy's near-impregnable weapons capable of staying at sea for months at a time.

Apart from the tremendous power and speed, Virginia Class subs boasted impressive firepower. They carried Tomahawk missiles that were fired via twelve VLS tubes, as well as Mk48 ADCAP torpedoes launched from four more tubes.

The advanced navigation allowed automatic control and the sub could patrol in shallow water, unseen and unheard. The ultrasophisticated antidetection capability enabled the sub to operate in hostile waters without being compromised and, coupled with the sensor arrays, gave it the ability to see and hear enemy mines and ships. It could hover motionless even in shallow water.

There was no conventional periscope. Instead, a state-of-the-art photonics system was installed, which enabled real-time imaging that more than one person could see at a time. In the control room, monitors mounted around the bulkhead walls were viewed by the on-duty crew, so they

could see exactly what was taking place outside the sub.
There were wall-mounted monitors in certain of the personnel quarters, as well.

Once on board, Phoenix Force was invited to the wardroom, where they were met by the sub's commander, Captain Deveraux, his XO and a third crew member.

McCarter was the first to step forward, holding out a
hand to the sub's captain, a man in his early forties, tall,
lean, fit looking. "You must think we're a pain in the butt,
Captain Deveraux. Waltzing in like a bunch of VIPs."

Deveraux returned the Briton's hard grip while his
steady gaze settled on McCarter's tanned features. The
captain saw something in the other's eyes that told him he
was dealing with someone not to be passed over lightly.
He saw honesty, as well as the measure of a man who had
been through all kinds of combat hell and had lived to tell
the tale.

Over McCarter's shoulder, Deveraux saw the same qual-
ities in his team: a group of men who went about their business without show, or any kind of macho posturing. These,
he saw, were real warriors who did not proclaim their skills,
because they had no need to.

"You obviously have strong connections," Deveraux
said. "I had a call from the Secretary of the Navy himself,
who it seems had a similar call from the Commander in
Chief." He caught McCarter's eye and grinned. "What the
hell. I can't argue with credentials like that."

McCarter thought it was sometimes a good thing to have
connections. In the case of the upcoming, highly illegal
mission Phoenix Force was about to embark on, having
those high-end connections was a real boost.

Deveraux got the team seated at the wardroom table,
making swift introductions to the two members of his crew
already waiting.

"My XO, Phil Jacobi. And this is Chief Rossi, who will be organizing your underwater gear. Tell him what you want, and he'll set it up for you." Deveraux made for the door. "I'll leave you in good hands. Time to get this operation underway," he said as he left the wardroom.

Rossi was a powerful-looking man with broad shoulders and an amiable expression on his face. "I heard from the Captain you're going to swim in along with your equipment."

McCarter nodded. "We had to make a quick choice, Chief. Going in by water seemed to be the best one."

"That's fine," Rossi said. "You all checked out with scuba equipment?"

"We are," McCarter said. "We'll appreciate any advice you have to offer."

Rossi nodded. "I'll run you through the procedures. We've got the best equipment the Navy has on its books, so you guys will be okay."

"I'd feel a lot better if you told me it was bulletproof," Hawkins said.

"We're not that advanced," Rossi said. "But working on it."

"I'll have to stand behind Gary again," Hawkins said.

"Why me?" Manning asked.

"You're big and brawny," Hawkins said. "You'll stop a bullet."

Jacobi, pouring coffee from an insulated jug, shook his head at the banter. "I take it you people have been working together a while?"

James took the offered coffee. "Thanks. And, yes, we have."

The XO handed around the rest of the filled mugs.

They spent a half hour discussing equipment needs and what they might expect when they reach the North Korean shore. Jacobi laid out a Navy chart and highlighted the section they were dealing with.

"From intel on the area," Jacobi advised, "we understand it's not all that heavily defended. Pretty remote area. Not much in the way of civilian population there. Couple small villages along the coast. Fishermen. We can check the area before we surface and drop you."

"But they do patrol the water?" Manning said.

Jacobi nodded. "Our people have logged in patrols, so we can pick our time. The NK keep to a rigid schedule out there. These guys are not very flexible. They have a course, and they stick to it like glue."

"Handy to know," Encizo said. "How close in can you get us?"

"That's where we score," Jacobi said. "Water's pretty deep along that stretch of coast. There's a natural trench that runs all along here." He traced a finger across the chart. "We'll stay submerged as long as we can and get you close into shore, so you only have a short swim."

"What about defensive measures?" McCarter asked. "No problem with mines? Detection equipment?"

"Unless they've planted them since a week ago, we haven't come across anything. Our equipment on board will tell us if anything nasty has been placed."

"Almost too good to be true," Manning said.

"How long do you figure to be ashore?" Jacobi asked.

"For as little time as possible," McCarter said. "In-and-out scenario. Depends on how it plays. No way we can pin it down to absolutes, but if we can hit hard and fast, catch the North Koreans off guard, we might be able to keep it short and sweet."

CHIEF ROSSI HAD all the equipment laid out for them: wet suits, bodyform thermal underwear and the scuba gear.

"This should keep out the chill," he said. "Worn it myself and it's pretty good."

"Not exactly going to make a fashion statement," James said.

"The ladies might go for the Jed Clampett look," Hawkins suggested.

"In case the NKs pick up this equipment, they won't find any manufacturing ID. This isn't the first time we've had to operate covertly. So it's all generic gear. No way it can be traced back."

"Handy to know," McCarter said. "Chief, this is bloody marvelous. So all we have to do now is slip into NK, blow up Major Choi's fun palace, and escape with the girl and her buddy."

"Sounds just like a James Bond movie," James said.

"Good luck there," Chief Rossi said.

He moved to the far end of the equipment displayed. "Rebreather units," he said. "You familiar with these?"

"They recycle the used air, clean it and let the diver use it again," Manning said.

"No telltale bubbles," Encizo said. "Means we don't have to wear heavy air tanks."

Rossi shook his head. "Anything you guys *don't* know?"

Hawkins held up a hand. "Yeah, how do we transfer out to a noncombat unit?"

"The question every swab jockey asks when a general alert sounds," Rossi said, a wide grin on his face.

Manning checked over the closest unit.

"Clean as you can get," Rossi said. "No manufacturers' markings. No serial numbers. These babies are as pure as the air we put in the tanks. You leave these behind, they could have come from anywhere."

"Really?" James said.

"Short of inscribing them with ET's home address, we try not to advertise."

"Chief, you could make a fortune working in a Chinese knock-off factory," Manning said.

"I've thought about that, sir, but my conscience wouldn't let me."

"Yeah, right," Hawkins drawled.

Rossi walked them through the rest of the prepared gear, watching quietly as Phoenix Force responded. He was quickly made aware the team knew exactly what they were dealing with. Once he had familiarized them with the equipment, they changed from their outer clothing and got into the scuba gear.

"Man, I'm glad none of my lady friends can see me in these LJs," James said. "It would really put a cramp in my style."

"Calvin," Hawkins said, "you do not have style. And pull that wet suit on, brother, before I go blind."

CHAPTER TEN

The sub had been rigged for silent running, coming in at just under a half mile from the North Korean coast. The word had come from the captain that they were as close as they could risk. The sub was resting on the bottom, all non-essential operations suspended to maintain absolute silence.

"You ready?" Deveraux asked.

McCarter nodded. "As we'll ever be," he said cheerfully.

"He likes to look on the bright side," Manning said.

"What bright side?" Encizo asked.

Phoenix Force was now clad in the wet suits Rossi had laid out for them, with the rebreather units strapped in place. Hawkins and Encizo carried the bulky pack-cloth waterproof bag holding their clothing, backpacks and ordnance. When they reached dry land, they would change into the combat gear and the bag, containing the underwater equipment, would be buried for later retrieval. The bag was equipped with buoyancy inserts to prevent it from sinking to the bottom of the sea once they were in the water.

"We'll stay on the bottom, within range of your transponder," Deveraux said. "Minute we receive your signal, we'll move in to pick you up."

"Sounds so simple when you say it like that," James said.

Deveraux smiled encouragingly. "We try our best."

They reached the aft section of the sub and the access hatch leading into the lockout trunk. The solid door opened with a hiss of hydraulics, exposing the interior. Phoenix

Force donned their swim fins before they eased into the chamber. With the addition of the equipment bag, it was a close fit.

Chief Rossi said, "I wouldn't like to try and slip a hundred-dollar bill between you guys. Good thing you know each other well."

"I'm okay," McCarter quipped. "Not so sure about these bums, though."

The chamber door swung shut behind them, a dull red light casting a baleful glow over the team. They heard the seals lock into place, and moments later, water began to flood across the base of the chamber. Masks were slipped on and mouthpieces adjusted. The chill water began to rise swiftly, as the pressure was increased.

It was handy that not one of Phoenix Force suffered from claustrophobia. If they had, the chamber would surely have triggered panic. The actual escape tube could only take two at a time, so the Force paired up to rise to the upper hatch. Encizo manhandled the bulky equipment bag up through the tube.

Phoenix Force finally eased out through the chamber and cleared the sub. McCarter, last out, swung the hatch shut with a solid thump and locked it, letting the sub know they were out. As he pushed away from the gray underwater craft, McCarter was able to view it in its entirety, realizing at that moment just how large the Virginia Class sub was. The huge bulk began to move aside slowly, not gaining any kind of speed until it was well clear of the area. As the distance grew, the sub became an indistinct shape before vanishing completely.

Phoenix Force formed into a loose group, James in front, guiding them through the murky water as they swam for the shore. He wore an illuminated compass on a wristband, using it to guide them in. The water *was* cold. They could

feel the chill, despite the wet suits and the thermal underwear, but at least their gear protected them from the low
temperature of the Sea of Japan. The movement of the restless surge churned up swirling banks of sand that formed
clouds across their path. James kept them on course, checking time and distance as they slid through the water.

The rebreather units worked well, scrubbing out the possible effects of used air and recycling it. It might not have
been the freshest they had ever breathed, but at least they
were not leaving behind a trail of bubbles to rise to the surface and possibly give them away.

The distance might have been under half a mile, but the
restless movement of the chill water made the going hard.
Not wanting to exhaust themselves, Phoenix Force took
it slowly. They maintained a steady pace. After a time,
McCarter and Manning took over from Encizo and
Hawkins, grasping the loops fixed to the sides of the equipment bag. Despite the buoyancy inserts, the bag was still
a solid weight, and they had to maintain a firm grip as the
moving sea tugged at the bag as they swam.

James led them up toward the surface as they neared the
shoreline. The murky water was not as deep now, and light
penetrated it the closer they got to land. They were also
experiencing the push and pull of the water. As it rolled in
against the shore, the waves strengthened.

Within twenty feet of the beach, the water became even
shallower. Pressure from the surge of waves threatened to
overpower them, and they had to physically resist, feeling
the sand under their feet moving in time to the breakers.

James was the first to put his head above water, bracing
himself against the slam of the waves. He saw the beach
ahead and made a quick scan.

A ragged stretch of sand and rocks gave way to tangled bushes and trees. It was already starting to get light,

the sky overhead streaked with clouds, and he could feel a cool breeze on his face. The area had a bleakness that was a long way from welcoming.

"What the hell," James muttered to himself. "We didn't expect a beach party."

The rest of Phoenix Force emerged, cautiously at first, until they got the all clear from James. Then they moved quickly from the water to the beach, and into the comparative protection of nearby rocks.

"We have a half hour before first light," McCarter said. "Time to get into our clothes and arm up. No time to waste. Get this stuff off and into the bag. We bury it, wait for Kayo Pak, then do the marching bit. Let's go, fellers. Cal, you stand watch for us."

James nodded, as he pulled one of the FN P90s from the weapon bag. He ran a quick check, set the selector to semi-auto and moved a few yards up the beach to stand guard, while the others disposed of masks and swim fins. They slipped out of the rebreather units. The wet suits were last. The camou BDUs were pulled on over the one-piece underwear, socks and boots next, then each man harnessed up. SMGs and handguns were checked, Tanto knives slipped into sheaths on their belts. As soon as the main group was ready, Hawkins took James's place while the tall black commando did his own quick change.

The scuba gear, including the rebreather units, went into the large pack-cloth bag. The watertight zip was secured, and the bulky bag was dropped into a hastily excavated hole well above the tide mark, dug using the folding spades they had brought along in the bag. The removed coarse sand was used to cover the bag and the location marked by its proximity to a low rock formation.

Hiko had been correct about the chilly sea conditions. The water had lowered their body temperature, and each man was forced the move around, flexing taut muscles until they increased their body heat.

They all donned their comm sets and ran checks on them.

"About ten minutes before we get full light," McCarter said. "Let's stay sharp, ladies. We don't know what kind of reception we might get, so let's go in ready. And remember we do not hesitate if a situation crops up. My rule is, take the shot before the other guy does. Understood? Five of us go in. I want to see seven come out."

He was referring to Kayo Pak and Li Kam not being abandoned in North Korea when the mission was over.

CHAPTER ELEVEN

The daylight spread as they waited, pushing away shadows that might have helped conceal them. Phoenix Force waited in silence. It was not the first time they had been forced to wait for the arrival of a local contact, and even though they might have been concerned, none of it showed.

Aware of Kayo Pak's situation as a covert agent, they understood the man's position. Pak could not simply stroll around and behave in a casual manner. He existed in a knife-edge world of deception, in one of the most restrictive regimes on Earth. There was not a man in Phoenix Force who envied the South Korean's undercover mission. North Korea, under the control of its fearsome leader, lived in fear of betrayal and harsh recrimination. Even in this remote region, the shadow of Pyongyang hung over it. Kayo Pak was in that shadow, day by day, and the men of Phoenix Force could do nothing less than admire the bravery of the man.

"You think he's okay?" Manning asked over the comm set.

"In his position," McCarter replied, "I reckon he can be forgiven if he's late."

"Let's hope that's all it is," Encizo murmured.

McCarter looked up as he heard soft footfalls in the brush just ahead of the Force's position. He leveled his P90, the suppressed muzzle locking onto the spot.

The brush parted and a lean figure clad in dark peasant clothing moved cautiously into view. Even under the cap the man wore, his face was recognizable as the one on the ID photo Hiko had showed them.

It was Kayo Pak.

In his early forties, he was on the short side. Thick black hair hung from under his cap, reaching his collar. His eyes flicked back and forth, as he scanned the beach and rocks. Pak carried a black handgun in his left hand.

"Kayo Pak," McCarter called out.

The figure turned in his direction.

"Coyle...Jack Coyle?"

McCarter rose to his full height and walked in Pak's direction. He held out his right hand, grasping the Korean's.

"There are patrols out," Pak said. "I had to make a detour."

"No need to apologize."

The rest of Phoenix Force emerged from cover to group around the Korean. McCarter took out a spare comm set linkup and handed it to Pak.

"Maybe they're nervous because of what happened in Hawaii," James said.

Pak nodded. "Exactly so. I offered Li Kam a small transceiver unit some time ago, only to be used in strict emergencies. Yesterday she did for the first time. Said Major Choi is agitated because of the accident on the ship. She also said he is desperate to find out how this happened."

"You think he might suspect sabotage?"

"Li believes that to be so."

"Then we need to get her out ASAP," McCarter said. "And you, Kayo. Time to call it a day."

Pak nodded. "I would be lying if I said I don't need a vacation from this place."

"Let's do it, then," McCarter said. "*Transceiver?* Bloody hell, that was risky."

"Our whole setup is risky. Li has to be so careful in case

she is discovered. Yes, it is very risky, but we needed to be able to get in touch."

"If everything goes well," McCarter said, "you'll be able to close that down for good."

"I look forward to that," Pak said.

"Kayo, cut the path for us, then. The sooner we get this bloody show on the road, the better I'll like it."

The Korean led the way, McCarter behind him and the rest of Phoenix Force in a line. Encizo brought up the rear, keeping a constant check on their back trail.

Off the beach they quickly moved into a landscape of gnarled timber and undergrowth, the scattered rocks lining the beach giving way to harsh grass and rutted earth. A steady breeze filtered down through the timber, bringing the threat of rain, and within ten minutes the first drops came. The wind curved in from the north, the increasing shower slanting across the terrain and hitting them head-on. The initial light shower increased quickly. The rain was chilled and showed no sign of letting up, as Pak led Phoenix Force on a northwesterly course.

The rain impacted against their exposed faces, sharp on bare flesh. If it hadn't been for the waterproofed outer clothing, they would have been severely tested. Despite that, the rain made for hard going as the ground underfoot quickly turned soft, the soil becoming little more than mud.

After forty minutes Pak raised a hand to stop them. McCarter closed in behind the man, as the Korean crouched in the cover of thick undergrowth.

"The road down to the harbor is that way. Through those trees. That's a couple miles away. If we move parallel, we should see the research unit directly ahead."

"How far?" the Briton asked.

"No more than a mile."

McCarter relayed the information to the rest of Phoenix

Force. He sent Encizo to run a check on the area and report any unexpected movements. The Cuban simply nodded and withdrew, easing into the undergrowth.

"Keep eyes open from here on in," McCarter said to the rest. "Remember what Kayo said about patrols. And don't forget what I said earlier. If there's a face-to-face, deal with it."

Pak said, "Good advice. Choi's men will be working on a similar rule. This facility does not appreciate visitors. Because of the Hawaiian strike, Choi will be anxious. If he feels the place has been compromised in any way, he will have given orders to shoot first and worry about the consequences later."

Pak's words were heard by the others.

At McCarter's suggestion, each man located the suppressors they carried in their backpacks, threading them on to the barrels of their P90s.

"We get the message," Hawkins said.

"Move on," McCarter said and tapped Pak on the shoulder. "Onward and upward."

Pak wasn't exactly certain what the words meant, but he decided they meant *let's go*, so he pushed forward.

THEIR TARGET LOOMED out of the persistent gloom and falling rain two hundred yards ahead.

A chain-link enclosure with a steel gate. Inside was a hybrid structure, part stone with added sections created from prefabricated material. There were two watchtowers that held manned machine guns. Each tower had a searchlight capable of traversing fully 360 degrees. They had been built on each side of the entrance gate. At the far side of the enclosure was a cleared area where a pair of MD-500 Defender helicopters stood. A number of military vehicles could also be seen, parked near the main entrance of the two-story central building. To one side was a large fuel-holding tank and a squat generator building. A cell phone tower could be seen at the rear of the building.

"Li has told me the lower floor is where the soldiers sleep. Choi has his office on the same floor. A cook house is situated at the far side of the building," Pak said. "All the research is done on the upper floor. That is where Li works alongside Absalom and the rest of the research team."

McCarter was studying the layout as Pak gave him the lowdown on the site.

"All the comforts of home," he said. "Pretty well self-sufficient."

"Done that way so there is little contact with the outside. Given the fact this place is a distance away from anywhere, the isolation works in Pyongyang's favor. Out of sight, out of mind. Choi can run his operation in safety."

McCarter said, "With a bit of luck we can change all that today." He glanced up at the heavily overcast sky and the increased rainfall. "This keeps up, it should help cover our way in."

That was not the way it went.

CHAPTER TWELVE

ABLE TEAM, HAWAII

Able Team picked up the SUV rental that had been left for them at Hickam Air Force Base as their transport to the hotel where rooms had been reserved for them by Price. Blancanales drove, Lyons at his side, while Schwarz reclined in the rear.

"Nice," Blancanales said as he glanced out the window at the sunny Hawaiian scenery. "Maybe we could have Stony Man move here."

Behind him Schwarz gave an amused chuckle.

"*What?*" Blancanales asked, sensing his partner was about to make some careless remark that would annoy Lyons.

"This brochure about the hotel. We could have a problem, Gadgets. It lists all the hotel amenities. But right at the bottom it says no pets allowed. I mean, what do we do with Carl?"

Lyons's shoulders rose a little as he heard the remark. He didn't do anything else. He was learning, albeit slowly, to not always react to his partners' comments, because, if he didn't, they lost some of the sting.

"I suppose he could bunk down in the car," Blancanales suggested. "We could toss him blankets and a pillow from the window."

Unable to resist a comeback, Lyons muttered, "I could suggest *something* being thrown out the window."

"I don't think we'll be getting much free time to sample the hotel amenities," Schwarz said. "We never do."

There was an easy silence as Blancanales negotiated the busy road. Honolulu was well known for having a heavy traffic problem. The highway buzzed with vehicles.

"So this Oscar Kalikani is with the HPD?" Schwarz asked.

"He's part of a special security detail team," Lyons said. "Task Force status. Hal wasn't all that forthcoming."

"Spooks," Schwarz muttered.

"Not CIA, I hope," Blancanales said.

"We'll see," Lyons said.

Blancanales signaled and turned into the hotel parking area. He found a slot and eased the rental into the space. The cool of the vehicle gave way to the Hawaiian heat as they climbed out. They grabbed their carry bags and crossed to the hotel entrance, went inside and found themselves in the cool again. As they crossed to the reception desk, a tall, lean figure rose from one of the easy chairs in the lounge area and intercepted them.

Oscar Kalikani was dressed in light-colored pants and a bright Hawaiian print shirt that covered, but did not completely hide, the handgun holstered on his right hip. His black hair was collar length, his light brown skin around his jawline showing a faint stubble. He was a good-looking man. He extended his hand to show the badge he held.

"Kalikani," he said.

Lyons introduced his team, then took the Hawaiian's hand. Kalikani led them back to where he had been sitting. When Able Team was seated, he waved a server across and ordered cold drinks for them all.

"You guys made good time," he said.

"Uncle Sam Airways," Blancanales said. "Never late."

Kalikani had an easy smile, and he had a casual look that stopped short of his intense blue eyes.

"We can move when you're ready," he said. "Don't want to sound pushy, but this thing is running hot."

"We know about the incident," Lyons said.

Their drinks arrived, tall frosted glasses holding chilled fruit juices.

Blancanales was the first to sample his and made an approving sound. "That is good."

"So what are we looking at?" Lyons asked impatiently.

If Kalikani noticed, he didn't let it show. "Since I got the call from the mainland, I started digging. I came up with a name known to me, a guy called Tomas Meeker. This *haole* runs close to the edge. Works both sides of the street, depending who holds the money. He gave me some information on a team working for some *pake*."

Lyons shook his head. "Translate."

"Sorry. *Pake* is Hawaiian for Chinese."

"Give us time and we'll catch on," Schwarz said. "So any particular Chinese?"

"Meeker wouldn't say too much over the phone. He gets a little paranoid. Thinks people listen in to his calls."

Schwarz smiled. "These days that isn't being paranoid."

"He wants to meet?" Lyons said.

"At the Maunakea Market. Across town. You guys ready for a fast tour of the city?"

"Give me five minutes to check in," Lyons said.

Their reservations were on the hotel system. Once they were registered, Able Team left their bags with the desk to be taken to their rooms, then followed Kalikani outside.

CHAPTER THIRTEEN

Maunakea Market was a noisy kaleidoscope of stalls and people thrust together in a crowded location. If Able Team had not been on duty, they might have allowed themselves to enjoy the surroundings. Despite that, they were unable to avoid the loud vocals.

"Makes Walmart look positively dreary," Schwarz muttered, as they stepped inside through the red brick entrance.

"Is this Meeker reliable?" Blancanales asked.

"I've done business with him before, but the guy operates for money. What can I say?" Kalikani jabbed a finger at the avenue between the stalls and said, "Along here."

"It always this busy?" Lyons said. He was uncomfortable in the closed area. The crowded stalls made the narrow walkways seem more closed in. Lyons kept his hand on the Python under his shirt.

"Today," Kalikani said, "is a quiet day." The Hawaiian slipped out his cell and keyed a number. He listened until someone picked up. "Kalikani. I'm at Maunakea Market with our visitors. Heading for a meet with Tomas Meeker. Have a couple units in the area to provide backup if needed."

"Are we early, or is your guy late?" Schwarz asked.

Kalikani made a soft sound in his throat. "I was just starting to wonder myself," he said. "He's usually on time. It's a thing with Meeker. Hates to be… Shit."

He snatched at his S&W, lifting it from the hip holster.

"We've been set up…"

Schwarz saw the armed figures emerging from between stalls ahead of them, weapons already swinging into position as they cleared the avenue. The lead guy was the first to fire, too soon and way off target.

Schwarz's hand pulled out from beneath his jacket, clutching his Beretta. He dropped to a semicrouch, holding the autopistol double-handed. His finger eased back on the trigger, and he sent 9 mm slugs at the lead guy. The Able Team shooter laid his first shot into the guy's throat, tearing out flesh and muscle. Blood spouted as the guy went down, dropping his SMG as he vainly tried to stop the rush of blood.

Lyons, drawing his loosened Python, turned the big handgun in a sharp arc and triggered two fast shots that targeted a burly guy in a flowered shirt. The heavy Magnum slugs caught the guy in the left side of his chest, traveling through his body. Kicked back by the force of the .357 Magnum slugs, the guy slammed into one of his own, knocking the man off balance. As he stumbled, the second guy pulled the trigger of his SMG and sent a burst that scored the concrete only feet ahead of Kalikani.

The Hawaiian cop returned fire and put a trio of 9 mm slugs into the guy that took him all the way to the ground. Without pause Kalikani adjusted his aim and put a single round through the guy's skull, sending a shower of bloody bone fragments into the air.

Panic had gripped the sellers and buyers in the crowded market. People scattered, some screaming in sheer terror at the sudden eruption of violence. They ran, jostling each other, tripping and falling, slamming into the stalls and spilling the displayed goods to the floor.

SMGs crackled as the surviving pair of hitters stepped

by their fallen buddies and made their try. Blancanales joined the fray, his Beretta firing as he gripped it in both hands and unloaded the magazine in an unending stream of 9 mm fire that targeted the pair. Blancanales kept firing until his slide locked back on an empty breech. The men on the receiving end of his volley never knew what had hit them. Blancanales dropped the empty magazine and slid in a fresh one without pausing for breath.

The area suddenly became very quiet, the near silence broken only by the groaning of wounded men. Able Team and Kalikani, weapons still held on the hitters, closed in to clear weapons, then check the shot men. Three were already dead. The surviving two were spilling blood across the concrete.

"I'll call it in," Kalikani said. He took out his cell and contacted his department. "This is Kalikani. Shooting at the Maunakea Market. Have patrol cars move in and send medical help. Three for the morgue. Two wounded. Patch me through to Tasker."

Captain Rudy Tasker was in charge of the special HPD department where Kalikani was housed.

"Welcome to Hawaii," Blancanales said.

"I thought the traditional Hawaiian welcome was girls in grass skirts and flowers," Schwarz replied.

Lyons glanced at them, a taut smile on his face. "You want dancing girls, come as a tourist," he said.

"That sounds boring," Blancanales countered.

Kalikani completed his call and lowered his cell.

"That was my department boss. He asked if you guys always get this kind of reaction wherever you go."

"Funny you should ask that," Schwarz said.

"Looks to me that we've already upset someone," Lyons said.

"Guys," Kalikani said. "I think we should go and talk with my informant. Tomas Meeker has some explaining to do."

TOMAS MEEKER WAS in no condition to explain anything. When Able Team and Kalikani arrived at the man's apartment in a down-market condo, HPD was already there. Kalikani showed his badge and led his guests into the apartment. They were directed to the main bedroom, where Meeker's body lay on the floor beside the bed.

He had been butchered. There was no other way to describe his death. The attending coroner had counted over thirty severe, deep cuts to his body; if the shock hadn't killed him, the massive blood loss would have. The body was soaked, as was the carpet on which the body lay. Blood splashes marked the wall and the bed. Brutal slashes across the back of Meeker's neck had almost severed his head.

"Overkill," Kalikani said.

"They got their information where the meet was from Meeker," Lyons said. "And whoever did this wanted us to know they don't screw around."

When Kalikani finished speaking to the cop in charge, he rejoined Able Team.

"Would you believe no one heard or saw a thing? Whole place is full of deaf, dumb and blind residents."

"So how come the police are here?" Blancanales asked.

"Anonymous call," Kalikani explained. "Just gave the address."

"A trace?" Lyons asked.

Kalikani shook his head. "We located the source but no good. Came from a pay phone on a city street."

"Anyone get the feeling we are being warned off?" Schwarz said.

Blancanales made a low sound in his throat at that, and

Kalikani glanced at him. The look on the guy's face told the Hawaiian that being warned off didn't go down well with the trio.

"I guess you guys don't back down from threats," he said.

"Oh, no," Schwarz said. "Backing down isn't allowed in our contracts."

Kalikani's cell rang. He answered and listened, a slow smile spreading across his face.

"That was the department. The boat that went down, called *King Kamehameha*, belongs to a local company. Fancy name for a down-market coastal tramper. Ownership is being checked out now."

He listened as the caller gave more information. He shut down the cell.

"Got the address. Take us twenty minutes to get there," he said.

"We need something to start us off," Blancanales agreed.

THEY RETURNED TO their vehicles, deciding to travel separately. Blancanales fell in behind Kalikani's official car, and they picked up the route. The cop drove fast, weaving in and out of traffic with ease.

"Doesn't waste time," Schwarz said, swaying as Blancanales pushed his foot down to keep up.

They stayed in sight of the water, passing through a warehouse district. Cranes and dockside equipment were skylined. Kalikani braked and swung in through the sagging, rusted-open gates in a corrugated sheet fence. Dust blew up from beneath his tires as he dodged stacked equipment and maritime spares, rolling to a stop outside an office block that had a distinctly scruffy look to it. Blancanales parked close behind.

Kalikani waited as Able Team joined him. His hand rested on the butt of his holstered S&W.

"Not what you'd call an upmarket spot," Schwarz muttered.

"Outfits like this are the workhorses of the ocean," Kalikani said. "They carry local cargo at rock-bottom prices. Anything for a dollar and not too many questions asked, if they can get away with it."

"So if somebody wanted to hire a boat and waved a thick roll of bills..." Lyons let the words trail off.

"No invoices. No tax. Easy money for an outfit like this."

"Let's hope it was a big roll," Schwarz said. "This charter cost them a whole boat."

They headed for the door, Lyons taking the lead, an expectant expression on his face.

"You think he's getting bored?" Blancanales asked his partner.

Schwarz nodded. "Nothing really exciting's happened so far. I guess you could be right."

Lyons reached out for the door handle. The door was jerked open a second before he touched it. The guy blocking the way was large, his big stomach hanging over his waistline. He wore work-stained jeans and an equally grubby gray T-shirt a size too small for his bulk. A stubby beard masked the rolls of fat beneath his chins, and his shaved skull gleamed.

"What do you want?"

"We need to speak to the man in charge," Lyons said.

"Maybe that's me."

"Okay, so can we do this inside?" Kalikani said. "Or we could go downtown and deal with it there."

"Says who?"

Kalikani produced his badge and showed it to the guy. "We going to make a thing about this?"

"Mebbe," the guy said. "What you come about?"

"How about the *King Kamehameha*?" Blancanales said.

If Blancanales had been expecting some kind of reaction, that was exactly what he got. The big man proved that size didn't always matter. He moved with unexpected speed, bracing his thick arms against the door frame and driving his booted right foot into Carl Lyons's chest, pushing the ex-cop clear of the door. As Lyons went backward a step, the guy slammed the door shut.

"Clear," Lyons yelled, hauling his Python from its holster.

The others took notice of his warning yell and moved away from the door.

Heavy autofire followed. The door was punctured by a burst of slugs that blew holes in the aluminum construction.

"Damn," Kalikani said.

"Check the rear," Lyons said.

As Able Team and Kalikani moved, Lyons reached for the door handle from the side and yanked it open. He was met by a prolonged burst of return fire.

Lyons crouched and angled his Python around the door frame, triggering two rounds. He heard a yell, braced himself and then lunged for the opening. He went in a low dive, on his left shoulder, telling himself it was a stupid move, but Lyons did not like being shot at, and his impulsive nature forced him to react.

Lyons rolled and came to rest on his front, the large revolver thrust ahead.

He caught sight of the big man, still standing, pawing at a bloody gouge in his left cheek. He held a squat mini-Uzi 9 mm in his right hand. The stinging wound in his face had him unfocused long enough for Lyons to take advantage. He didn't hesitate. Lyons had learned a long time ago that distraction, hesitation, a pause in the heat of a combat situation, was the sure and certain way to get yourself shot. Dead was dead, and there was no forgiveness in a bullet.

He angled the Python up and put a solid shot into the man, aware of the guy's bulk and muscle. His only saving grace was the fact he was wielding a .357 caliber Magnum; the 158 grain Hydra-Shok slug possessed solid stopping and penetration power. The office echoed to the hard sound of the blast, and the heavy pistol jerked in Lyons's grip.

The slug hit deep within the guy's chest, targeting the heart. It cleaved its way through and punched a bloody hole in his back on its way out. The big man twisted under the impact, breath gusting from his mouth as he staggered, colliding with a desk. He rolled half across it, his trigger finger curling and sending a burst of 9 mm slugs into the timber floor. His massive bulk toppled to the floor, and the whole building shook as he slammed down.

Lyons pushed to his feet, staring around the room. There was another door in the back wall, and it was swinging back into position.

In the time the big guy had been inside the office, he had been able to warn others, and *they* had left in a hurry.

Lyons crossed the room, kicking the door wide and bursting through.

He caught sight of distant figures vanishing in among stacks of wooden pallets. They were spread out under an open-ended, roofed shed that ran along the edge of the dock, the water of the Pacific below the ten-foot drop.

Lyons heard footsteps behind him. He turned and saw Schwarz, Blancanales and Kalikani coming up fast.

"In there," Lyons yelled and set off in the direction of the shed.

He didn't hesitate. Lyons's reputation as a hothead when roused wouldn't allow him too much caution. His teammates knew that and fell in behind to cover his actions.

Reaching the carport-configured shed, Lyons caught sight of shadowed figures ahead. One turned, and the Able Team commander saw the wink of flame as the guy opened fire. Wood splinters exploded in Lyons's path as the hastily fired volley chewed at the pallets close by.

Lyons dropped to one knee, raised his Python and returned fire. He used his last three shots, clawed a fresh speed-loader from his pocket and made a fast change, aware that his partners were near, their own weapons firing.

Blancanales understood the mechanics of a firefight. There was little time to stand back and make plans. When the enemy was intent on shooting you down, there was only one response. Stay on line, hope to avoid being shot yourself and take the fight to the enemy. He followed Lyons into the shed, realizing the problems ahead as he scanned the rows of stacked wooden pallets, the crisscross tangle of shadows thrown by the stacks as sunlight speared in through the open sides. Ahead he spotted darting figures, the occasional flash of gunfire, followed by hearing the thump of slugs hitting the timber.

He knew Schwarz and Kalikani were somewhere in the vicinity and picked up the noise of their returning shots.

He had chosen to act as backup for Lyons, knowing the blond berserker would be closing in on the opposition with his usual disregard for his own safety. It was the way Lyons operated. He moved with deceptive speed, almost like some human missile, locked on to his target, as if he had a tracking device implanted in his skull. There were times when Blancanales wished Lyons would hold back, assess, before he bulldozed in for the kill. He knew that was a forlorn hope. Carl Lyons would never go for the softly, softly option. It was head down, all guns blazing, once he hit the speed button and fired on all cylinders.

CHAPTER FOURTEEN

Lyons picked up on the fleeting shadow from the corner of his eye. He made no indication that he had seen the movement but simply kept moving forward, as if nothing was amiss. He passed through a patch of shadow thrown across the storage shed floor. As he cleared the blackness and stepped into the light again, he saw the first of the crew tracking him.

The guy was short, stocky, with wide shoulders and a shock of thick black hair over his broad face. He carried a stubby SMG, and the moment he locked eyes with the tall American, he threw the weapon up.

Carl Lyons responded, the .357 Magnum on track in a millisecond. Lyons stroked back on the trigger and placed a heavy slug in the guy's left shoulder, higher than he had anticipated. Despite being off target, it blew apart the guy's shoulder; flesh was torn and ripped, and the bone disintegrated into multiple shards. A spurt of macerated flesh and blood exploded out his back, as he was turned around under force of the slug. With all coordination gone, he fell facedown, slamming into the concrete floor with a solid thud, screaming in pain.

The day blew all to hell after that.

Lyons heard a guttural yell from his left, turning in time to see another shooter emerge from cover. The guy opened up with his own SMG. The burst cleared Lyons with inches to spare. Lyons crouched, cupping his left hand under the butt of the Python to steady it as he tracked the shooter. He eased back on the trigger and laid a pair of slugs in the target's thick chest. This time his shots hit where they were supposed to. The guy was stopped in his tracks, then kicked back by the solid mass of the Magnum's power. His feet left the concrete as he toppled, landing on his back, his weapon bouncing from his grip.

Lyons didn't stop to check him out. Lyons was on the move again, well aware there might be others around.

It turned out he was correct, as his way was blocked by an armed pair. Lyons took evasive action, turning on his heels and taking a wild dive through the row of stacked pallets. He threw his arms in front of his face, as he struck the pile. Wood splintered, as his muscular form hit. Lyons managed a reasonable shoulder roll, once he landed on the concrete, knowing he wasn't going to have much time left, before his attackers altered course and came seeking him. Even as he gained his feet, he picked up the angry shouts as his pursuers came looking for him.

Lyons used his clear seconds to check his surroundings, then caught a glimpse of one of the enemy pushing his way through the stacked crates. He leveled the big revolver, tracked the figure partly concealed by the boxes and put two of his remaining shots into the moving target. The Magnum slugs powered through the flimsy timber, filling the air with dusty splinters, then cored in through the guy's chest, toppling him in a flurry of arms and legs before his bloodied form hit the concrete.

There was a strained silence that followed Lyons's shots. The Able Team leader flipped out the Python's cylinder and ejected the loads. He slipped a fresh speed-loader from his pocket and inserted it into the cylinder. With the revolver fully loaded again, he moved from his position and crouch-walked away.

He had seen two shooters still alive, so there had to be one more around. Lyons accepted there might even be more, who hadn't shown themselves yet.

He thought, Hell of a day, Carl; then added, And it isn't over yet.

Easing his way through the lines of stacked pallets, he picked up the scent of old fruit still lingering in the air. The smell came from wooden crates nearby. The concrete under his feet was wet. The air humid. As the final row of pallets confronted him, Lyons saw the open outer wall of the shed.

His ears picked up the slight scrape of shoes on the concrete at the far end of one stack of crates. Lyons peered through the slatted pallets, searching for movement. His vision was hampered by the dark and light strips of sun. It didn't prevent him from catching the brief gleam slanting off metal.

The metal from a handgun?

The identifying noise of a shot reached him—the loud crack as a bullet was expended from the barrel he'd just spotted. Lyons was showered by wood splinters. His right cheek blossomed with blood from a three-inch-long gash.

"Son of a bitch," he growled.

The flash of pain brought a rapid response from the Able Team top man. His revolver snapped into position; he had cupped his left hand under the butt of the weapon, holding it steady. Lyons triggered three fast shots through the flimsy wooden barrier between him and his opponent, and two of his .357 slugs were directly on target. They impacted with the guy's head, the heavy caliber bullets slightly deformed by their passage through the wooden crates.

One ripped into the target's left cheek, splintering bone and cleaving its way to emerge behind the ear. It tore a gaping hole in the back of the guy's lower skull, amid a bloody spurt of flesh and bone. The second shot hit just above the nose, tunneling through and into the center of the skull, where it ripped into the mass of the brain and lodged there. The guy went over backward, dead before he slammed to the floor, body convulsing briefly as his nerve functions slowed, then stopped completely.

The dead guy still had his weapon gripped in his hand. Lyons bent over to clear it, picked up a whisper of sound behind him as he jerked the pistol free from slack fingers. He began to turn, sensing a moving presence.

He saw a dark shadow on the concrete. Someone was moving in fast.

Heard someone grunt with effort.

Then something hard clouted him across the side of his skull. The blow drove him to his knees. Lyons tried to resist. A second hit dropped him to the concrete, and his senses faded as a third blow slammed him facedown. His revolver slid from his fingers.

Close to being unconscious, Lyons felt hands grip his arms and drag him across the concrete. Voices sounded, unclear, so he couldn't understand what was being said. He was hauled upright, then thrown bodily forward, and he realized he was being manhandled inside a vehicle.

"Go, bro, fucking go."

Those were the first words he heard clearly. Doors slammed. An engine swelled with sound and tires screeched. Lyons was thrown against the back of a seat. Hands pressed him down. The hard, cold muzzle of a weapon was jammed against the side of his skull.

"Stay down, asshole," somebody said. "Mess with me and I'll burn a hole through your brain."

Lyons's urge to fight back was diminished by the pain from the blows to his head. Yet in his weakened state, he was able to understand his current position. There was no way he could retaliate. If he did, he was simply going to put himself in harm's way. The sensible thing, which went against his nature, was to do as he was told. At least for the time being. His chance would come.

THE UNCEASING CRACKLE of autofire delayed Lyons's partners and Kalikani from closing in on his position. There were at least three separate shooters, raking the area with heavy fire. Slugs ripped into the pallets, filling the air with chunks and splinters of shredded wood.

Both Schwarz and Blancanales were concerned about Lyons. His wild man charge toward the opposition was a typical Ironman maneuver. He was never a man who came along at the rear. Lyons always had to be in front, taking the battle forward. He wouldn't have been Lyons if he held back.

The three shooters kept up their relentless attack.

"This is crazy," Schwarz yelled.

"We should have brought heavy ordnance," Blancanales said.

Schwarz made a sudden move, angling around the stack of pallets he was using for cover. He vanished from sight around the end of the stack, crouching as he worked his way along the length of the row.

Blancanales and Kalikani kept up a steady rate of fire to cover his move. They kept a low profile themselves, not wanting to present easy targets.

SCHWARZ HELD HIS Beretta two-handed as he eased his way along, the sound of autofire growing louder as he closed the distance. He could hear the single cracks of return fire from Blancanales and Kalikani.

Peering between the slats of the pallets, he made out the shooters. Two were close to his position. The third guy was twelve feet off to the right.

One of the gunners near Schwarz dropped an exhausted magazine from his SMG and went to snap in a fresh load. Schwarz pushed his 92F through a gap and zeroed in on the man. Whether his move caught the guy's eye, Schwarz never knew, but the shooter froze for a second, then turned his head.

Seeing the muzzle of Schwarz's pistol, the guy opened his mouth the yell. That was when Schwarz double tapped the Beretta's trigger, fast, and placed a pair of 9 mm slugs into the guy's surprised expression. The impact collapsed his face, seeming to push it in on itself, before flesh and bone was blown apart.

As the man went down, face a bloody, raw mess, Schwarz angled his weapon at the second shooter. This one was much too slow, and he had barely registered his own partner's demise before Schwarz put three quick shots into him. They took him in the side, shattering ribs and tearing at his heart. The guy went over uttering a single croaking sound.

BLANCANALES AND KALIKANI heard the shots. When they saw the two shooters go down, they moved instantly, angling toward the shed to confront the surviving gunman, who opted to quit the scene now that he was on his own. He had barely taken three steps when the combined force from Blancanales and Kalikani hit him, twisting him off his feet. He crashed heavily to the concrete, spitting blood and arching his fatally hit body.

There was no sign of Lyons.

The sound of rubber squealing on concrete resounded within the shed.

Schwarz was closest to the far end of the shed, and he ran toward the sound in time to see a large dark maroon

Suburban picking up speed, as it turned around the building and vanished.

Schwarz took off after it, his nostrils picking up the smell of burned rubber. Rounding the end of the storage shed, he caught a glimpse of the 4x4 as it swung around their own parked cars. Dust rose from the tires as the Suburban made a swaying left turn, then cleared the gates and sped out of sight.

"I think they have him," Schwarz said, as Blancanales joined him.

Blancanales didn't say a word but simply held up Lyons's discarded Colt Python.

Kalikani walked on by, making for his own car. He opened the door and leaned inside to call on the radio. He was still speaking as Blancanales and Schwarz reached him.

"I guess no one tagged the plates?" he said.

The Able Team pair shook their heads.

"Let's go check our perps," Schwarz said. "See if one of them is alive. Maybe we can get some answers about this damned setup."

"I won't hold my breath on that," Blancanales said.

CHAPTER FIFTEEN

Lyons woke to find he had one hell of a headache. There was blood down the left side of his face, still slightly moist, so he figured he hadn't been unconscious overly long. As his awareness slowly returned, he realized he was no longer in the vehicle that had transported him.

He was sitting on a wooden chair, his wrists bound together with a plastic tie, lying on his lap. His jacket had been removed but his shoulder rig left in place, minus his sidearm; he recalled having dropped the weapon during the firefight back at the dock.

He was able to feel the warmth of the sun down his right side so it was still daylight. The floor underfoot felt hard, and wherever he was being held had a musty odor in the air. Lyons kept his head down to give himself time to recover his senses. The blows that laid him low had skewed his reflexes, and he needed time to let them reset.

He listened for sounds. Occasionally he picked up the distant hum of passing traffic. But he was unable to work out if he was still in the city or had been removed to some isolated spot.

He heard a man's voice close by. Another answered. They were not speaking English. Lyons recognized it as Chinese.

If nothing else, it seemed he had found the people they were after. Not the way he would have chosen to find them, but what the hell, maybe he could fool them into believing they had the upper hand.

Lyons smelled tobacco smoke. By its pungent odor, someone was smoking a cigar.

"Time to stop pretending you are still unconscious, Matthews. I know that is not who you really are. Just your—what is it you Americans childishly call it?—cover name."

Lyons slowly lifted his head; the ache inside his skull was still too fragile for quick moves.

He realized his name had been used.

When he slowly opened his eyes, he found himself facing two casually dressed men. He took his time checking them out.

The one smoking the cigar was Chinese. He was young, lean, with slicked-back black hair. He had a semblance of a smile on his lips. The smile did not reach his eyes. He carried a heavy autopistol in his left hand. The guy next to him had a broad set to his face and body. His hair was cropped close to his angular skull. The heavy cheekbones and thin-lipped mouth suggested Korean heritage. Neither man was more than average height.

"What do I call you?" Lyons asked. "Yin and Yang?"

"We are not here to trade witty remarks. Or exchange banter. At this moment in time, Matthews, you are close to becoming dead. Make no mistake. It doesn't matter to me if you die in the next few moments. My companion, who does not understand English, will kill you if I tell him to."

"Is this going to be one of those question-and-answer things?" Lyons asked. "If it is, just get on with it."

"Why so much interest in us?"

Lyons shook his head. "Now you're insulting me. You *know* damn well why. We're interested in someone screwing around with NNEMP technology. Setting off a test firing that affected a small area here in Honolulu. It brought down a search-and-rescue helicopter and left the crew dead. Same launch backfired and sank the boat carrying the equipment. That *was* your boat that sank in the water just off the coast. You hit us with the NNEMP. That's the bad part. But your ship was sunk. That's good. Yin and Yang."

"I can see," the Chinese said, "that you persist in trying to provoke me, when all I require from you is a little information. And to put right your error, the vessel that sank belonged to the North Koreans, *not* the Chinese. Something you did not know? Not that it really matters. However I am interested in knowing how you located where the boat came from. Obviously your information was firsthand."

"I've only been on the islands for a short time. What can I tell you?"

"The extent of your involvement with Oscar Kalikani. What else you have learned, if anything, about our presence in Hawaii. And, of course, who you people really are. Things of small importance."

"So small you send out your hit teams to try and kill us? I figure maybe you're running a little scared." Lyons nodded in the direction of the silent Korean. "Does he speak?"

"Only his own language. But he understands me, so we have no problems. He is nothing but a *heavy*. Another American word. He will, if needed, provide the muscle. Not very pleasant for you, if it occurs."

"Their game and you're along to lend support? The North Koreans are way ahead with the NNEMP technology. That must piss you off. You're way behind. You Chi-Coms have been spending too much time making washing machines and computers for the rest of the world. Took your eye off the ball there. But you're throwing big money at the Koreans. Am I right?"

For the first time the Chinese allowed a flicker of emotion to shadow his bland features. Lyons knew he had scored a point.

"Very perceptive, Matthews. However, you are still tied up and resisting answering my questions. It will not do you any good, so why continue?"

"Maybe I'm stalling for time. Waiting for my team to burst in and kick your skinny Chinese ass. Face it, you have me tied up. Not going anywhere. You can finish me off anytime you want. So why would I want to make it easy for you? You certain you have the hang of this interrogation thing?"

The Chinese turned and said something to the Korean. The guy took a swift step forward and launched a fist that caught Lyons across the side of his face. The blow was delivered with full force. It rocked Lyons's head. The Korean used his other fist to slam against the opposite side of Lyons's face. They were solid hits, hard, and Lyons gasped under the stunning blows. He rocked back on his chair, spitting blood from his mouth.

"Do we start talking again?" the Chinese asked. "Or is there more of your comic routine to come?"

"If my hands were free, I could do a few card tricks," Lyons said.

The muffled sound of a cell phone interrupted him. The Chinese took the phone from his pocket and answered the call. He spoke in rapid Chinese, his annoyance clearly visible in his actions and the tone of his voice. He turned to the Korean and snapped out brief instructions before returning his attention to Lyons.

"Consider this a short reprieve. I need to attend to something. I will leave you in Yun's hands. He might decide to work on you some more, so be careful how you act toward him."

He put away his weapon, turned and walked off, leaving by a thick wooden door. Shortly Lyons heard a car fire up and move away.

The Korean, Yun, circled Lyons's chair. Lyons could hear him muttering to himself in a low voice. When he moved back into view, the first thing Lyons saw was he now had a pistol in his right hand.

An added complication but not something Lyons was about to quit over.

Time drifted by. Too long. Yun was becoming restless. He checked over his shoulder a few times, clearly expecting the Chinese guy to return.

This, Lyons decided, was not going to end well. Unless he pushed someone's buttons.

Lyons watched as Yun moved again, walking around the chair and then confronting his captive. He began to speak. This time his voice raised, and he kept jabbing a thick finger at Lyons. The tone of his voice warned him Yun was working up to something, so it was time to make his move.

A cell rang. Yun pulled it from his pocket and listened. He replied, his tone angry. He shut off the call and pocketed the cell.

The Korean started to harangue his captive.

"Yun," Lyons said loudly. "Shut up."

Lyons had a powerful voice when he chose to use it. The outburst had a brief effect on the North Korean. He stared at Lyons, unable to understand what the American had said.

That hesitation offered a thin window for Lyons. He realized he was about to get one chance.

And being the Ironman, he took that opportunity, coming up off the chair in a powerful lunge. His right foot, clad in a tough boot, swung up and struck Yun between his thighs.

Kicking a man in the testicles was a precise art; make contact off center and the pain would be minimal, but catch the target correctly and there would be catastrophic results. Carl Lyons understood the concept and delivered a blow 100 percent accurate that drew a high screech of anguish from Yun. The Korean went up on his toes, the cry of pain trailing off into a whimpering whine.

Lyons gave him no time to recover. He delivered a second kick, directly over the site of the initial strike. Yun sagged at the waist in an instinctive and protective move. Lyons had been hoping for that. As Yun doubled over, Lyons dropped his bound hands over the man's head, gripping the back of his thick neck and pushed down hard. Yun's unprotected face met Lyons's solid knee, as it swept up. The brutal impact flattened Yun's nose. Cartilage was crushed, and Yun's nose streamed thick gouts of blood.

Keeping a tight grip on Yun's neck, Lyons slammed his knee into the Korean's face three more times. Yun dropped to his knees, his face a ruined mass of torn flesh and shattered bones. Blood gushed down his chin and soaked his shirtfront. The pistol had slipped from his fingers, and Lyons nudged it out of reach.

Without hesitation Lyons swung around to stand behind the Korean's kneeling figure. He dropped his bound hands over Yun's neck and hauled back, cutting off the air to the man's lungs. Lyons slammed a knee into Yun's upper back.

Already half conscious from the heavy blows, Yun offered only token resistance. As Lyons increased the pressure he heard a soft crunch of spinal bones. When he heard that whisper of sound, Lyons held his position until he felt the man's body lose all tension. He freed his arms and let Yun drop facedown on the floor.

Lyons sucked air into his lungs. His head and face hurt from the earlier blows to his skull and the recent punches Yun had delivered, and his mouth was bloody on the left side.

He picked up the pistol Yun had dropped. It was a P226. He glanced around and saw where his own jacket had been thrown on the floor. He went through the pockets, found his cell and took it out. He pushed the P226 down the waistband of his blood-spattered pants, then awkwardly—because of his bound wrists—speed-dialed Blancanales's number.

"That you?" Blancanales asked. "Carl?" He missed using Lyons's cover name, but Lyons overlooked it.

"It's me," he answered.

"You hurt? You sound weird."

"*Yeah?* Could be because I got hammered in the mouth."

"Hell. Where are you?"

"No idea," Lyons said. "Let me get outside and I'll figure it out."

Lyons crossed to the door where the Chinese guy had exited. It opened to bright sunlight that hurt Lyons's eyes. He leaned against the door frame as he took in the scene. He saw warehouses. It looked deserted. All the buildings had a shabby, unused look to them. Lyons scanned the area. He spotted a sagging sign on one frontage.

"Someplace called Pacific Rental, Warehouse 35," he quoted to Blancanales.

He heard Blancanales relay the message and picked up Kalikani's affirmative response.

"We should be with you in twenty," Blancanales said.

"I'll wait around," Lyons said drily.

The area was quiet. No movement. And no sign of his Chinese inquisitor. The guy had disappeared. Whatever had taken him out of the warehouse had removed him from the vicinity, leaving Lyons alone with his silent guard. Lyons didn't see the man returning. The phone call Yun had received must have advised of that fact.

He leaned against the warehouse frontage. After a minute he decided it would be more comfortable if he sat down.

He kept Yun's P226 in his hands. Hawaii, he decided, was showing itself to be somewhat less than paradise. The sun was strong. It hurt where it burned against the gash in his skull but Lyons couldn't be bothered to move. He was suddenly very tired. It was becoming hard to keep his eyes open and after a while he didn't bother trying....

CHAPTER SIXTEEN

Dr. Emanuel Absalom sat facing his team across the conference table, his body in the room, his mind elsewhere. Physically he presented the archetypal scientist from popular fiction; in his late forties, tall, lean, with pale skin and thick white hair that he wore long. His keen eyes stared out from behind glasses he was always pushing into position while he considered a complex problem. His dress code was expensive crumpled, and even the white lab coat he wore hung loosely on his spare frame.

Outward appurtenances aside, Absalom was a man who understood his business; his knowledge of physics and the application toward pulse technology was unrivaled. Absalom could have held any number of prestigious positions throughout the scientific world. Instead he enjoyed the excitement that came from selling his skills to less-than-favorable clients.

He barely acknowledged the presence of the other three men and one woman. When someone placed a cup of coffee in front of him, he made no move toward it, which in itself was unusual; Absalom was a coffee addict, and normally he would have immediately consumed it.

That fact alone alerted the team to the seriousness of the situation. They were all aware of the malfunction of the equipment following the NNEMP dispersion in Hawaii. Though the main part of the test had worked, the secondary burst that had destroyed the delivery vessel had been

totally unexpected and was the cause of Absalom's intro-
spection. His team understood his dismay. Absalom was
a man who took even a partial failure as a disaster, which
was troubling him.

It also troubled Major Ri On Choi. The forty-three-year-
old North Korean army officer was there as the research
center's controller. The research facility's top man. His task
was to oversee the NNEMP project and keep the higher
command updated on its progress.

Major Choi was ambitious to the extreme. In his eyes
every delay, failure, breakdown applied to the project—
code named Cobalt Blue—reflected on him. He understood
the need for the creative input of Absalom's team, yet at the
same time, he felt their caution a hindrance. Choi wanted
results. Positive results he could present to his peers that
would reflect positively. The test firing that resulted in the
breakdown of the Coast Guard base had been tainted by
the destruction of the ship. In Choi's estimation that was
inexcusable.

"Well?" Choi snapped, directing his question across the
table in Absalom's direction. "What have you got to say
for yourself? This incident is not acceptable, Absalom."

As Absalom did not speak Korean, the major used English, as did all of Absalom's team.

Absalom looked up, meeting Choi's angry glare. His re-
fusal to be intimidated by the uniformed man only served
to increase Choi's anger.

The physicist had no love for Choi. He found the North
Korean insufferable. The man was nothing more than a cog
in the North Korean machine, an arrogant individual so in
awe of his own self-importance that he imagined himself
to be the lord over all he surveyed.

During the physicist's career, wherever he went,
Absalom had come in contact with Major Choi clones.

Given a degree of power, they thought they stood head
and shoulders above every other mortal, and took great de-
light in using, *abusing*, their power. Ignoring any physical
size, these people, to a man, were small individuals. They
imagined they were indestructible, persons of high intellect; when, in fact, they were far from that ideal.

Emanuel Absalom understood Choi's limitations, but he
was unable to resist a degree of insubordination when confronted by someone like him, especially in an instance like
the present situation. The unexpected development with the
NNEMP weapon had puzzled even Absalom.

The firing had seemed to go without a hitch. The sudden
power kickback had left the whole of his unit mystified.
Absalom felt sure they would get to the root cause. Given
the mass of recorded information, it would take time to
sift through the whole database. It was large, and the task
would proceed slowly. If just a single piece of code was
overlooked, they might have to go back and start again.

That was the reality.

It was also a reality that the military brain of Major Ri
On Choi would not—could not—grasp. He would *never*
grasp it.

"Acceptable or not, Choi, it happened. It really did happen."

"We are all acutely aware of that," Choi snapped. "And
my rank is *Major*."

"As mine is Doctor, if you wish to play immature games.
As to your earlier query, I have little to say at this time. Be-
cause, Major Choi, we are still looking into what occurred.
These matters take time."

"We brought you here to ensure our weapons system
could be brought successfully online sooner rather than
later."

Absalom allowed a weary smile to edge his lips. "Science

does not perform in order to satisfy time schedules. Regardless of what is written in your manifesto, the weapon will be ready when it is ready. You as much as anyone should understand there are no such things as miracles."

Choi's rigid face flushed with anger. He sat upright in his seat and pointed a finger at Absalom.

"Be careful what you say, Doctor. Men have been executed for less."

"Ah, the ultimate threat. And what would that achieve, Major? My death would gain you nothing except more delays. Steps back in the development. I was invited here to help your people get what they want. My work on NNEMP is way ahead of the Chinese *and* the Americans. North Korea chose me because my knowledge is invaluable.

"If killing me will satisfy you, then go ahead. Just remember I carry more in my head than there is on paper or in your computers. And I am sure your superiors in Pyongyang would not be happy if you wasted all the money they paid out to get me here."

Absalom paused, holding the Korean's angry stare. "The fact that the test *did* actually produce results seems to have been forgotten. Now if there is nothing else, *Major* Choi, we have work to do.

"The destruction of the delivery vessel needs to be analyzed, because if this cannot be resolved, we may have an ongoing problem with future larger-scale tests to carry out. Until, and if, the equipment is located and returned, all we have is our computer backup here.

"It may give us some answers, but we need to do a full breakdown of the program to attempt to determine how this happened. We will have to duplicate the launch mechanism and run lab tests on that. We may come up with a solution. So our work must go on without interruption."

To his credit Absalom faced the Korean without flinching. "Major Choi, my responsibility is to develop the NNEMP. Which I *am* doing. I am a scientist, not a soldier. Security is in your hands. You are fond of telling me to do my job. I will. Now *you* do yours."

"Are you telling me how to perform my duty?"

"Right now we are all concerned over what happened," Absalom said. "Solving the matter is something else, because it should not have happened."

"Exactly so," Choi said. "Which is why I need to understand. When I speak again to Pyongyang, I will be expected to detail *why* this disaster took place."

"I would not call it a disaster, Major. In essence we achieved what we set out to do. The pulse did work. Admittedly to a lesser degree than we had hoped, but it *did* work. The reversal of the electromagnetic pulse effect weakened the burst. That is my real concern. Until we work out why it happened, we cannot risk any further field trials. It would be rather counterproductive if the same thing happened each time we fired our device."

"Are you telling me that this team of yours, much vaunted by yourself, is unable to explain what happened?"

Choi was showing signs of impatience. Not a good thing. Failure reflected on his command and Major Ri On Choi refused to become the scapegoat because of the failure of others.

Choi knew how Pyongyang would react. Their anger would be directed at him. He was the man in charge, so he carried the responsibility. Choi knew he would not be able to avoid that. He showed a brave face to the world. Inside there was fear, and it would not go away until the matter was resolved.

It was Li Kam who spoke up.

"Please understand, Major. The science of these procedures is both difficult and challenging. We are dealing with a complex mix of circuits that combine linear and semi-conductors. This is electronic engineering at the highest level. Our need is to bring these matters together in a manageable form that allows us complete control. It requires a delicate balancing of all the functions. We enter them into the computer system and merge them into what we hope will offer us the function we require."

"Our calculations," Absalom said, "gave us the readouts we hoped for. On paper, as they say, we had our system blueprint. It is incredibly complex. Until we go through everything, we will not come close to understanding why we experienced the reversal that generated enough power to sink the launch vessel. We are prepared to work day and night while we investigate. But it will not—cannot—be an instant response.

"No matter how much Pyongyang shouts, there is no quick fix. Without question they could push us aside and send in more people to take over. By all means send for them, if you believe they can do better. I assure you, they could not walk in here and find a solution faster than we can."

Choi stared around the table, pausing on each face. He quickly realized, as irritating as the doctor was, that Absalom was correct. Choi was not graced with a scientific mind. He was, after all, a soldier. Give him a rifle, and he would strip and reassemble it in the dark. But here, among Absalom's computers and his talk of electronics and pulses, Choi was lost. Grudgingly he was forced to accept what Absalom and his team told him.

"I need... I *want* answers," he snapped. "Find out how this error occurred. And do it as quickly as possible. Believe me when I say that I—and Pyongyang—will not wait forever. The successful development of this weapon is vital."

Major Choi stood. He once more glanced around the

table at Absalom's team, who remained silent and passive. All except Li Kam, who sat upright, facing him with her unflinching stare. He straightened his uniform jacket and swept his cap off the table.

"Keep me informed of developments," he said. "I want to hear the minute you have anything."

"Of course," Absalom said evenly, rising himself.

He watched as Choi crossed to the door and left, the heels of his polished boots snapping against the floor.

There seemed to be a collective sigh of relief around the table at Choi's departure.

"Would someone bring me a fresh cup of coffee, please," Absalom said.

Li Kam picked up his cup and crossed to the side table to freshen his drink. She was young, slim and feminine, and she deferred to Absalom. But unbeknownst to the man, only on the surface. Her real feelings were kept hidden. She was aware of her vulnerable position. One slip could expose her real agenda, and everything that had gone before would be wiped out. Li Kam understood the fragile path she trod. As matters moved toward the inevitable conclusion, she had to stay in control to see them through.

"You should be careful," she suggested. "Choi is not a nice man. He will remember what you have said to him today. He is a hard-line member of the party. Very strict when it comes to…"

Absalom smiled at her hesitation. "When it comes to daring to mock him?"

Li nodded.

"If I have insulted any of *you*, then I apologize. The last thing I want is to disrespect my team," the physicist said.

Gok Tang, one of the male members, shook his head. "Don't concern yourself with Choi. The man is obsessed with the project."

"I thought we all were," Absalom said. "Was I wrong?"

Tang said, "There is obsession, and there is *obsession*. Choi is more self-obsessed than anything else. He sees this project as his opportunity to higher promotion. To help him climb the ladder within the military. If this project fails, so does he."

"He has ambition," Absalom said. "In itself not a bad thing."

"But Choi takes it to extremes. He uses his power to intimidate," said Tang. "If we succeed in developing the project, Choi will take every bit of the credit, and we will be forgotten."

"What are you thinking?" Absalom asked.

Another team member, Ki Yen, said, "That we make certain we do not find ourselves pushed into the shadows."

"But I was under the impression that being loyal party members, you were doing this for North Korea. Without personal gratification."

"Of course," Li said, "but we also want to be alive at the end." She gave Absalom a glance that told him there was more to the young woman than simply a desire to demonstrate her blind loyalty to the NK regime. "Explain to us, Dr. Absalom, why *you* came here to develop the NNEMP process."

"You know why."

"To help our country develop a weapon we can use to make North Korea stronger? Able to show the South, and its capitalistic ally, America, that we here in the North are capable of greatness?"

"Said like that, I almost forgot I came for the money your people offered me," Absalom said, smiling gently. "Politics do not interest, or influence, me. The petty squabbles between countries are beyond me. I work for my science."

He added, "But do not forget I am a capitalist, and I do like my financial rewards."

Li nodded. "*You* almost forgot," she said. "You came for the money. We want the success that creating the weapons will offer. If we perfect the process, we four will enjoy a better standard of living. You must understand the strictures under which we exist. A shortage of food. Barely sustainable lifestyles. The country dies on its knees while the rulers live in luxury. We are not so naive as to let ourselves be manipulated by all the propaganda. Is that so hard to understand?"

Absalom shook his head. "No. It's not hard to understand at all. My own childhood was far from pleasant. But I learned at an early age that I had a better brain than most. I excelled in mathematics. The sciences. And I used those skills to better myself. The sciences were my way out of poverty.

"I also saw fit to make those skills pay. Not to labor in some dull job where I would barely make a decent living." He smiled. "I realized I could use my skills by selling myself to the highest bidder. The world has a need to create bigger and better weapons of destruction. My creativity was my way out. And it has enabled me to lift myself from the ranks of the poorly paid."

Yen said, "And when your work here is done, you will be able to move on. We have to stay."

"As much as I sympathize, Yen, there is little I can do about that. It is out of my hands."

"Yen, the doctor cannot be held responsible for our problems," Li said. "You know that. The work we do here may advance our own situation and offer us some security."

"Only if we make this project a success," Me Sang, the final member of Absalom's close team, reminded them all.

Absalom took a drink from his cup. "In that context I

am as tied here as you. Success for us all depends on that system. We have to make it work." He placed his cup back on the table. "So let us go to the beginning and review the Hawaiian test firing. In all the feedback we got from the computer link, there has to be the answer why the pulse reflected back to the ship and caused that explosion."

While Li and Absalom sat at the table, bent over the printed feedback, Tang, Yen and Sang returned to their own monitor screens and began working through the mass of stored data that had been transmitted from the ship during the test firing. The input had been steady and had only ceased the moment the NNEMP burst had reversed itself and struck the ship.

They all were aware of two important things.

The days and night ahead of them were going to be long and stressful.

And with Major Choi overseeing their every move, they were on a ticking clock.

CHAPTER SEVENTEEN

Her name was Li Kam and she was twenty-eight years old. Her late parents had been fishers from South Hamgyong Province. Li was their only child.

From a young age, she had showed promise and had been recruited into the government educational program after her three-year compulsory military service. Her natural ability had been studied as the years passed, and her aptitude for science—and especially the study of physics—meant the young Li was recruited into the applied physics courses.

She had had no choice when she was taken from her family and housed in a government dormitory building with other students; where day after day she was schooled in the subject, her instructors keeping a close eye on the bright and articulate young woman.

Life for Li Kam was by no means perfect. As a gifted student, she was housed and fed by the state. The apartment she shared with two other girls, clean and reasonably comfortable, made her feel uncomfortable when she thought about the crude, basic hut her parents shared. It made her even more awkward when she admitted there was nothing she could do about it, apart from taking small gifts whenever she managed to visit them.

Within herself she felt a strong urge to rebel against the stringent and authoritarian regime that forced the larger part of the country into silent sufferance, while those in positions of power resided in comfort, had plenty of food and lived a lifestyle of comparative ease.

The deaths of her parents had shocked Li. But her separation from her parents and the hard life in the government compound had made her realize she had little control over her own life. It was a simple choice. To maintain her status, she had to publicly condemn her parents and maintain her status as a true member of the regime. She became an obedient citizen and did as she was told.

To do otherwise would have destroyed her cover. So she held her tongue, kept her thoughts to herself and waited for the chance, any chance, to rebel. And while she showed a loyal face, inside she refused to forget her parents and the way they had died.

The injustice gnawed at Li. The anger inside grew, and when she was approached by Kayo Pak, she had responded eagerly to his suggestions. She listened to what he had to say. He had, he told her, noticed her impatience with the current status of the country's majority, and if she wanted to do something about it, he could introduce her to his covert group.

Despite her need to strike out, Li was wary. She knew how the state set traps for the unwary, using their own agents to test loyalty. Anyone who was caught uttering antigovernment propaganda would be arrested, given a so-called trial and then summarily sentenced; the punishment could be death, which was often looked on as preferable to being sent to one of the dreaded labor camps.

There, caged behind barbed wire, the victims of the regime's oppressive code would work out their lives at hard labor, in squalid conditions where life meant nothing. Very few escaped the labor camps. If they did break free, they were hunted down and then usually shot. Or as in the case of her family, treated in such a way that death became the only way out.

Li's intelligence and her skill in her chosen field resulted in her being seen as a valuable asset. When she was placed in the isolated research facility, Li was more than pleased, though she simply accepted the position with humility.

Her insight into the work they were doing, gained by her interest in the use of nonnuclear electronic pulse technology, brought her on board when Emanuel Absalom recognized her potential. He had asked for her, and she was placed within his department.

Li fitted into the small unit well. Once installed, she learned even more about the application of the developing NNEMP research. As she worked daily beside Absalom, her quick brain grasped the fact that she was now not only working for the North Koreans on an important project but was at the same time able to siphon off data that she smuggled out to her contact in the South Korean security agency.

For her SK contact, Kayo Pak, Li's recruitment into the NNEMP research facility was an unexpected coup. He had been hoping she would be placed in an important position, but even he was pleasantly surprised at her appointment.

The NNEMP development was something South Korea had been viewing with mounting suspicion. If North Korea could create a workable weapon, it would become a real threat. Pak's bosses had been trying to get a foot in the door, but until Li Kam's appointment, they had not been successful.

When Pak reported Kam was in, the South Korean administration informed him that he could write his own ticket to help the young agent make the most of her new assignment. Pak remained calm and made it clear to Li Kam that she should proceed with caution. He demanded that she should do nothing to upset the status quo. He wanted results. Solid results, not quick results.

They might never get another chance, so he made Li understand she had to stay calm and wait for the right moment. Her main task was to play the devoted party member, to work as part of the team but also to pass as much information as she could to Pak and covertly attempt to sabotage the development.

When Absalom joined the unit, Li simply reported the fact to Pak. He managed to convince her to continue watching and waiting. As the months passed, Pak had to brush off the impatience from his superiors, while instilling into Li Kam that the scraps of data she was able to pass him were all helping in allowing South Korea to build a picture of the emerging NNEMP system.

Li Kam's first practical initiative came when she had learned about the upcoming trial. Just Major Choi and Absalom were in the know as to the actual target. The only scrap of information that was passed to the team was the fact the trial would be *away* from North Korea. It was a practical decision in case there were any repercussions.

She took it on herself to write and insert the computer code into the launch equipment. It was designed to initiate a failure in the NNEMP probe. Her skill with the computing side of the work allowed her to create a block of code, hidden within the main computer text, that would in effect disable the launch sequence once the NNEMP missile was in the air.

In fact the sequence did not have quite the effect Li had been anticipating. She learned later that, although the launch had gone ahead—and it was only then she learned the target had been Hawaii—and had been successful, the code she had inserted into the system had caused a kickback. The result had been the explosion that had sunk the launch vessel and killed a number of the North Korean crew.

Li's concern was that Major Choi would be doing his best to find out what had happened. He would dig and probe. He would question, badger, even without understanding what he was looking for. He would not be satisfied until he had proven to himself someone at the facility was responsible. And he would fret until the launch unit was recovered and sent directly to the North Korean facility.

Choi's investigation would sweep through Absalom's department. Each member would be under suspicion, even Absalom himself. Li was hopeful she had covered her tracks, that she had not left any trail that could be traced back to her. She was not naive to believe she was in the clear, and her thoughts were directed toward Kayo Pak. The sooner he arranged to take her out of Choi's reach, the better. Her time here was done. Whatever success she had achieved would have to be enough.

Until that happened, she would have to maintain her cover. She understood that was going to be doubly difficult. Major Choi would not rest until he got to the bottom of the matter. His investigation would encompass the whole of the research facility, and they would all be under the spotlight. Li realized she would need to remain in control and not allow her inner feelings to show.

CHAPTER EIGHTEEN

Rafael Encizo crouched in the shadows thrown by a couple of close standing trees, his trained eyes checking the back trail. He had been monitoring the sparse conversation reaching him from McCarter and Pak over his comm set. While he listened, he scanned the area, keeping in mind the possibility of roving sentries. If this Major Choi was as keen as Pak suggested, then it would be expected the man would maintain an armed presence to watch over the installation.

Encizo's vigilance paid off when he caught a glimpse of movement some yards away to his left. He focused in and spotted the outline of two armed and uniformed figures checking the area.

The North Koreans wore camou-style dress and carried Type 68 auto rifles, a copy of the Soviet AKM. They also wore steel helmets and had waist-length waterproof slickers. Neither man looked as if he was enjoying patrolling in such poor weather, and as they advanced through the trees, Encizo could see they were discussing something. One of them kept pointing at the ground, which suggested to the Phoenix Force pro that they had seen something that had caught their interest.

Encizo didn't take too much time speculating. This area was isolated and most likely off-limits to anyone not part of the research establishment. As far as he could work out, the two Koreans had picked up on something out of place.

His suspicions were further heightened when the two soldiers raised their rifles and increased their pace.

One reached for something under his cape and his fingers emerged clutching a handset.

He wasn't about to call in anything trivial.

Encizo couldn't let him make the call.

He shouldered the P90, aimed and put a short burst of suppressed 5.7 mm slugs into the Korean's chest. The ammo raised spurts of blood as they cored in. The guy toppled sideways, banging against his partner.

As the first man dropped, Encizo arced his weapon a few inches to the side and hit the second guy. His aim was higher, the burst impacting with the side of the target's head below the rim of the steel helmet, spinning him around, then depositing him on the rain-soaked ground. Before the bodies had stopped moving, Encizo closed in, standing over the pair and firing again into each man to ensure his kills.

Encizo heard McCarter's urgent call in his earpiece.

"Fredo?"

"I just took out a pair of sentries. Looks like they had picked up our tracks. One was about to call it in. He didn't make it. Both down."

"They on their own?"

"Far as I can tell. But there have to be more in the area."

McCarter said, "We have sight of the installation."

"I'll stay back a ways. In case there are any more in the area. But I'll work around in your direction. If you need me up close, just yell."

"You good?"

"I'm fine. Go ahead. I'll watch your backs."

"No worries, then."

Encizo smiled. He slid into deeper cover and watched the surrounding area…

"FIRST CONTACT?" JAMES SAID over his comm set.

"Mmm-hmm, and it won't be the last. Rack it up, fellers, the party seems to have been cracked open. Kayo, you ready to play?" McCarter asked.

"I am ready, but this is not a game, is it?"

"I keep forgetting you might not understand my humor."

"When we have time, perhaps you can explain it to me," the Korean said, his face expressionless.

McCarter found himself not sure he could, so he shook his head. "Lock and load," he said over his comm set. "Let's pay this Major Choi an unexpected home visit. Spread out."

THE WATCHTOWERS HAD sloping covers to protect the machine gunners from the regular rainfall that plagued the area. It kept them and their weapons dry, though it did little to protect them from the cold. While they were reasonably isolated from the downpour on this particular day, the guards found the heavy rain reduced their visibility.

Beyond the fence, leading up to the dense wooded terrain, the steady curtain of water dropping from the leaden sky made it hard for them to see more than a misty image. The thick undergrowth at the base of the trees simply added to the confusion. Bending and swaying under the downpour, the thick greenery fooled the eyes into imagining there might be someone looking back at them. A second glance and the imagery had vanished.

As PHOENIX FORCE expanded their area, Manning dropped back to check the wider aspect. The rest of the team had moved on ahead, when Manning made eye contact with a single armed sentry who had maintained a watch from his position. The guy had his Type 68 slung over his right shoulder, his face turned away from the wind-driven rain still whipping in from the punitive sky. It was the fact he had his face turned that created the eye contact. He reacted quickly, dropping to a crouch, as he slid his autorifle free and swung it in Manning's direction, his finger finding the trigger even as the weapon lined up.

Manning jerked to the side, bringing up his P90, aware that the Korean had reacted extremely fast. The stuttering crackle of full-autofire was loud in the comparative quiet of the area.

Manning hit the ground, rolling on his stomach. The 7.62 mm slugs struck the earth inches away, geysering up mud.

McCarter's voice came through the comm set. "What?"

"I've been made," the Canadian told him.

His suppressed weapon kicked out a burst at the Korean, forcing the guy to jerk aside, briefly losing his firing stance. That gave Manning the thin window to take steady aim and trigger a second time. He saw the enemy soldier pull almost upright, his throat and lower jaw bursting apart as the 5.7 mm slugs hit. He arched over onto his back, legs going into spasms.

Manning pushed upright and pulled back into tree cover, as he spotted more armed figures clustered at the enclosure's metal gates. Hard autofire followed him, the copper-jacketed 7.62 mm slugs whacking into the thick trunk, sending bark and splinters into the air.

In the brief moment when the gunfire ceased, Manning risked a look and saw the gates being swung open. A tight group of North Korean soldiers spilled out, breaking apart as they cleared the gates.

"Just great," Manning muttered as the armed figures began to advance on his position.

He leaned out from cover and opened fire, hoping to scatter the advancing figures. He saw one Korean stumble, then drop to one knee, clutching at his side. Manning fired again, putting the man down for good. The others hesitated for a few seconds, allowing Manning the chance to pull farther back into the timber. He knew the stalling action wouldn't last for long.

As he pounded into the shadows, he heard more hard firing from the North Koreans' weapons and picked up on the solid chunk of slugs hitting tree trunks around him. The Koreans were firing blind as they followed him into the timber. That might easily change as they worked their way deeper.

This was *their* home ground, and they would know the forest. If they picked up sight of him, took their time aiming before they fired, Manning might suddenly become the preferred target of the day.

He was depending on his team backing him, hoping they had taken up positions ahead and would track in on the Koreans, if they continued to follow the obvious trail he was leaving for them.

A crackle of shots sent more slugs in Manning's direction. A number of them were too close. He felt flying wood chips patter against his BDU jacket. He felt suddenly very exposed.

Too exposed.

The Canadian spotted dense and tangled undergrowth ahead. He crouched and pushed his way into the greenery, feeling the tendrils claw at his body. Spiky lengths drifted across the side of his face, a thorny end scraping his cheek. Manning knew it had drawn blood. He ignored the sting. An advantage of the steady rain was its effect on his cut. The blood was washed away quickly.

Now he could hear raised voices behind him, the thrash and scramble of the North Korean soldiers as they stayed on his trail. Persistent if nothing else, he decided.

As if to make him realize they were still there, the Koreans opened up, raking the greenery with autofire. The slugs zipped through the air, chopping and slapping at the undergrowth, slamming into the trunks of trees. Luckily for Manning none came too close, but he knew he was not going to shake off the pursuing soldiers so easily.

Manning pushed on, working an M-69 fragmentation grenade from his harness. He slung his P90 around his neck, letting it dangle free, as he gripped the smooth shape of the fourteen-ounce grenade. Manning gripped the sphere in his right hand, fingers of his left pulling the pin. He stopped running, pivoted and faced the enemy he couldn't see clearly through the foliage, pinpointing them by the sounds they were making.

"Catch this," Manning mouthed as he tossed the grenade into the dense greenery.

The metal spoon sprang free as the M-69 curved through the air and the internal fuse activated and detonated the tightly packed Composition-B inside the metal casing. Manning had already dropped to a crouch, clear of the blast radius. The grenade blew with a solid crack, sending vicious fragments of metal in a deadly swathe. On the tail of the explosion, Manning heard at least one agonized trailing scream as the grenade found a target.

The vibration from the blast was still radiating out as Manning gained his feet and moved on, repositioning his line of travel to take him back to the group. He moved fast, ignoring the drag of heavy foliage. The grenade he had dropped on the enemy soldiers might only hold them there temporarily, so he had to make the best use of his time.

Manning grasped his P90 to stop it from bouncing around and held it close to his body, ready to use if needed.

It seemed he was moving for an eternity, but in reality he had covered only a short distance.

He could hear raised Korean voices behind him now. It

was as if the opposition was coming out of the woodwork in hungry packs.

Autofire sounded. Slugs shredded the foliage. He felt one slug slice through his sleeve.

That, Manning thought, was cutting it too close.

"Take a dive," a voice he recognized came through his comm set.

Manning didn't need a second warning. He threw himself forward and down, hitting the rain-sodden forest floor full-length. Despite the soft landing, Manning felt his breath burst from his lips on impact.

Over his prone body, a concentrated rattle of autofire drowned the hiss of the rain. The burst felt as if it went on for a long time, but Manning realized it was over in seconds. There was some return fire from the Type 68s.

Manning felt the slap of rain hitting his clothing as he raised his head. The firing had ceased. He pushed up off the ground and saw his team emerging from the undergrowth, weapons up and still ready if needed.

"Hey, man, you look a sight," James said.

"More leaves on him than the rest of the forest," Hawkins observed.

Manning turned his face to the sky and let the falling rain sluice the mud from his face.

"Took your time," he said as McCarter appeared.

"We had to be sure they were in range," he observed.

"In range? They were so close one of them was ready to go through my damn pockets."

"He gets an easy job, and all he does is complain," McCarter said. "Just no pleasing some people."

"It might not be as easy to deal with the ones still inside the fence," Pak said.

"When their buddies don't come back, they're going to be harder to crack," Hawkins said.

"So let's not give them too much time to think about it," McCarter said. He spoke into his comm set. "Fredo, join us."

They waited, crouched in the shadows of the foliage until Encizo rejoined them.

"Fredo. Landis," McCarter said. "You circle around to the rear and put those choppers out of commission."

Manning slid his backpack free and opened it. He reached inside and withdrew a trio of prepared C-4 blocks with battery-powered detonators already attached. He handed them to Encizo and James.

"Place them inside the engine compartments. Timers are set for two minutes. Activate and then get the hell clear."

Encizo and James took the explosives and slipped away through the trees.

"You have enough for the main event?" McCarter asked.

Manning nodded. "No problem," he said.

"You people always this busy when you go out?" Pak asked.

"They don't pay us to sit around drinking tea and cracking jokes," Hawkins said.

"Well, not the part about drinking tea," McCarter said.

He jerked a hand in the general direction of the watchtowers and the machine guns. "Our first priority," he said.

Manning closed his backpack and slid it over his shoulders again.

"Allen, those machine guns are going to be a regular pain in the arse when we try to breach that fence," McCarter said.

Manning scanned the tall towers, assessing distance and angle. They were well within the range of the P90 he was carrying. He watched as the gunners swung the weapons back and forth, aware they could fully traverse across any approach.

Hawkins's whispered voice reached McCarter's ears.

"I'll take one," he said. "If I can't hit one of those jokers from here, I'd turn in my sharpshooter's badge."

"You saying you have a badge?"

"No, boss, but if I did, I'd hand it in if I missed. Can't say better than that."

"Cheeky sod," McCarter muttered. "Okay, cowboy, you're on."

"Left or right?" Manning asked.

"Left," Hawkins said.

THE ROUND OF autofire exchanged deep in the trees had alerted the watchtower guards. But the rattle of shots were not within their view, so the pair of machine gunners were helpless to help their comrades in the wooded area. They knew something was happening, yet it was hidden. The guards exchanged glances, frustrated. Until someone actually came within their range, they could only wait and listen.

Their fellow foot soldiers had rushed through the gates and into the trees. Gunfire had erupted once more. Faded to silence. No one came back. All the two guards could do was watch until the enemy showed. Then they could employ their weapons.

They never got their chance. Saw no sign of any enemy. Only heard the distant gunfire, and when the silence returned, the guards went back to passive observation.

It stretched out...

ENCIZO AND JAMES ended any conversation as they made their way through the greenery surrounding the perimeter fence. The teeming rain helped to cut down on any sound they made as they traveled. That would also work against them. The deadening rain covered any sound the opposition made, as well. Neither Phoenix Force warrior liked the situation, but all the technical gadgets in existence couldn't control the weather. They stayed within the natural protection of the undergrowth, which helped hide them from sight.

They reached the farthest point around the perimeter of the fence. The forest had been cleared for the construction of the helicopter pad, leaving an open area that would provide little or no cover for their final approach. The landing patch stood inside the perimeter fence.

Crouching, the Phoenix Force pair scanned the way ahead. They had already counted the four-man team covering the choppers, on the alert since the earlier gunfire.

On the far side of the helicopters was the fuel tank.

Encizo watched the cautious movement of the helicopter squad. He glanced over the roof of the main structure to where the outlines of the pair of watchtowers showed.

"We're in position," he said into his comm set and received McCarter's brief response.

"LET'S DO THIS," Manning said to Hawkins.

They set the P90s to single shot, taking up positions just inside the timberline. The targets were obliging by not moving around inside their roofed boxes. If they had been alerted by the flurry of gunfire, they were content to wait until they had visible targets rather than spray the trees with random fire.

Hawkins aligned his weapon on the chest of his chosen target, waiting patiently until he heard Manning's whispered command to fire.

Hawkins stroked the P90's trigger, felt the soft kick against his shoulder. He fired a second shot close after the first. It struck the unsuspecting guard a half inch from Hawkins's first. The guard fell back out of sight.

Beside the younger man, Gary Manning had fired two

quick shots. The second guard toppled back and leaned against the rear box surround, blood trickling from the corner of his mouth.

NEITHER MAN HEARD the suppressed shots offered by Manning and Hawkins. Able to see the towers over the roof of the main building, Encizo and James did spot the reaction as first one, then the second tower guard, was hit. Both men fell out of sight in the tower boxes.

"Let's do this," Encizo said.

He shouldered his own P90 and drew down on one of the closest guards patrolling in the vicinity of the helicopters. Beside him James did the same. They fired within seconds of each other, the suppressed shots hardly heard above the rain. Encizo saw his man jerk sideways as 5.7 mm slugs hammered into his chest. He fell without a struggle. Only feet away, the Korean James had fired on stepped back as the pair of 5.7 mm slugs dug in through the side of his skull and shut down his brain in an instant.

The other two sentries, attracted by the falling bodies, rushed forward to determine what had happened. They ran into the next round of shots coming from the Phoenix Force pair. Caught unprepared, the Koreans were put down quickly.

Encizo left his partner to stand watch as he pulled a fragmentation grenade from his pack. He pulled the pin from the M-69 and signaled for James to move away. Once James had cleared the fence, Encizo let the spoon go and dropped the grenade at the foot of the chain-link fence. He beat a hasty retreat and followed James down onto the ground. The grenade detonated, and James and Encizo felt the shock wave pass over them. As the sound faded, they scrambled to their feet and headed for the torn gap in the fence.

They cut across to where the pair of helicopters stood.

While Encizo handled the explosives Manning had provided, James yanked open the covers of the MD-500 engine housings. Encizo wedged the activated packs into the body of the power plants.

"Let's move," he said to James.

They were about to head for the generator housing for cover, when armed figures appeared from around the far side of the research building. The hammer of autofire reached them, and they sought immediate cover, ticking off the countdown of the explosive packs. They had chosen to move on the far side of the helicopters, using the aircraft as cover. Behind them the angry yells of the Koreans could still be heard.

James spotted a slight depression in the ground and the two Phoenix warriors launched themselves in hurried dives for the promised cover. They hit the water-soaked earth seconds before the helicopters blew. Flame and smoke obscured the bulk of the machines as the powerful explosives ripped them apart. The ground underneath James and Encizo shuddered.

Fragments of shredded metal were hurled in all directions and caught the milling Koreans too close and in the open. Razor-edged shards ripped into clothing and flesh, taking off limbs and turning living flesh into bloody chunks. The wash of heat from the blazing fuel added to the chaos and pain.

As the sound of the blast began to fade, the Phoenix Force operatives were able to hear distant autofire, this time from somewhere on the far side of the building.

"Let's get out of here before they regroup," James said.

As they moved around the large tank that held the fuel for the site, James paused to pull the final explosive from his backpack. He clamped it under the base of the tank, setting the timer for forty minutes, then pressed the button. "Give them something else to think about after we're gone," he said.

"Nice thought to leave them a parting gift," Encizo said.

The pair moved away to rejoin the rest of the team.

It appeared the battle for the research site had been fully engaged, and there would be no retreat.

CHAPTER NINETEEN

Unaware of the events about to unfold, Major Ri On Choi waited for the technician to make his report. The slim white-coated man, plainly nervous at being put on the spot by Choi, looked around with obvious unrest as he stood in the major's office.

"Well?" Choi snapped.

"I…"

"Do you think I might shoot you, if I receive the wrong answer?"

The tech gave a halfhearted smile. "You might," he ventured.

"Is my reputation considered so bad?"

"You are known not to favor fools, and any kind of failure you look on as betrayal."

For the first time in days, Choi actually smiled. He knew that every person within the facility feared him. His command of the establishment was without equal. Yet even Choi had not realized just how strong his reputation had grown. It pleased him. He turned his attention back to the tech.

"Ki Yen, I admire a man who is not afraid to speak his mind. So tell me what you have found. I promise not to shoot you."

"Even if my answers are not what you are seeking?"

Choi considered that. "Probably not. But don't try my patience by giving me all negative ones."

Yen decided he had little choice now. "The signal the

launch mechanism delivered from the ship would appear to have been infected with a code intended to render the NNEMP sequence unstable. It was meant to disable the missile and make it harmless. However, this did not happen. The missile overrode the instruction and continued to its target. It released the NNEMP blast, which in turn *did* create the desired effect. I have analyzed everything in the computer system, and this is the only conclusion I can see. The system was sabotaged."

"So Absalom's calculations were correct? The electromagnetic pulse *is* workable?"

"Yes. Within the constraints of the launch equipment, it was a successful trial, although the overall power of the pulse was weakened."

Choi raised a hand, finger extended. "Then why did the sabotage fail?"

"My thoughts are that, although the code inserted into the launch computer was activated, the NNEMP pulse reversed the polarity and sent it back to source, that being the launch unit. The powerful electronic feedback created must have increased in strength as it returned to the unit and resulted in the sinking of the ship." Yen added, "The NNEMP technology is powerful and is something we are still looking into."

"So my priority is finding out who did this. I have a whole unit of possible suspects, Yen. All of whom are capable of inserting the code into the program." Choi managed a wry smile. "We know the good doctor is an amateur when it actually comes to using a computer, so unless he has been fooling us all this time, he would not have the skills to carry out this sabotage."

"That is true," Yen said. "Absalom may be a genius with the theory, but he needs guidance to enter the calculations."

"There are going to be questions from Pyongyang," Choi

said. "Answers will be demanded, and if I fail to provide the correct answers…"

"It puts you in a difficult position, Major Choi," Yen said.

"Tell me something, Yen. How do I find out who did this? Think about it. How would you go about sabotaging the equipment, writing in the code sequence to compromise the program?"

Ki Yen became nervous again. It was the way Choi was looking at him, a glint of malice in his gaze. A sudden thought occurred to Yen.

Did Major Choi suspect him?

He almost blurted out that he was innocent of any wrongdoing. He forced himself to remain silent. Any sudden denial might draw unwanted attention. Yen had no hand in the crime. He only wished he could convince Choi of that. But how to do it without sounding guilty? Yen decided to stay silent. To gain Choi's trust by working *for* him and not *against* him.

Yen allowed the empty silence to drag on for a while. He turned to face the computer sitting on Choi's desk, studying it intently as his mind worked at a furious pace. He knew Choi would be following his every move. He moved closer to the computer and ran his eyes over the equipment. He heard the hard sound of Choi's boots treading the floor behind him as the major moved closer.

"Major, may I show you what I am thinking?"

Choi nodded. He followed Yen from his office and up the stairs that led to the research lab. It was deserted at the moment because Choi had canceled all work, while he began his investigation.

The faint glimmer of an idea had permeated Yen's conscious thoughts. He considered the idea and allowed it to grow in his mind, as he scanned the room, his gaze moving from unit to unit. He finally stopped, as he stared at the metal door at the far end of the lab.

It was of heavy construction, with a thick glass viewing window in the upper half. A secure unit that held the master computer, fed from every station within the research labs—in fact from all equipment within the building. Its digital memory banks held a record of every command and every piece of information put into each individual unit. It was a secure receptacle. In simple terms: a gigantic memory bank. There was no access to the storage except through Major Choi, who held the electronic access code.

"Major," Yen said, "I believe I may have a way of finding out who put the code into the system."

"Yes?"

Yen pointed in the direction of the steel door and said, "We will find the identity of the traitor in there."

Choi moved so he could see Yen's face. "Tell me."

"The master memory system records every keystroke, gives it a time and date number. If we go though the digital log, it should offer us the code that was entered into the NNEMP's launch sequence."

"It can be done?"

"Yes. But it could take time, Major. With all the keystrokes enabled every day, there must be hundreds, if not thousands, of lines of memory."

Choi nodded. He picked up one of the phones and tapped in a number. When it was answered, he spoke rapidly, ordering one of the guards to come to him. He crossed to the door and entered a code number into the pad on the wall. The steel door clicked, a light coming on inside the room.

"There you are, Yen. Ask for whatever you need. I will supply it. Find me that entry. I don't care how long it takes.

Just identify that code. No one will interrupt you. I am posting a guard at the door. If anyone tries to get inside and disturb you, he will have orders to shoot them."

Yen nodded. He understood the enormity of the task ahead. He also knew he could complete it. This would be his chance to prove himself to Major Choi. His success could lead to bigger things, to a chance to be promoted to a better position.

"Major, I need a starting point," Yen said.

"Explain."

"The date when the NNEMP trial was announced. I am making an assumption that, once the field trial was given the go-ahead, the saboteur would make the decision to insert the sequence code. If I have that date, I can work forward from there."

"Good thinking. The trial was announced six days before. That was when I instructed Absalom to inform his team. But only Absalom and I actually knew *where* the trial would take place. It was a simple safety precaution."

"Of course."

Yen was thinking the secrecy over the location was because Major Choi did not trust anyone on the team. The man believed traitors were waiting behind every door.

On this occasion he had been correct and someone *had* attempted to disrupt the trial.

The man was paranoid—but his paranoia had a basis in reality.

Yen crossed to the door and pulled it open. The solid steel structure moved easily on balanced hinges. As Yen stepped inside the room, he became aware of the electronic hum of equipment. He also felt the light caress of fresh air coming from the ceiling. The room was temperature controlled.

Until this moment only Major Choi himself had ever

been inside the room. Entry was forbidden to everyone in the unit. Choi guarded this sanctum obsessively. Yen considered himself privileged to be allowed inside.

There was a bank of monitor screens, with a working area and keyboard. A comfortable-looking high-backed chair was situated in front of the display.

Yen sensed Major Choi behind him, so he quickly sat down, feeling the contoured seat grip him. He rolled it forward until he was comfortable, pulled the keyboard to him and began to tap in commands.

"I will go back six days, then begin to scan the retained data," Yen said. "I will create a search parameter to seek out what could be considered *unusual* entries. It should help to eliminate *normal* requests."

Choi turned as a uniformed, armed soldier appeared at the open door. He snapped out his instructions, and the Korean took up his position to one side of the door.

"There is a phone on the desk. Press number one to reach me. I don't care if it is in the middle of the night. You will report anything you find."

"Yes, Major."

"I will have refreshments sent to you. Is there anything you need right now?"

"Just some bottled water, sir."

"Thirsty already, Yen?"

Yen did not tell the major his thirst was more from fear than anything else. He had committed himself to giving Choi what he wanted. It would not sit well for Yen, if he failed to deliver.

"A little, Major."

"I will have some brought to you."

Major Choi turned and walked out, leaving Yen alone, partly closing the steel door. A sense of relief washed over the tech. He had asked for water, because his throat had become very dry, and he knew it was due to the realization that he was, without a doubt, still under the watchful eye of Major Ri On Choi.

HIS SUPPLY OF bottled water was brought in a few minutes later. Yen broke the seal on one of the bottles and swallowed some of the chilled water. He set aside the bottle and began to work at the keyboard, tapping in the commands, as he created his search program. Depending on how smart the saboteur had been, Yen couldn't guarantee his attempt to isolate the individual's record trace would work.

Not working would be unacceptable to Major Choi. As far as he was concerned, Yen had made a promise. Choi would expect that promise to be honored. In theory Yen's idea *should* work. Somewhere within the multitude of computer lines was the one that would identify the saboteur.

Yen simply had to find it.

He noticed his hands were trembling as they hovered over the keyboard. He clenched and unclenched his fists a few times, willing himself to calm down. The trembling ceased, and Yen took a breath.

You can do this, he told himself. They are just lines of code. All you need to do is unravel them.

He completed his input and activated his program, then watched the monitor in front of him as columns of digits flashed by.

The flow was interrupted every minute or so, as blocks of text were separated. He had asked that anything out of the ordinary be moved to a fresh cell to be displayed on one of the other monitors. As each block was checked and cleared, Yen felt his spirits sink. He realized the process could take hours, and all he could do was sit and wait.

The first hour passed and still the backup files produced nothing abnormal. They appeared to comprise tedious day-to-day records of the research lab's work. Nothing that should not have been there.

Into the third hour Yen was starting to believe there was no trace to be found.

Perhaps the saboteur had been smart enough to write the code sequence in such a way that it was able to fool the computer into believing it was an acceptable string and would be overlooked by his program.

Staring fixedly at the monitors strained his eyes. His body became stiff from being immobile. Yen felt the screen images blur.

He almost missed it when the second monitor suddenly flashed a section of numbers. The block sat on the screen, and Yen's concentration on the main monitor prevented him from picking it up for a minute, until his eyes caught the text. He turned and stared at it for a while. His fingers reached down to the keyboard and quickly hit the save symbol.

He studied the data and read through it, seeing the subtle way it had been written, cleverly constructed to blend into the already programmed instructions for firing off the NNEMP projectile, yet artfully worked out so as to override the safety protocols and reverse the launch codes. Yen realized he would, after a careful analysis, be able to determine how the alphanumeric string had failed and countered itself.

A clever plan that had backfired in more ways than one. In retrospect, Yen decided, it must have been planted too quickly and errors in the program had not been strong enough to fully maintain integrity. The NNEMP burst had proved Absalom's work. It had inflicted damage to the American target but had been tampered with.

The final result was that the delivery system had been sent to the bottom of the ocean. Even Yen realized the danger behind that. If the Americans got their hands on the launch equipment, they would be able to point the finger directly at North Korea. And also offer them valuable technical information.

The saved data filled the screen. Yen read through it and then ran his diagnostic, bringing up the information that told him the computer station that had generated the sequence. Each member of the research team had his or her own station, accessed by individual names and a personal entry code. This was a safeguard to maintain overall control of the data input. It took no more than a few keystrokes to bring up the computer station and the person assigned to it.

Yen spotted something else. The mass of collected data on the NNEMP system had been downloaded onto removable drives. Something that was not sanctioned. Someone had been stealing the research data.

Yen tapped in the override code that would display the identity of the guilty person.

The name that flashed on the screen, with the security photo image, was Li Kam.

The last person Yen would have expected to see.

But then the very nature of being an undercover operative was that of being the most unlikely one to commit any criminal activity.

Yen sat back, groping for his bottled water. He took a long swallow. His mind was still having difficulty absorbing what he was seeing.

In the end he had to accept the inevitable.

Li Kam was the traitor.

There could be no mistake. Her code had been entered to allow access to her computer station. Only she was permitted to use that particular unit. If someone tried to use someone else's machine, the physical presence would have been noticed. If work had taken place on Li Kam's computer, it could only have been done by Li Kam herself.

The evidence was unshakable.

There was no way around it.

Li Kam was the guilty one.

Yen reached for the phone on the desk and punched in the number that would connect him to Major Choi.

"Yes?"

"Major, it is Ki Yen."

"You have good news I hope."

"Yes. I have the name of the person who programmed the code inserted into the launch program."

"Tell me," Choi said in a remarkably calm tone.

"Li Kam."

"You have no doubts?"

"I have the inserted code isolated on a monitor in front of me, along with the relevant information on the individual who placed it in the computer. It was Li Kam. Something else, Major. The system shows that data has also been downloaded onto removable drives."

Major Choi found he was not entirely surprised. Li Kam was not simply bright. She had a sharp intellect and a way about her that made Choi feel there was more going on inside her head than simply the apparent devotion to her work. Now, it seemed, her outward loyalty to the state was nothing more than camouflage. While she carried out her role as one of Absalom's assistants, she had also been creating mischief; mischief that had caused a partial failure in the Hawaiian strike and the sinking of the launch vessel, bringing long-term problems for North Korea if the NNEMP equipment fell into American hands.

It was good that there was a North Korean presence in Hawaii, a covert team placed to oversee the results of the strike. Now that team would be tasked with recovering the equipment and returning it to Korea, out of enemy hands. Hopefully the equipment could be investigated and data recovered. The NNEMP research would not end with this catastrophe.

Choi sat for a moment, digesting the information, before he spoke.

"Very well, Yen. Make certain that evidence is saved and stored. I will be with you shortly."

The phone call was ended.

Yen replaced the receiver. It was out of his hands now. Major Choi would deal with the matter.

Li Kam's fate, and her life, lay in the man's hands.

Yen was considering what his revelations to Major Choi might mean for himself, when there was a rattle of gunfire coming from outside the building. It sounded like automatic fire. The shooting increased. Then there were heavy explosions that made the walls shudder. A window shattered…

CHAPTER TWENTY

Able Team took time out for Lyons to have his wounds treated. Kalikani had directed them to the closest hospital, using his official status to get priority emergency help. Thereafter Kalikani excused himself to check with his unit. Outside the emergency entrance, he keyed his cell and spoke with his department.

"Heard about your little escapade," Tasker said. "You got time to take a message?"

"Go ahead."

"That skinny guy, Mojo," Tasker said. "He called at least three times in the last half hour. Guy is all over the place."

"I don't have time for Mojo right now."

"Maybe you should hear what he has to say. He won't talk to anyone except you. Says he has information you need to hear. About your run-in over the *King Kamehameha*."

"How in hell did he get to know about that?"

"Oscar, he's a smart guy. Has a bead on everything going down. You told me that yourself."

Kalikani debated what to do.

He looked back over his shoulder to the treatment room where the American team was.

"*Oscar?* You want to deal with this? Mojo won't talk to anyone else."

"I want backup," Kalikani said. "Have a cruiser meet me at the edge of the location, ready to move in if I call."

"You think it's necessary? Mojo seemed determined he only wanted to see you."

"After what happened already today, I take no more chances."

"Oscar, you're sounding almost smart."

"No one ever told me that before."

"I'll have a unit join you. I just don't want Mojo taking off, because you have someone else along."

"I'll make sure the backup stays out of sight."

"Don't screw this up."

Kalikani walked out of the hospital. His mind replayed the conversation he had just had with Rudy Tasker. The captain had seemed almost reluctant when Kalikani had requested backup. With the way things had been playing, Kalikani was simply being cautious. Tasker should understand that. Kalikani, like any HPD cop, knew budget restraints sometimes forced themselves on operational procedures, but asking for a backup car wasn't about to break the bank.

So why was Tasker acting like he had a bug up his ass?

Kalikani found the conversation weird.

He made his way to the parking lot and climbed into his vehicle. As he fired up the engine, his radio buzzed and he picked up the handset.

"Kalikani."

A voice he recognized came over the speaker.

"Hey, O. You need backup? Tasker called me."

As Kalikani cruised out of the lot, he smiled. The young female cop on the radio was Jenny Lopaka, a twenty-nine-year-old Hawaiian he had worked with on a number of occasions. She was a cop who he had no problems having as backup.

Almost from the first time he had met her, Lopaka had addressed him as O. Never Oscar. Or Kalikani. Simply O.

"So you going to babysit me today?"

"No one else wants to do the job," Lopaka said lightly. "Looks like I got the really short straw."

"I'm on my way to the location right now. I want you to hang back, but keep your ears open for my call if I need you."

"No lights, no siren," Lopaka promised.

"You hear about earlier?"

"Uh-huh."

"So these people are not playing games, Jenny."

"Just what I like, O, my man."

Jenny Lopaka had a reputation as a tough street-smart cop. In a few short years, she had worked her way up to sergeant and had a long list of solid busts on her sheet. As well as being a crack shot, she was also a ranking martial artist. Kalikani had personally seen her take down a six-six solid hardcase with nothing more than a few quick moves. Having Jenny Lopaka as your backup was akin to having a SWAT team on your six. Added to that, she was also a stunning young woman who didn't feel the need to compete with anyone.

"Where are your new buddies from the mainland?"

Kalikani negotiated a snarl of traffic. "One of them got a couple of whacks on the head during the takedown this morning. Had to leave them at the hospital while getting him doctored up. If Mojo wants an urgent meet, it can't wait, or he'll decide to go native and hide out. If Mojo hides, even *Hawaii Five-O* couldn't find him."

"Tasker said the meet is at the old Wiseman apartments. Even I know that is a bad place to go in solo. You sure about this, O?"

"No. But with you at my back, I feel safer."

"Brother, you have great faith. I'll try not to let you down."

Kalikani guided his vehicle through the late-afternoon

traffic. He hit the AC button and felt the chilled air start to blow.

He recalled what Lopaka had said about the location for the meet. She was right about it being a tough spot. He appreciated Mojo not wanting to meet in a busy place, where he might be seen talking to a cop. In all the years he had known Mojo, they had kept to quiet spots, but never one as remote as the Wiseman scene. Kalikani shook his head. Tasker had said Mojo needed the meeting urgently, so he was going to have to suck up his doubts and make it.

"Lopaka, when we get to Wiseman, you hang back but stay on the ball. Okay?"

"Hey, I'm not about to drop to sleep, O. Your back will be covered."

"I can be sure of that?"

Lopaka laughed. "O, believe me. I'm a cop."

IT WAS STARTING to get gloomy as Kalikani rolled his cruiser off the main highway, and bumped over the cracked and uneven strip that led to the meeting place.

The area was in the early stages of falling apart, a collection of empty apartment buildings that was waiting for the wrecking crews to start tearing them down. In the years they had stood empty, the buildings had been subjected to vandalism, used as crack houses, refuges for the homeless and somewhere for low-rent hookers to take their unsuspecting johns.

Kalikani headed his car across the empty lot fronting the buildings, searching the shadows. He saw nothing except the derelict building and the burned-out shell of an automobile. Beyond the trees behind the apartment blocks, he made out the haze of city lights coming on in the distance. Over there was noise and people. Here it was another world—shadows and near silence with only the occasional hum of a passing vehicle on the highway.

Kalikani stopped the car and turned off the engine. He was about to step out, when caution dictated his actions. He loosened his autopistol in the holster on his hip, then opened his door ready to climb out. Kalikani reached across and pressed the transmit button on the handset, leaving the channel open.

"You still hearing me, Jenny? I'm leaving the channel open so you can monitor."

"Got you loud and clear."

He hadn't seen or heard anything—but he began to experience an uneasy feeling in the pit of his stomach. He had been a cop long enough to heed those feelings.

Experience was clicking in.

The sensation of something being off-kilter grew stronger.

He stepped out, pulling his S&W and holding it parallel with his pants leg, as he walked to the front of the auto. The shadows, deeper in the trees, stopped him seeing anything in detail, but he was sure he could see someone standing directly ahead of him. The figure looked familiar.

"That you, Mojo? Step out here. It's Kalikani. You wanted this meet. So here I am. Let's do it, brother."

Kalikani reached the front of the auto. He saw the figure start out from the shadow of the trees and undergrowth. His trigger finger tapped repeatedly against the side of the S&W. That told him he *was* uneasy.

"Hey, Mojo, don't screw around, man. I got other things to do."

That was when the moving figure stopped, and even at the distance they were apart, Kalikani saw the man's head move to one side.

In the pale light he saw the man was *not* Mojo.

Warned, the Hawaiian cop began to turn as he picked up a whisper of sound close by.

There was a flicker of movement behind him. He saw a heavy figure closing fast. Then the blur of something slicing through the air a second before Kalikani felt a solid blow that slammed across his left shoulder. The blow stunned him. Enough to make him tip sideways, and it was only the bulk of the car that kept him from going down. Tears of pain filled Kalikani's eyes. He slid along the hood of the car. A second blow landed, his legs almost giving way under him.

Kalikani tried to stay on his feet. He knew, if he went down to the ground, he was finished. He turned his body to face his attacker and saw the dark bulk as the guy moved in for another strike. He heard someone yell, picked up the thump of booted feet on the ground as the first guy moved to join the fray.

A third blow cracked ribs on his left side. Kalikani gasped. The pain was intense.

Son of a bitch.

He was inwardly calling himself every kind of an idiot for walking into this. With eyes wide open. Like a newly badged rookie. The morning's incident had been bad enough. Now he had been suckered into a fake meet that might easily turn into his premature funeral.... He had no idea what was really going on. All he did know was somebody was working hard to keep him and the team from the mainland from getting too close.

He had to do something before the second guy reached him. Two of them pounding away at him and he was finished.

Through watering eyes he made out the new guy, wielding what looked like a baseball bat. That was a moment before his original attacker delivered the fourth blow. It cracked across Kalikani's left arm, just below the elbow, and Kalikani heard bone snap. A burst of pain exploded.

Kalikani managed to bring his pistol up from where he had been holding it concealed between his leg and the side of the car. There was no hesitation in his action as he swung the S&W on line and eased back on the trigger. The pistol cracked twice. The range was short by this time—no more than a couple of feet—and both 9 mm slugs slammed into the attacker's chest. He stumbled forward a couple more steps, the bat slipping from his fingers, then he toppled forward and hit the ground on his front, his face slamming into the hard earth. His slack body bounced as he hit.

Kalikani heard the roar of a car and knew Jenny had heard the attack over the open channel and was coming in like the 7th Cavalry.

Tires burned on the concrete.

Kalikani heard Lopaka's voice as she left her cruiser.

His senses were all over the place, pain overriding everything else.

"Police. Lay it down," Lopaka yelled at the second guy.

Kalikani saw the swinging baseball bat arcing in again. He tried to duck but the tip scraped across the right side of his jaw, blood welling up from the tear in his flesh.

Then he heard the rapid burst of fire from Lopaka's Beretta. At least a half dozen 9 mm slugs blasted into the hitter's face, obliterating his features and twisting him off stride. The guy didn't even have a chance to yell as his head was snapped back under the close range of Lopaka's burst. Dark gouts of blood erupted from the back of his skull as a couple of the slugs powered through.

The swinging bat lost its momentum, slamming across the auto's windshield, leaving a starred pattern.

The shot guy went down, and his body wriggled for a while before it became still.

Kalikani slumped to the ground, his entire body burning with pain. He could taste hot blood in his mouth where the inside of his cheek had caught against his teeth.

"Hey, you still with me, O?"

Kalikani blinked away the tears from his eyes and stared up into Jenny Lopaka's face. Her concern showed as she helped him lean against the side of his vehicle.

She keyed her comm set and asked for medical assistance. She gave their location.

"On its way," she told Kalikani.

He was trying to get up but she forced him back down.

"I need to see who these guys were," he said. "We might get something from them. We don't have time to waste...."

"I'll check them out. You stay where you are, O."

Kalikani saw her push to her feet, casting around in the gloom. He kept his S&W in his right hand, pushing back the pain threatening to overwhelm him as he covered Lopaka's back.

She checked the guy she had shot. He was dead. Then she moved to the one Kalikani had dropped, crouching to find a pulse.

"He's gone," she called.

Lopaka holstered her pistol, then she frisked the dead men expertly, coming up with a few items she brought back to Kalikani.

"Wallet," she said. "Full of money. All hundred-dollar bills. A lot of them. Looks like they got paid in advance. Driver's license. Says the guy is Ritchie Stroud. Hell, I know that name, O. He's a lowlife. Hangs around the docks. Done time for petty crimes. Offer him cash, and he'd mug his own grandmother. Last time I saw him, he was on his way to do six months in the slammer. Other one is Ben Loki. Similar rap sheet as Stroud."

LOPAKA WAS AT Kalikani's side as the medic team stretchered him into the ambulance. The two bodies were being placed in the medical examiner's vehicle for transport to the morgue. She had spoken to the cops who had turned up and given a statement. She would have to show up later at the station and speak to the incident team.

"It won't cause you any problems," Kalikani said. He was groggy from the sedative the medics had given him, but refused to give in. "This was a righteous shooting. I'm involved, as well, so we look out for each other."

Lopaka said, "What are you? My dad?"

Kalikani winced as pain from his cracked ribs flared.

"You wish," he said.

One of the medics said, "We need to get moving."

"I'll see you there," Lopaka promised and headed for her cruiser.

KALIKANI WAS TAKEN to emergency for X-rays and treatment. Before he was wheeled away, he told Lopaka about Able Team and their own presence at the hospital.

"Go talk to them. An update."

"Leave it with me, tough guy."

"Compared to you, I'm a pussycat."

Her laughter trailed down the corridor.

LOPAKA FOUND WHERE Able Team was gathered, drawing appreciative glances when she stepped into the room.

"Sergeant Jenny Lopaka, HPD. Kalikani asked me to drop by. He…he's been hurt."

She told them what had happened, filling them in on the incident.

"How bad?" Blancanales asked.

"Looks like a broken arm. Maybe cracked ribs and a bad scrape across his jaw."

"You took both perps down?" Lyons asked.

Lopaka shook her head. "I handled one. O dropped the other."

"What started it all?" Schwarz asked.

"One of O's informants asked for a meet, insisted he had to see him about that boat involved in the Coast Guard strike. Had the name. When we got there, the snitch wasn't around, but two guys with baseball bats attacked O."

"Not entirely successful by the sounds of it," Blancanales said.

"This takedown," Lyons said. "Lethal?"

Lopaka nodded. "They should be in the morgue by now."

"Who were they?"

"Couple local hard guys."

Blancanales said, "Not hard enough, huh?"

"This was a setup," Lyons said. "What is it with this place? Everyone wants us out of the way."

"I think you've made someone very nervous," Lopaka said. She looked Lyons over. "How're you feeling?"

"Headache and a bruised jaw. I'll live. We should go check on Kalikani."

"I'll take you to see him."

Able Team followed the young woman. After a few yards, Blancanales pushed ahead so he could walk beside her.

"I'll bet his pulse rate just shot off the scale," Schwarz murmured.

By the time they reached the treatment room, Blancanales and Lopaka were conversing like long-lost friends.

"Why O?" he asked her.

She glanced at him.

"Just a little joke between us," she said. "Happened the first time we paired up, before I made sergeant. He gets impulsive. Did things on the beat that would surprise me, and I'd say *oh*. And he would respond, like I'd called his name. It kind of stuck. So that's what I call him now. Just O. Kind of stupid, I know, but that's it."

Blancanales said, "Nice."

ABLE TEAM HUNG around until they were able to step inside and see Kalikani. The cop had his left arm in plaster and his ribs were taped up. He also had butterfly strips over the injury to his jaw.

"We always thought Matthews was the one who dived in regardless," Schwarz said.

Kalikani grinned, then winced as his sore jaw reminded him what had happened. He had to speak slowly. "I guess I walked into this with both eyes open."

"Any thoughts on who might have set you up?" Lyons asked.

Kalikani nodded gently. "Some thoughts I need to keep to myself, until I'm sure. But it has to do with what we're dealing with. The message I got mentioned the *King Kamehameha*."

"Which got your attention," Schwarz said.

"I took the bait..." Kalikani said.

"And got hooked," Lopaka added.

Kalikani extended his right hand. "Did I mention Lopaka here helped me off that hook. Don't get her mad, because she's a mean shot."

"That coming from the guy who had just taken a beating and still managed to put two rounds into the perp who did it."

"I'm not going to get out of here anytime soon," Kalikani said. "Not going to be much help on the street for a while, so I'll stay office based. You'll still need a guide around the island, so I'll let Lopaka stand in for me. Any objections?"

"No objections," Blancanales said a little too quickly. Then he continued, "Officer Lopaka will be a great help."

So Sergeant Jenny Lopaka, HPD, became a temporary assistant for Able Team.

CHAPTER TWENTY-ONE

Macklin saw the approaching vehicle through binoculars. It moved slowly as it negotiated the winding road. There was a lead car in front and a backup behind the main vehicle. Macklin watched as the small convoy came in their direction.

"Get ready," he said.

Borgnine nodded. He reached across the seat and picked one of the pair of LAWs lying there. Spelman picked up the second one.

"This should be easy," he said. He caught Borgnine's eye. "Which one do you want? Front or rear?"

"Never thought about it."

"I'll take the lead car, then," Spelman said.

They were parked in a rest area off the road. Thick stands of greenery hugged the back of the area and a rented panel truck was waiting alongside the big 4x4. There were two more of Macklin's men in the van.

Macklin pushed open his door and climbed out, Borgnine and Spelman following. They stayed behind the 4x4, waiting for Macklin to give them the signal. He stood casually leaning by the big vehicle, smoking one of the big cigars he favored, a cell phone held to his ear.

When the lead car showed, Macklin maintained his pretense, letting the car cruise by. The HPD armored truck containing the package followed twenty feet behind. The backup car was twenty feet behind the truck. As the truck drew level with Macklin, he lowered the cell and called out to Borgnine and Spelman.

They moved from cover, Borgnine from the rear of the 4x4, Spelman the front. They shouldered the LAWs and targeted the cars, firing within a second of each other.

The 88 mm rockets burst from the launch tubes with a throaty *whoosh* of sound, leaving identical trails of smoke. They hit the cars and detonated. The vehicles vanished for seconds as the high-explosive warheads turned them into fiery balls of flame and smoke. The concentrated blasts tore apart the cars, metal and human debris scattered across the road. The rear backup car was lifted off the ground and flipped over on its side, burning fuel spilling out across the tarmac.

The waiting panel truck broke cover and wheeled across to block the truck, Macklin's men emerging, carrying 9 mm SMGs. They hit the tires with concentrated bursts, shredding them.

"Borgnine," Macklin yelled. "The pair in the cab. Fix it."

The driver had kicked open his door and emerged cradling a pistol in his hands. He walked directly into a volley of autofire that dropped him to the ground. Borgnine stepped over his jerking body and leaned in the open door, firing at the driver's partner as the guy attempted to get out, slamming him against the far door. He slid into the foot well in a twisted heap.

"Quit screwing around, Jake," Macklin called. "Get back here."

Borgnine and Spelman joined Macklin as he approached the back of the armored truck. He banged on the rear door.

"Come out fast," he said. "Make it hard for us and we will make you suffer."

The rear door rattled as the handle was released. The door swung open and a subdued figure emerged, arms partly raised. He stepped out, looking between the armed figures waiting for him. He was a broad-shouldered native Hawaiian, sweating from being confined inside the body of the truck.

"Hot in there, bro," Borgnine said.

The guy looked at him, frowning at the remark.

Spelman leaned in to check the interior of the truck.

"It's there," he said.

Macklin threw his cigar into the flames of the second car as the Hawaiian stepped by him. He slid his 9 mm Beretta from his belt. The muzzle brushed against the back of the guard's skull as he pulled the trigger twice, one slug blowing out through his forehead. The guy jerked forward, dropping to his knees, then flopped to the ground, his body going into a spasm.

"Let's go," Macklin said.

The pair from the panel truck handed their SMGs to the others and climbed inside the truck. They freed the restraining straps and manhandled the square metal unit to the door, then eased it out. Borgnine stepped in to assist, and they carried the unit from the truck to the nearby panel van, where they slid it inside and secured the rear doors.

"Let's get out of here," Macklin told them.

Once the panel van had exited, Macklin, Spelman and Borgnine climbed into the 4x4 and drove off.

The hijack was completed. Successful. Carried out with the minimum of fuss and full use of the time available.

As quickly as that.

The wrecked cars were issuing dark smoke that swirled up into the clear Hawaiian sky. It was at least twenty minutes before a car appeared, coming to a hurried stop so the driver could use his cell to call the police.

CHAPTER TWENTY-TWO

ABLE TEAM

The first responder was followed by a fire truck and an ambulance. The burning cars were beyond help as were the occupants. The passengers in the burned-out cars had been killed by the rocket blasts, and their bodies badly burned in the resulting fires. The only survivor was the truck driver's partner. He had four 9 mm slugs in him, but he was still alive. Barely, but he was not dead yet.

With the arrival of nighttime, lights were set up to illuminate the scene. The area swarmed with police, fire officials and medics.

BY THE TIME the information got back to Oscar Kalikani, the trail was cold. No one had witnessed the attack, and there were no traffic cameras in the area that might offer some clue as to who had mounted the attack.

He called Carl Lyons's hotel from his office and gave him the details.

"These guys were well organized," he said. "We'll keep looking. Maybe we'll get a break somewhere along the line. Matthews, you don't need to remind me that we're on a deadline here. If they have the item, they'll be wanting to get it out of the country fast."

"The guy from the truck? Did he stay alive?"

"Yeah. He's in intensive care. Got him under armed guard. Why?"

Kalikani suspected what Lyons was about to ask.

"Maybe he can give us something. Right now he's our only witness. We need to see him."

"Last I heard the guy is still unconscious." There was silence on the line. "Okay, Lopaka can direct you to the hospital. But don't yell at me if the docs won't let you in to see him."

"Thanks, Officer O," Lyons said quietly. "You take it easy. Let us handle things for the moment."

JENNY LOPAKA HAD a grin on her face when she picked up Able Team.

"You win the lottery?" Schwarz asked as they joined her in the HPD vehicle.

"Good as," Lopaka said. "Kalikani was telling me you called him O." She was looking directly at Lyons.

He shrugged. "He's had a rough time since we got here."

From the rear of the 4x4, Blancanales stifled a laugh. He tapped Lyons on the shoulder. "You called the guy by Lopaka's pet name? That crack on your head must have softened your brain."

Schwarz said, "If he starts giving me goo-goo eyes, I'm taking the first jet home."

They entered the hospital, and Lopaka directed them to the unit where the guard was being treated. An HPD officer was seated on a chair outside. He stood up when Lopaka approached.

"What's the situation?" she asked.

The cop glanced by her at Able Team.

"It's okay, Stan. These are special agents from the mainland."

The Stony Man team showed their badges.

"This is Officer Stan Benson," Lopaka said.

Introductions were made and Lyons asked, "How's our patient doing?"

"Would you believe they took four slugs out of him, and the guy is already sitting up?"

"We need to talk to him," Lyons said.

The cop hesitated, unsure how he should handle the situation. "I was told…"

"Right now that guy in there is the only survivor," Lyons snapped. "We're out here wasting time when he could be handing us something we can use."

"I…"

"I understand your position," Lyons said. "I was a cop myself with LAPD. I'm not trying to make trouble for you, Stan. But I need to speak with that guy."

"He has clearance that goes above anything we have," Lopaka said. "He'll take responsibility."

"His name is Joe Matson," Benson said. He flipped the door handle and pushed it open, then stepped aside, nodding at Lyons.

"I don't want to crowd him," Lyons said. "You all stay out here."

He didn't wait, simply stepped into the room and closed the door.

The blinds were half-closed, leaving the room in shadows. Lyons picked up the subdued hum coming from the monitoring equipment attached to the patient. Matson was propped up on pillows, tubes taped everywhere and an oxygen mask over the lower part of his face. His eyes were fixed on Lyons, as the Able Team commander crossed the room.

"I'm Joseph Matthews. From the mainland," Lyons said. "I'm with the Task Force looking into what happened. Right now, Joe, I need your help, because we're in a bind. I don't have much to go on, so anything you can tell me is going to be a help."

Matson turned his head slowly so he could keep Lyons in his line of vision. "They tell you about my partners?" he said.

"Bad break."

Matson nodded slowly. "I want you to catch these bastards."

The guy reached out a big hand and laid it in Lyons's arm, fingers tight. When he spoke, his words were muffled by the oxygen mask, so he peeled it away, took a pained breath.

"They were waiting for us. Hit the escort cars with LAWs. Recognized them just before they fired." He sucked in more oxygen from the mask. "One of them headed for the cab and shot Max when he opened the door. Then the guy came for me. It happened smooth. Like a military operation. I was in the service, and the way they operated was just like they trained us. They moved fast." He took more air. "That son of a bitch just hit me. There were bullets flying all around me. I expected more, but someone called him off to help with the rear door."

"You remember what was said, Joe?"

"Damn right. His name was Borgnine. Like the movie actor. *Borgnine*. I was already down when someone called him a second time. First name. Could have been Jack. Jake. Jerry. That was all I got before I went under. Man, I figured that was it for me." Matson added, "Just before that asshole fired on Max, I spotted a white panel van parked across from us. No markings on it."

Lyons let Matson replace his mask and flop back against the pillow. The man's face glistened with perspiration.

"Thanks for that, Joe. It'll help. We'll get them. Promise. Now take it easy."

When he left the room, Lyons quietly closed the door.

"Anything?" Schwarz asked.

"Couple things," Lyons said. "He told me that he thinks they might have had military training. Said the operation was smooth and fast. They knew what they were doing. Took out the escort cars with LAWs. Had the truck caught between them, then hit the truck cab and moved to the rear to get the inside guy out. And the guy that shot him was called Borgnine. He also heard a first name for the guy. Jake, Jack, something along those lines."

"Borgnine? Like the…" Benson said.

"Yeah," Lyons said. "Like the movie actor."

"I can get Kalikani to run the name through the system," Lopaka said and moved off, using her cell.

Lyons glanced at Benson. "Thanks for your help, Stan. We have to go."

Lyons led Schwarz and Blancanales along the corridor, passing Lopaka, who was still on her cell.

When they stepped outside, Lyons took out his own cell and tapped in the speed dial for Stony Man. Price came on.

"I need Bear to run a name," he said. "Borgnine. And before you ask, yes, like the actor. Also first name's along the lines of Jake, Jack, Jerry. Got this from a survivor of an attack. The hit was professional. Run like a military operation, so check into service personnel. If you come up with anything, run a secondary check for possible connections to other military types. See what the cyberjockeys can find. If you get a hit, it might link with buddies he served with."

"I'll call back if we hit pay dirt. You need anything else?"

"Not right now."

Lyons ended the call, not wanting to get into any protracted talk with Price. There was too much rattling around

in his mind, and he still had a headache from the batter-
ing to his skull.

Jenny Lopaka rejoined them; her cell remained in her
hand.

"O will let us know if his trace picks anything up," she
said.

"Looks like we're on a loose end until then," Schwarz
said. "Why don't we grab some food while we wait?"

"Sounds good to me," Blancanales said. "What do you
say, boss?"

Lyons glared at him. "As if I have any choice. This pair
would put WW3 on hold so they could fill their stomachs."

"Now, boys, no sulking on my watch," the Hawaiian
cop said. "Let's do it."

SHE TOOK THEM to a seafood snack bar just off Waikiki
Beach. Lopaka ordered for them. She obviously knew the
owner, and he provided a spread of local prawns and crab,
fresh snapper and a bowl of salad. There was fresh pine-
apple and bread. A pitcher of chilled fruit juice was placed
on the table.

"Go ahead, guys, no need to be shy. This is Hawaii,
food to be enjoyed."

There was little argument from Able Team. Despite the
urgency of their ongoing mission, they used the opportunity to indulge.

"This is only reinforcing my belief we should relocate
here," Schwarz said. "What's not to like?"

"We still get shot at," Blancanales pointed out.

"Not-so-nice neighbors," Lyons said.

"Hey, you guys. Don't make it sound so bad," Lopaka
said.

Schwarz told her, "This is a great place, really."

"What made you want to be a cop?" Lyons asked.

"You really want to know?"

"Sure."

"I look good in the uniform."

Blancanales grinned. "You certainly do, Officer Lopaka."

"Apart from that, I always wanted to be a cop. Since I was twelve years old."

"Not so long ago then," Blancanales said, always the politician. Blancanales's easy manner had earned him his nickname, *Pol*.

"Is he always like this with the ladies?" Lopaka asked.

"Always the charmer," Schwarz said. "So be aware— be very aware."

A little while later Lyons's cell rang.

He listened as Barbara Price gave him a verbal rundown of the facts the cyberteam had unearthed. She ended by telling him the full facts were being downloaded to his phone. "Hope it helps," she finished.

"It will," Lyons said. "And thanks."

He heard his mail app ring and opened the download. Along with the text, there were a couple photos.

"Jake Borgnine. Ex-military. Army. Now a freelance security operative. His sheet is saying he's basically a mercenary. Gun for hire who'll work for anyone with the right amount of cash. Works under his former unit commander. Major William Macklin. According to info here, Macklin is a hardcase who clashed with top brass, because he liked to do things his way, not the Army's way."

Lyons read through the files, then gave a concise briefing to the others.

"Just the kind of guys to run that hit on the convoy," Schwarz said.

"First we go back and show Joe Matson this photo, see

if he recognizes Jake Borgnine. If he does, we've got him nailed down," Lyons said.

"All we have to do after that is find him," Lopaka said.

Lyons drained his glass of juice. "Let's go."

MATSON LOOKED AT the image for no more than a few seconds, before he nodded.

"That's the mother. A face I won't forget ever." He switched his gaze to Lyons. "You guys don't waste time."

"It's the one thing we don't have much of."

"Hey, did I help?"

"Damn right, Joe. You opened this investigation up for us."

Now, Lyons thought, it's time for us to close it.

CHAPTER TWENTY-THREE

NORTH KOREA

Choi was not fully aware what was happening. He started in alarm when the explosions filled the air with sound. Windows behind him blew in, sending glass spinning across the room, and he even felt particles strike the back of his jacket. As the echo of the blast began to fade, he heard the staccato crackle of autofire. He recognized the hard pops of his men's Type 68s. There was answering fire from other weapons—those he did not recognize but assumed they were weapons belonging to the strike force.

"The helicopters have been destroyed," one of the soldiers said, his face glistening from the rain as he ran inside. "We have intruders."

Choi managed a wry smile, as he faced the man. "Then why are you in here and not seeking out these people?"

The soldier stood, hesitant, lost for words. And then he turned around and ran back out the door. Choi followed, leaving by the main entrance, and hurried around to the far side of the building. He stared in disbelief at the sight of the blazing helicopters.

He slid out the cord attached to the communication set tucked into his uniform top pocket and turned it on. Then he inserted the earbud and angled the thin microphone into place.

"This is Major Choi. Someone tell me what is happening."

All he heard was a buzz of static.

Major Choi saw his career stalling because of this attack. His superiors in Pyongyang would see the failure of his command, and there would be severe recriminations. The North Korean structure left no breathing space for such things to happen. Especially to special projects like Cobalt Blue. By placing the research station here, on this isolated section of the coast, the thinking had been that no one would connect the dots. Choi and his team would be able to carry out their research into NNEMP development away from interested eyes.

Pyongyang had been hoping the weapon would be perfected long before anyone became aware of its existence. That seemed to have been wishful thinking. The dramatic occurrence in Hawaii had done little to keep the secret. Cobalt Blue had been compromised. And now Choi and his team were under attack.

His earpiece buzzed as a voice came through his comm set.

"Major, this is Zang. We have located a small force inside the compound. Three, maybe more. They have blown the helicopters…"

"I have already been informed. Where are they now?"

"They have been spotted going in the direction of the research lab…and…Major, Li Kam is with them. She is carrying a weapon. Major, she is not a hostage…"

"I understand that already. She is working *with* them. Li Kam is the one who interfered with the field trial in Hawaii. She planted the virus that was supposed to destroy the NNEMP firing."

"*Major?* What are your orders?"

"Idiot, what do you think? Stop them. If Kam is leading them to the research lab, they are going to destroy the project. Take them, preferably dead, but stop what they intend doing."

Choi heard more autofire. The sudden blast of a grenade.

If the research lab was destroyed, Choi might as well use his last bullet on himself. There would be no moving forward from such a disaster. Even connections he had in the capitol would sever their contacts. They would not want to be associated with him. Major Ri On Choi would suddenly find the world a cold and inhospitable place.

Choi was a true follower of the regime, and as such, he would not go down without a fight. The training hammered into him as he had progressed through the ranks left him with a single purpose: uphold the commands of the Leader. Protect the ideals of the nation. Nothing else mattered. No sacrifice was too great.

But at that precise moment Choi concentrated on the matter at hand.

His location was under threat from enemies. His responsibility was to protect it. To stop anyone from destroying the project. Nothing was more important than that. Choi did not care where the strike force came from or how strong they were. He would throw the full force of his men at them. Pyongyang would expect nothing less. And Major Ri On Choi would not back down from that. He owed his life, his very existence, to the state. The state was all that mattered. Nothing else.

Yet behind all that was a secondary concern. Something that Choi was unable to erase from his mind.

The betrayal by Li Kam.

A supposed loyal party member, who had been given such responsibility by the state. North Korea had trained her at great expense. Given her the opportunity to serve her nation, and she had worked against them. Her knowledge had allowed her to turn her expertise into an act of betrayal. She had sabotaged the Hawaiian strike. Had made an attempt to wreck the trial. It did not matter that the overall result had been only partially successful; the loss of the NNEMP equipment had been a disastrous blow.

Li Kam had to be made to pay for her treachery. No matter what else happened, the woman had to be captured and held responsible. Choi recalled her attitude toward him. The brazen way she had spoken to him, while all the time she had been the cause of the NNEMP mishap.

There was no way back for her now. Choi would find her. He would beat her into submission and make her confess her disloyalty. Her suffering and most likely her lingering death would at least go partway to erasing her disregard of his authority and her rejection of the state.

RI ON CHOI came from a family of good background. His father, now dead, had been an official in the Ministry of Propaganda. A dedicated acolyte of the Supreme Leader— Kim Jong Il. For Ri On Choi it had been an honor when he had been introduced to the Supreme Leader when Choi was sixteen years old.

He had been brought up in the strict regime of North Korea and was totally dedicated to the ideals of the country. He had been conscripted into the army, and from day one, he realized this was where his future lay. Serving the leader and the country. Nothing else mattered.

Choi was a good recruit. He excelled in everything and was rapidly pushed through the ranks. He was skilled in military functions. A fearless leader of his men. It was no surprise when he was promoted to major.

He commanded by his devotion to duty. He was intelligent but had an arrogant style that often stood him apart from fellow officers. That did not worry him. Choi knew he was a good officer. His superiors trusted him and approved his dominant style.

Though Choi was aware of his accepted status, he did not allow himself to be fooled into believing he was untouchable. Pyongyang would praise a victor. It would also quickly and mercilessly condemn and brush aside someone who failed to meet their demands.

On more than one occasion, Choi was given command of special projects. He knew how to focus on his given responsibilities. He drove himself as hard as he drove his men. They feared him. Respected him.

During a training exercise, the helicopter he and his small squad were in developed a fault, and came down in a remote and inhospitable region. Choi and five of his men were the only survivors. There was no way to contact their base. Their equipment was basic and even the wireless communications failed. It was the middle of winter. They were over sixty miles from any military base. The only option was for them to walk to safety. If they didn't, they would have surely died, frozen by the elements.

Ri On Choi ordered his men to march. He led the way, his mind set on one thing—to survive and bring his men out alive. When his dispirited crew began to falter, Choi urged them on. He coaxed and bullied and threatened. When a man fell down, Choi dragged him upright and ordered him on.

The weather was terrible: freezing temperatures, heavy falls of snow and biting wind that blinded them with its ferocity. Through it all Choi kept his small band on the move.

Hope that rescue might come faded after a time. Day and night passed, and Choi's command struggled on. Whatever his men felt, Choi urged them on. More than once, a man would be ready to give in, but Choi kept them going. He would not let them give in.

They were doing this for the Supreme Leader, he told them. Keeping the spirit of North Korea alive. Struggling through adversity, just as Kim Jong Il expected of them.

They were lost for days. Weak, emaciated, cold and struggling to stay alive. Yet they did. Because of Ri On Choi's urging. Because of his unshakable belief in his Supreme Leader and the example he showed to the nation.

When they finally stumbled into the remote base, they were greeted with cheers. Given up as lost and dead, no one had expected them to return. It took them weeks to recover.

When Kim Jong Il made an unexpected visit to see them in the hospital, to praise them as high examples of the dedication he expected from his military, it had been the greatest moment of Choi's life.

His men were honored, given medals and held up as heroes of the state.

Ri On Choi received the highest award the Supreme Leader could bestow. With his President on one side and his beaming father on the other, Choi could not have asked for more.

He was given a posting to a section of the military that came under the heading of Special Projects. It was a prestige posting. The unit oversaw the development of advanced weapons, and Choi immersed himself in the various enterprises. He understood the need for North Korea to advance superior ordnance. South Korea, along with the connivance of America, was provoking possible future conflict. So the North had to adopt a similar attitude.

America fed billions of dollars into its weapons divisions. It supplied the South with ever sophisticated armaments. North Korea retaliated by doing the same, though with its much weaker economy, it had a difficult time keeping up with the Americans.

China—its own eyes on the future—helped by injecting financial aid to its poorer neighbor. Beijing watched the North-South competition and knew that it needed to keep North Korea's head above water. China wanted greater control in the Pacific Rim arena. There were strategic implications in play. So assisting North Korea was in China's interests.

Ri On Choi was given command of North Korea's development of the burgeoning NNEMP research. North Korea's research had taken a number of leaps forward, so a concentrated effort was in full swing. Choi was sent to the remote facility, given total control over the site. His orders were plain. Push the research forward. Bring the pulse weapon on line. To do this, North Korea poached Dr. Emanuel Absalom and placed him as head of the special team.

It had been learned that Absalom was one of the foremost experts in the field. Other governments had considered his talents, but none had made any firm commitments. With an unexpected and bold stroke, procurers working on behalf of North Korea stepped in and spirited Absalom from his university appointment in Germany, and brought him to the Korean site. Absalom, though a dedicated physicist, had a weakness. He liked money. So North Korea offered him a great deal. Pyongyang considered the inducement cheap, if Absalom got them what they wanted.

And he did. Far quicker than anyone had anticipated.

When a trial was decided on, the American puppet state of Hawaii was chosen. A date set.

Then the sabotage, the sinking.

Matters were escalating quickly. And not in the way that Choi would have anticipated or would have chosen.

A traitor had been uncovered within the research unit.

And now Choi's command was under attack from armed intruders intent on causing even more unrest.

It could not, would not, be allowed to succeed.

CHAPTER TWENTY-FOUR

The gates were partway open, left in that position by the first of the North Koreans to search for the intruders. It allowed Phoenix Force to enter the compound without having to blow them, but not to avoid more of the defenders.

As the trio of Stony Man warriors—Kayo Pak moving with them—breached the gates, they saw grouped soldiers rushing in their direction. It was not the time for any kind of finesse.

Hawkins and Manning both produced fragmentation grenades and pulled the pins, tossing the handheld ordnance in the direction of the NK soldiers. They had timed the throws well, and the grenades detonated seconds after dropping in among the charging group. The HE explosives scattered the grenade fragments through the Koreans, the deadly shards tearing at clothing and the flesh beneath. All but two of the group went down, bloody and torn. Briefly disoriented by the twin blasts, the surviving Koreans had no chance to bring their weapons into play and were hit by concentrated P90 fire from McCarter.

As the North Koreans were driven to the ground and Phoenix Force advanced, Kayo Pak keyed the compact text unit he carried. It was a simple means of passing a brief command to the unit Li Kam carried.

He had told her to always have the compact unit and to act immediately on any commands it gave.

Outside. Now was all the text showed.

LI KAM FELT the small unit vibrate in her pocket. She palmed the device and saw the two-word text on the tiny screen. She understood what it meant, and the sounds of grenades going off—first at the rear of the building and now below her—told her the time had come to move.

She slid the message unit back inside her lab coat pocket. As she did, she sensed movement close by and, looking up, saw Ki Yen staring at her.

He was looking at her, as if he had never seen her before. A total stranger.

"What are you doing with that? You know it is forbidden." A triumphant smile curled his thin lips. "I already know you are the saboteur. I traced your computer log. Now you are communicating with other traitors. Major Choi knows what you have done, too."

Li found courage she didn't know she had, as she faced Yen.

"And what are you going to do about it, Yen? Go running to your master like a little pet dog?"

The building shook as twin heavy blasts from the exploding helicopters sent out concussion waves. Glass shattered. Stone cracked. The floor shook.

Li reacted quickly, snatching up one of the tubular chairs and swinging it at Yen as the tech ran at her. The chair slammed into him chest high, knocking him off balance. Yen twisted away from her, throwing up an arm to protect himself from the unexpected attack.

Li maintained her advantage, swinging the chair again and again. She opened a bloody gash across Yen's face, as he screamed violent invectives at her. He fell back, catching a heel in the leg of a bench, and Li drove in at him again, knowing her time was running out. One of the armed soldiers could appear at any moment, and the chair she was using as a weapon wouldn't do her much good if that happened.

She made a final swing, the chair cracking hard against Yen's neck. He gagged, spitting blood, and went down hard on the floor, hands clutched to his crushed throat. He writhed on the floor, gasping as he tried futilely to suck in air. Li slammed the chair on the back of his exposed skull, and Yen dropped facedown on the lab floor, blood gleaming where Li had struck him.

She threw aside the chair and ran for the exit, pushing the door wide and running fast. She half tumbled down the stairs, her only object being to get clear of the building. In her white lab coat, she was simply one of the group who was also trying to get clear. She unbuttoned it and shrugged it from her shoulders, letting it fall away.

And then she was outside—rain striking her as she stood, quickly soaking through her clothing—momentarily unsure what to do as she looked around.

There seemed to be a great deal of confusion around her. Other white-coated techs were running blindly in every direction. Smoke was rising over the roof of the research building. She heard shouting and then the muted howl of a warning siren.

Li stared, surprise on her face when she actually saw Kayo Pak running toward her. He was carrying an automatic weapon and three uniformed non-Asian men were with him.

"Li," he called. "Here…"

She ignored the rising cacophony of noise around her and joined the group.

"Major Choi knows about me. One of the techs told him that I was responsible for the sabotage."

McCarter said, "No time, then. Can you show us where the research lab is? I'm Coyle and this is Allen."

Li nodded. "It's the building behind us. Come this way."

She realized they would be foolish to go back inside by the normal entrance, so she chose the only other way to enter the building. The others fell in behind her, and Li directed them along the side of the building.

A soldier appeared from the corner they were heading for, his weapon rising as he saw the intruders. McCarter already had his P90 up and ready, and he triggered a burst that spun the North Korean off his feet and dropped him on the wet ground.

"Keep moving," the Briton yelled.

As Pak reached the downed soldier, he scooped up the man's autorifle and thrust it into Li's hands. She took the weapon, nodding without breaking her stride.

McCarter, Manning, Hawkins, Kayo Pak and Li Kam skirted the side of the main research building. She pointed to the metal stairs attached to the rear outer wall and ran up the swaying metal structure, Manning close behind, while McCarter, Hawkins and Kayo protected their rear from the base of the stairs.

"Go and do what you have to," McCarter said. "We'll cover. Just make it fast."

Li had reached midway up the stairs, when the door at the top burst open and an armed soldier pushed through onto the square landing. Li angled her Type 68 and opened fire, catching the Korean before he could bring his own weapon into play. Her hasty burst tore into his left hip, ripping through flesh and bone. Manning tracked in with his P90 and hit the guy with a second burst, high up, and the soldier was tipped back against the metal rail. He held there for a few seconds, then fell out of sight.

"Inside," Li called as Manning joined her. "We can reach the main lab from here."

She vanished through the door, with Manning on her

heels, his P90 raised, scanning the passage they were moving along. Li kept to one side, leaving a clear field of fire for the Canadian.

The short passage opened up onto a large room crammed full of electronic equipment, including a number of high-spec computer terminals and monitors. It was the main research lab. At the far end a wide door led from the room. As Manning and Li entered, they caught sight of the uniformed soldiers pushing to get inside the lab.

Manning sighted his P90 in that direction and fired off bursts that drove the soldiers back. One took a full hit in the chest, slumping against the wall, and Manning freed a grenade and threw it the length of the room. It glanced off the door frame and into the passage beyond. Manning caught hold of Li's collar and pulled her below the level of the workbench they were standing by. As they dropped into cover, the grenade detonated. Manning heard someone scream. Debris was flung back into the lab as a thick wreath of smoke coiled through the door.

Li indicated the steel door at the other end of the lab.

"That is the door to the room where the memory bank is housed. The digital log of everything created on all the computers within the facility. All the work done on the NNEMP development will be in the memory." Li was unable to prevent a smile of regret showing. "It must be where they discovered I was the one who entered the code into the NNEMP program. Foolishly I had forgotten it recorded all entries."

"Don't worry about that," Manning said. "Hell, nobody's perfect," he added, grinning at her.

Manning slipped his backpack to the floor and opened it. He took out a prepared explosive pack and studied the door for a few seconds. His expertise gave him the answer to where he needed to place the device to open the door.

"Li, keep your weapon on that far door. Anyone shows their face, open fire. Keep them busy while I fix this to the door."

Li nodded and turned to face the far door.

Manning cleared the end of the bench and crouchwalked to the door, shielded by other work units. At the steel door, he placed the pack close to the lock mechanism, where it was held in place against the metal by the thin magnetic strips attached to the underside. He tapped in a ten-second countdown and activated the detonator. He turned about and made his way back to where Li knelt. He grabbed his pack and Li's arm and pulled her toward the entrance of the passage they had used to breach the room. He was mentally counting off the seconds as he moved her along the passage.

Nine…ten…

The explosion was not as loud as Li had expected, but she felt the floor and walls quake under the concussion of the blast. A thick rush of smoke filled the passage. Splintered stone pattered from the ceiling. A few of the monitors were shaken from the workbenches.

Manning ignored the smoke, leading Li back to the lab where he positioned her against the end wall and instructed her to watch the far door again. As the smoke and dust thinned out, she could see that the door to the memory bank hung partway open, metal bent and twisted, blackened by the heat of the blast.

"One more visit, then we're gone," Manning said. "Just keep that far entrance covered and shoot anything that moves."

He extracted a couple more explosive packs, and without hesitating, plunged into the misty fog still hanging in the air. He reached the blast-loosened door and eased inside the room.

The backup unit stood against the far wall. Made of

metal and plastic, it would be no match for the powerful explosive Manning was about to attach to it. The high-intensity compound would rip the unit apart and destroy the digital memory circuits inside. Within the confines of the small room, the blast would be concentrated and undiminished. Manning clamped two identical packs to the metal casing and keyed in ten seconds, then pressed the activation button. As he turned away from the unit, he took hold of his P90, then slipped out through the door.

A burst of autofire from Li's position told him the North Korean soldiers had braved the door again. He heard a man yell. Following that, a concentrated salvo sent streams of slugs across the lab. Manning had dropped low the moment Li opened fire, so the burst intended for him slammed into the wall over his head. With the knowledge of the ten-second countdown still ongoing, Manning stayed low and crawled across the floor, letting his weapon hang by its strap again, and ignoring the bite of debris against his hands as he supported himself. Partly protected by the workbenches, he ignored the gunfire over his head, concentrating on reaching the passage where Li was concealed and still returning fire.

Manning pushed Li away from the opening and tumbled against the passage wall himself a scant second before the double explosion rocked the lab again. The heavy blast blew the already damaged steel door off its hinges, sending it spinning across the room. The tumbling door ripped its way across the workbenches, wrecking monitors and computer towers in its path. For the second time, a thick mix of smoke and dust filled the room. There was a sudden groan of loosened stone as the ceiling began to sag, followed by a rumbling sound as it collapsed into the lab. Chunks of stone and splintered wooden beams dropped, crashing down hard and creating a solid barrier across the middle of the lab.

Manning had already urged Li into retreating along the passage. As he made to join her, he slipped his two remaining explosive packs from his bag, set them for twenty seconds and placed them on the passage floor.

She was staring at him through the dusty air, eyes flicking from him to the explosives, then back.

"Shouldn't we get away from here?"

"Oh, yes," Manning said and caught her arm, hustling her along the passage to the outer door. As they emerged onto the metal landing, the heavy rain caught them again. It felt pleasant after the dust and smoke inside.

McCarter, Hawkins and Pak were holding fast at the base of the steps, driving back any of the Koreans who risked sticking their heads out from cover. McCarter glanced over his shoulder as Manning and Li hurried down the stairs.

"About bloody time," he said. "I was about to come…"

"You want to give it a second," Manning said back.

The final twin explosions rocked the building.

The door and the windows above their heads blew out, showering them with glass and toothpicks of wood. The very wall bulged under the pressure of the blast, stone crumbling. The metal stairs shook and twisted, as bolts securing the structure were blown free.

Manning and Li were pushed off balance as they kept moving down the swaying steps. They managed to stay upright and took the final steps in ungainly lunges, stumbling as they reached ground level. McCarter reached out and caught hold of Li as she started to go down.

"Thanks," she said.

"I'm okay, too," Manning said.

"That's fine, then." McCarter grinned. "Now let's get

the hell out of here before Choi and more of his boys come running."

Li indicated they should go back the way they had come, so that was the route they chose.

Thick smoke was pouring out of the upper windows and the roof where the explosions had disturbed the tiles. The orange glow of rising flames was visible.

"Lot of timber in the old construction," Li pointed out.

"Burn, baby, burn," Manning murmured as they skirted the wall of the building.

"Choi will make it his life's work to stop us now," Pak said.

"Let's hope it's a short one, then," Hawkins said.

The crackle of autofire was followed by the slam of 7.62 mm slugs striking the stone wall. Stinging chips peppered them, and McCarter waved Manning and Li to ease back.

McCarter raised his P90 and returned fire on the moving soldiers. He then led his SMG on the closest man, as the guy paused in order to settle his aim. McCarter fired first, his shots on target, the 5.7 mm slugs piercing the man's combat jacket and into his chest. The North Korean stumbled and went down on his face.

The moment he fired on the first, McCarter swiveled the muzzle of the P90 and stitched the second attacker across the middle. The guy had dropped to his knees, his finger jerking on the trigger of his autorifle and sending a burst of fire into the ground. Seeing the guy was still alive, McCarter again raised his weapon and put a short burst into the man's head, the impact kicking the Korean backward, his skull bursting apart in a bloody explosion.

"Let's move it," McCarter yelled above the sudden crash of collapsing stone overhead from the building behind them.

Flames rose, crackling fiercely. Dust and smoke swirled across the area, reducing visibility.

They angled away from the spot, cutting across an open section of ground, and merged with the parked vehicles that provided the closest cover. Raised voices behind them indicated they had been spotted. Autofire sparked, but the only hits were to the vehicles.

"Now that isn't the smartest thing to do," Manning observed, as he heard a tire burst under the impact of loose fire. "Blowing holes in their own transport."

The thud of shots hitting vehicle bodywork continued as the Koreans kept up steady fire. Crouching in the lee of the parked trucks, McCarter, Hawkins, Manning, Pak and Li returned fire, driving the exposed soldiers back. One went down clutching a shattered hip. A second tumbled from concentrated fire that punched through his clothing and into his body.

Li called out, "There—it's Major Choi."

McCarter followed her pointing finger.

At the front of the building, in among a group of advancing soldiers, was a figure in the uniform of a North Korean officer, his drawn pistol being used to wave his men forward.

McCarter plucked a grenade from his harness and pulled the pin. He held for a few seconds before throwing the grenade in a long curve that dropped it close to where the North Koreans were clustered. The fragmentation bomb detonated with a harsh sound, the scattering metal pieces scything through the Korean military men.

When the smoke drifted away a number of soldiers were down, the others backing up.

Choi was among them.

"Missed the bugger," McCarter grumbled.

"Maybe we get him next time," Pak said.

"Move out," McCarter ordered. "Time to leave."

He led the way past the parked trucks and out through the open gates in the perimeter fence.

The deluge of rain drowned any sound they might have made as they ran away from the defined path, and eased into the tangled undergrowth and trees. The ground underfoot was sodden, and they left tracks as they moved along. That fact concerned McCarter, but he knew there wasn't a thing he could do about it; he could only hope that the still-falling rain might wash away most of the boot prints from the soft earth.

They moved fast, without any pause, wanting to gain some distance before Major Choi reorganized his force and came after them. McCarter was under no illusion. The strike against the research lab would incense Choi, and regardless of any subsequent punishment he received for allowing the attack, the man would be desperate to gain some kind of success from the affair by capturing or killing the people responsible.

The North Korean command didn't tolerate failure, so Choi would be in deep trouble. There would be no excuses his superiors would accept. The loss of the NNEMP research and the lab would set the Koreans back. If any success had been achieved from the experimental strike in Hawaii, the destruction of the lab would wipe it out. The elimination of the covert team that had penetrated into North Korea was all Choi had left to offer the high command in Pyongyang. He had to have something to show them, when he went cap in hand.

"Spread out," McCarter ordered. "Bunched together, we're going to offer Choi and his mates an easy target."

Phoenix Force went in different directions, their intention to converge when they reached the beach jumping-off spot.

Li and Kayo Pak stayed on McCarter's six, as they forced their way through the thick greenery.

The rain showed no sign of easing off. The forest floor underfoot had turned to a spongy carpet, dotted with gathered pools where the ground could not absorb any more water.

Glancing down at his P90, McCarter saw the ammo magazine showed he was almost out. He released the translucent loader and cast it aside. He slid a hand into one of the pouches on his harness and pulled out a fully loaded fresh magazine. McCarter snapped it into placed and primed the SMG.

A raised voice sounded above the pounding rain. It came from McCarter's left. He turned his head and spotted a uniformed figure keeping pace with them.

"Hey," McCarter shouted a warning.

"See him," Pak said.

The North Korean soldier was shouting into a handheld comm set.

"He's telling his mates where we are," McCarter said.

He slithered to a full stop, raised the P90 and fired a short burst that hit the radio spotter in the side. As the guy went down McCarter saw other uniformed men crowding in behind their comrade.

Both Li and Pak opened up, their respective weapons spitting out lethal fire. With McCarter's contribution they dropped the bunched Koreans.

"Keep moving before any backup shows," McCarter said.

With Li and Kayo Pak close, McCarter led the way.

A bubbling rush of water barred their path. Normally only a stream running through the forest, it had turned into a wide, frothing runoff.

"That's a bummer," McCarter commented. "We're going to get wet wading through there."

The off-the-cuff remark, normal for the Briton, hung in the air for a moment before Li Kam laughed.

"I think I could get to like you, Coyle," she said.

While Pak stood watch, McCarter and Li waded through the cold water. It reached waist high in the middle, the current strong. They hung on to each other to stay upright. Once they had reached the other side, Pak made the crossing, forcing his way across.

"I do not think I will ever be dry again," the Korean said.

"Any chance of Choi calling in additional troops?" McCarter asked as they pushed on.

"If he did, it would take time," Pak said. "This is a remote area. The closest army base is at least three hours away by helicopter."

"Choi would not be happy having to ask for help," Li said. "This place is his personal responsibility. To ask for more soldiers would go against his pride."

"Let's hope you're right. Last thing we need is a full battalion of North Korean regulars on our tail."

THEY TRAVELED ANOTHER half mile before McCarter called up the rest of Phoenix Force on his comm set. He picked up responses as they came back within range and relayed their positions.

"Close in," McCarter said. "I want to be able to see your ugly mugs again. What's your sitrep?"

"We have a number of North Koreans on our heels," James said. "Still a distance away, but I have a feeling they're not going to back off."

"Rain is slowing them," Pak said. "Ground underfoot isn't going to hold our boot prints for long, so they'll need to move slower in order to stay on track."

"I was wondering about that," McCarter admitted.

"Just be grateful for the bad climate this time of year," Pak said.

"Let's cut around and head for the shoreline," McCarter said. "We need to get to the rendezvous point and retrieve the scuba gear."

James said over the comm link, "We're closer. Let us scout ahead and advise if there's a problem."

"You do that. We'll move in and wait for your intel."

Encizo said, "We planted our last explosive pack under the main fuel tank. Set it for forty minutes. Which should be coming up pretty soon."

THE EXPLOSION SOUNDED just over a minute later. The solid blast was followed by a massive swell of orange-red flames that surged skyward. It spread and boiled in an orgy of destruction, the flames searching outward as well as up. Anything within its range was incinerated. A number of the base's parked vehicles were turned into blazing wrecks. As the flames rose, so did a thick mass of swirling blackness that threw a dark blanket of shadows over the base.

JAMES AND ENCIZO headed for the spot where Phoenix Force had originally come ashore. They moved fast, constantly aware that Choi's search teams were still around. Their shoreline ingress location was the closest to the research facility, and it was entirely possible the NKs might have been checking the area.

It turned out the enemy *had* been thinking ahead.

"Landing site is well and truly compromised," James said over the comm set. "We have a reception committee waiting for us to show up. Don't know how they figured it out, but they did."

"Hang tight," McCarter said. "How many?" he asked.

"I see at least five," James answered. "They have our goody bag dug up, as well. Wet suits and all spread over the sand."

There was a pause before McCarter spoke again. "Pull back. Head for our location. It looks as if we actually do have a Plan B."

CHAPTER TWENTY-FIVE

HAWAII

"That Korean's actions have made things worse," Xian Chi said. "Hiring local thugs to deal with the police and those agents has not done anything positive. Now they will be out in force looking for answers. Looking for us."

"Then the sooner we get the package off the island the better," Macklin said. "The longer we hang on to it, the more chance it might be discovered."

"Tak will be thinking the same. Has he contacted you since you took it?"

"No, but I figure he soon will. For now it's secure. My people will have eyes on it." Macklin paused. "You said you were going to deal with Tak."

"Yes," Chi said. "The matter is well in hand."

"Glad to hear it."

Chi glanced at the American. "Are you worried your final payment might be compromised, Mr. Macklin?"

"Can't deny the thought has crossed my mind, but that isn't my main concern. Tak is no fool. I'm suggesting you take care. He's suspicious by nature. If he even *thinks* something is wrong…"

"Your concern is noted. I know Tak. The man would not trust his own mother. And in matters concerning the state, he will be extravigilant. However, I am not without guile, so dealing with Tak will be handled quickly, and he will

not be expecting it. What is that Western saying—yes—
he won't know what hit him." Chi smiled at his own wit. "I
rather like the concept."

"Contact me as soon as you complete arrangements to
move the item," Macklin said. He stood, pushing back the
chair, and left the hotel lobby.

Chi leaned back. Only a short time ago he had faced
Tak, who had been sitting in the same chair Macklin had
just vacated.

So much had happened in the time since then. If matters took their course, the mission would be completed.

Tak would be dead, and the package would be on its
way to Beijing.

Chi raised a hand to a passing server and ordered more
coffee. If he was summoned back home, one thing he would
miss would be American coffee. He had grown to like it.
Chi sighed. A small thing perhaps, but his indulgences did
add a bit of pleasure to his busy life.

He took out his cell and tapped in a number, then waited
for pickup.

"Ah, Tak, we need to meet. Final arrangements to make.
Where?" Chi smiled at the Korean's suggestion. "Good. An
hour? Very well. I will see you there."

Chi watched as his coffee was delivered and placed on
the small table in front of him. He signed the bill, poured
himself a fresh cup, raising it in a mock salute.

"Thank you, Tak, for making this easy for me."

He phoned Kai Yeung, and told him to bring the car
around to the front of the hotel. He strolled outside and
waited until the car arrived, then climbed into the rear
seat. He told the younger man where to drive. If everything went as planned, another part of the operation would
be complete.

Tak removed once and for all.

A step closer to Chi taking over the operation completely, sweeping away the deadwood, as it were. He smiled.

Deadwood seemed to describe Tak, the North Korean, so lacking in any kind of finesse. Chi had never taken to the man, to his dour personality and his mind-numbing adherence to North Korean dogma. The man had no redeeming features to his personality. The sooner he was eliminated, the sooner Xian Chi could move on.

Tak's own suggestion as where to meet had been ideal—a storage facility on the edges of the warehouse district, overlooking the Pacific. The Korean had used the place for clandestine meetings with his hired people and to house equipment. It was isolated. A shabby, run-down area that not even the local derelicts bothered with. Darkness would also help, as the evening brought shadows to the area.

Chi arrived well ahead of time. Yeung dropped him on the perimeter, then drove away. Once he had dealt with Tak, Chi would call his driver and arrange to be picked up some distance away. The service road leading to this section of the waterfront was quiet during daylight hours. At night even more so.

Chi had dressed down for the occasion. Dark clothing, topped off with a leather jacket, one of the deep pockets concealing the 9 mm automatic pistol, already fitted with a suppressor; it was a new weapon, never having been fired before, so there would be nothing on record for the police to link up with.

He reached the storage building and stood outside, waiting. As usual Tak was exactly on time, driving himself in a Ford sedan. The headlights picked up Chi's waiting figure. They flicked off as Tak stopped the car and climbed out. He wore the same suit he had had on when he and Chi had spoken in the hotel.

The man never relaxes, Chi thought. Even in Hawaii, he dressed as if he were at a board meeting.

"Where is your car?" Tak asked, staring around the area.

"Kai Yeung brought me," Chi answered honestly. "He will collect me later."

Tak considered the explanation. Then his head moved.

"We should go inside, so we can't be seen. In case someone walks by."

Chi couldn't imagine anyone wanting to take a leisurely stroll through such a dilapidated area. He didn't press the point. He let it go as just another of Tak's paranoia episodes.

"Yes."

Tak pushed open the side door and stepped inside the building.

As Chi followed, his hand dropped inside the pocket of his coat, gripping the pistol.

Tak said, "I will contact Pyongyang as soon as we…"

Chi was directly behind him.

He drew the pistol, raised it and pressed the tip of the suppressor against the back of Tak's head.

Tak's words trailed off. He made a soft, breathy sound, as he realized what was about to happen. It was far too late for him to do anything about it.

There was no hesitation in Chi's actions as he pulled the pistol's trigger and fired twice. Both 9 mm slugs hammered into the Korean's skull. The second one went all the way through and exited from Tak's left socket, taking the eye out in a burst of blood and fluid. The shots destroyed Tak's brain, and he dropped without a murmur, slamming facedown on the dirty floor.

Xian Chi dropped the pistol back in his pocket and quickly left the building, closing the door behind him. He crossed to Tak's car and saw the keys still in the ignition. He pulled on the gloves he carried in his pocket and sat inside the car, starting the engine. He released the hand brake and dropped the selector to Drive.

As the car started to move, Chi spun the wheel and aimed the vehicle for the edge of the dock. He let it roll, then quickly exited the car and closed the door. He stood watching as the car cruised to the water's edge. It was moving slowly and for a moment it seemed it wouldn't make it, so Chi leaned his weight against the trunk and pushed. The car gained enough momentum to teeter on the edge for several long seconds before the weight of the front did the trick and it fell, scraping the wall of the dock as it dropped. The splash when it hit the water seemed incredibly loud. Dark water foamed up around the car as it finally slid under the surface, wide ripples spreading out. Then the water settled and calmed.

Chi turned and walked away, back across the dock. He called Yeung and told him to pick him up. Minutes later he was settling in the rear of the car, on his way back to the hotel, allowing himself a faint smile of satisfaction.

One more problem out of the way.

But Xian Chi was wrong.

His problems were far from over.

CHAPTER TWENTY-SIX

"HPD called this in an hour ago," Kalikani said over his cell. "Harbor patrol boat spotted an oil patch near the dock in the abandoned warehouse district. They took a look and spotted something under the water. Diver went down and found a late-model car on the bottom. Nobody inside. Vehicle was newly dumped. When the registration was checked, it turned out to be a rental from a company one of the hotels uses."

"They find out who the driver was?" Lyons asked.

His cell was on Speaker so they all could hear.

"You'll like this," Kalikani said. "Car was booked to a guest at the hotel by the name of Soon Il Tak. North Korean."

"O," Lopaka said, "I know that tone. What else aren't you telling us?"

"Give a guy his moment, girl. The harbor patrol called HPD, and a cruiser made the scene. Checked the area. They found a body in the building right where the car went into the water. Double tap to the back of the head. Identification in the pocket was for Soon Il Tak. His photo matched what was left of his face. His passport was in his pocket. What are you supersleuths going to make out of that little mix?"

"This is getting weird," Lopaka said.

"You think?" Blancanales said.

"I'll call home," Lyons said. "Send me what you have, Oscar."

"I'll get the crime scene cops to push the dead guy's picture through."

Blancanales said, "You say he had his passport on him?"

"Yes."

"Maybe he was getting ready to leave," Schwarz said.

"Might not have been the way he expected," Kalikani said, "because now he's *really* gone."

Twenty minutes later Lyons was forwarding all the data they had to Stony Man and asking for a quick result.

"This guy was North Korean," he said. "How likely is it we can get any useful data from him?"

"It's going into the system as we speak, my impatient brother," Kurtzman said lightly. "My equipment is fast, but I still need to feed it first."

Lyons grunted and ended the call.

"Let's get back to our hotel. Wait it out until we have some answers. Right now we don't have squat on who else is mixed up in this."

"I'll get back to the station," Lopaka said. "Check in with O and see if he's found anything."

She returned to her HPD cruiser.

Watching her go, Blancanales said, "She makes me want to break the law, just so I can get arrested."

"That's recognized as dirty-old-man talk," Schwarz said.

"Really?" Blancanales said, smiling. "But not so much of the *old-man* part."

CHAPTER TWENTY-SEVEN

ABLE TEAM—ASSAULT

Jenny Lopaka crossed the office area and homed in on Kalikani's desk. She perched herself on the corner of his desk.

"Hey, O. Anything for me?"

Kalikani eased his swivel seat around, wincing slightly when even that small effort gave him discomfort.

"One of the bonuses of being confined to this damn seat," he said, "is it gives me time to think."

"I have a feeling something bad is coming," Lopaka said.

"Maunakea Market. Those guys were waiting for us. Knew we were coming. Same with the Wiseman thing. Setups, clean and simple."

"I think we all got that."

"So the next step is *who* gave out the locations?"

"Not to sound a little simplistic, but it had to be someone who knew in advance."

"Exactly. These meetings were not publicized. As far as I can figure, there was a single source with that knowledge."

Kalikani let the words go and leaned back.

Realization dawned on Jenny Lopaka's face. To her credit, she maintained a neutral expression as she leaned forward.

"The department?"

Kalikani nodded briefly. "I can't pin it on anyone else. The information had to be leaked from in here."

Lopaka's expression changed as she said, "The convoy. Everything about the transport detail came from here. Those six cops died because somebody passed on the schedule."

"Looks that way. Keep calls to the department to the minimum. Use my personal cell. You got that?"

Lopaka acknowledged. She said, "Who would do this to us and get our own killed?"

"I'll find out," Kalikani said. "You get back to Matthews."

As she slipped behind the wheel of her cruiser, Lopaka had to push back the anger she felt over the possibility of a department member being responsible for the deaths of the six cops. Discovering who that person was would be down to Kalikani. She had no doubt he would succeed. Oscar Kalikani was a good cop. He knew his job, and his own anger would push him to the limits. Kalikani would not stop until he exposed the one responsible.

Back at Able Team's hotel, Lopaka reported what Kalikani had told her.

"Fits," Schwarz said. "An insider with knowledge. Tipping off the opposition."

"For money? Blackmail?" Lopaka asked.

"There are always reasons for people to go rogue," Blancanales said. "You mentioned money. Blackmail. What about political convictions? Ideological leanings? Revenge?"

"I can relate to that," Lopaka said. "It's buzzing around inside my head right now."

"Don't get mad—get even," Blancanales advised.

"Aren't they the same?"

"You let emotions take control, it can lead to you losing

focus," Blancanales said. "You get even by concentrating on the facts and working on a reasoned response."

"He gets on one of his considered arguments, you end up falling asleep through sheer boredom," Schwarz said. "When you come round, you've forgotten what it was all about."

Lopaka caught the playful tone in Schwarz's voice.

"You guys," she said.

Lyons's cell buzzed. He answered and listened to the caller. The call was long.

"It'll be his mother," Blancanales said. "She gets worried when he's away. Be checking he's changing his underwear every day and not staying out too late."

Lopaka was still smiling when Lyons ended the call.

"I know what you were saying," he said.

"Did Mom say hi?" Blancanales said.

"No, but she did come up with some helpful information. Our friend Borgnine showed up here a few days ago. Flew in from San Francisco along with his old buddies, Spelman and Macklin."

"So all we need to know is where they're hanging out," Schwarz said.

"That's no problem. Mother used her home computer to hack into the airport camera system. Our three suspects took a cab from the airport to an address outside the city. Turns out it's a rented property without any close neighbors."

"Nice touch using a cab," Schwarz said. "No contact with their employers in a public place. Keeps it all low-key."

"You located all this using your base?" Lopaka asked.

"Most anything we need," Lyons said.

"Your people can do all that?"

Schwarz nodded. "Let's say Mother has a few electronic tricks up her knitted sleeve."

"I believe you," Lopaka said.

"Let's go make a house call," Lyons said.

LOPAKA LED THE way out of the city and into the hills that flanked it. Able Team followed in their own vehicle, Schwarz driving.

They turned off the main road, and Lopaka took them along a narrow side road until she pulled into a wooded area and stopped. Schwarz braked and shut off the engine, while they saw the HPD cop climb out and walk to the rear of her cruiser.

Lopaka reached inside the Crown Vic's trunk and took out a Benelli M1 auto-shotgun. She quickly loaded seven 12-gauge cartridges into the underbarrel tube, then six extra shells into the side-saddle carrier fixed to the receiver. She checked her S&W 9 mm issue pistol, slipping a couple extra 15-round magazines into side pouches on her HPD gun belt. She pulled on a department protective flak jacket and zipped it up. Finally she hung a compact pair of binoculars around her neck.

"You sure you have enough there?" Blancanales asked as he joined her.

Lopaka said, "My training officer told me that you can never carry enough when going into a tricky situation."

Lyons reached into the rear of Able Team's SUV and hauled out the ordnance bag they had brought with them.

"She talks my language," he said, as he pulled out a Franchi-SPAS combat shotgun and began to load it from the supply of 12-gauge shells Stony Man had provided.

"Well, at least our fearless leader is happy," Schwarz commented.

"So, you guys really do like each other, yeah?"

Schwarz and Blancanales exchanged stone-faced glances that forced a chuckle from the HPD cop.

A pair of 9 mm Uzis were loaded by Schwarz and Blancanales. They fed 30-round magazines into the SMGs and added extra mags to their own flak jackets.

"Been around for a while," Lopaka said, indicating the Israeli SMGs. "Fired one at the range once. Good weapon."

"It does what it says on the box," Schwarz said.

"Target is about a half mile in that direction," Lopaka said.

They moved off, Lopaka in the lead, taking them through the lush vegetation by the shortest route.

"Bet my next month's paycheck that this place is teeming with every kind of beetle, bug and snake ever created," Blancanales muttered.

"Could be a few," Lopaka said. "Old Hawaiian saying. If you come face-to-face with anything, just stare it down, and it'll back off."

"That true?" Blancanales asked.

Schwarz could see her face over Blancanales's shoulder, and though she didn't flinch, he noted a mischievous glint in her eyes.

His partner hadn't seen that and took her pronouncement seriously. Then said, "Are you kidding me?"

As usual Lyons saw through the female cop's remark. "She is yanking your chain, Comer. Who the hell ever heard of a bug backing off?"

Lopaka gave a soft chuckle. "Sorry," she said. "I couldn't resist."

"So what should I do?"

"Just give a girly scream and run like hell," Lyons said.

"That usually works for me," Lopaka said.

"You people are so not funny," Blancanales said.

Lopaka moved slightly ahead, with Lyons close behind, Schwarz and Blancanales at the rear.

Under the canopy of vegetation, the air was humid, the

ground underfoot soft. The dense growth of trees deprived them of full daylight, shadows gathering in pools along their path. The occasional squawk from some distant bird broke the silence.

"This is like *Jurassic Park*," Blancanales said. "You certain you don't have raptors?"

"I still think a full-on approach would have been a damn sight faster," Schwarz said. "Big car and going in all guns blazing."

"You just don't like the forest," Blancanales said.

"Got that in one." He glanced at his partner. "Coming from you, that is priceless."

Lopaka raised a hand, her black-clad form dropping to a crouch. Able Team gathered close. The female cop parted a mass of ferns. A hundred yards ahead, where a slight downgrade leveled out, they could see their target—the sprawl of the big house. A number of vehicles were parked in the driveway that fronted the building. Among the collection was a panel truck.

"That could be our panel truck," Lyons said.

Schwarz sighed. "This could be where we do the *all guns blazing* part."

"I don't think those people down there are going to raise their hands and surrender," Lopaka said.

Lyons placed his hand against the dressing on his head. "All I've had since we got here has been grief. Shot at and given a hard time. I don't have a great deal of sympathy for these perps."

Lopaka had passed her binoculars across to Schwarz. He was scanning the area. He locked on to a couple figures coming into sight from the side of the house.

"Is it normal for Hawaiian householders to walk around with autorifles?" he asked conversationally.

"Not really," the cop said.

"Then we either got someone playing around, or this is crunch time."

"You see any others?" Lyons asked.

"Not right now," Schwarz said. "But that doesn't mean there aren't any. Inside the house. Out back. Take your pick."

Lyons took the binoculars Lopaka now handed him and zoned in on the rear of the truck, making a note of the license plate. He quoted the number to Lopaka.

"Call Kalikani. Ask if he can trace the number."

Lopaka nodded and started her call to Kalikani's personal phone.

Lyons was staring down at the scene below, his expression studious.

"What are you thinking?" Blancanales asked.

"That maybe the truck down there is a blind. These guys were sharp enough to take the unit and get away. What are they hanging around for and leaving that truck in sight?"

"Doesn't make too much sense," Schwarz agreed.

"Make sense of this," Lopaka said. "Kalikani sent me a text message. The license number belongs to a rental company. They deal in commercial vehicles. O got the details of the renter. An Oriental food distributer with dealings in the city."

"That sounds all legitimate and open," Blancanales said. "Could be a nice cover. A way of staying under the radar."

"Kalikani found out that the same renter also hired a second vehicle. Same day. Different color."

"Two trucks? I only see one," Schwarz said.

"Jenny, call Oscar back," Blancanales said. "Get him to scan traffic cameras. Any cameras he can. See if they can spot that second truck. Where it might be. If Honolulu is like mainland cities, there should be cameras on every street. We might get lucky."

"What are you thinking?" Lyons asked.

"That the hijackers took the package from the convoy. The panel truck down there headed back toward the city. My guess is the plates were changed before the hit, then changed back. And the package could have been transferred to a second vehicle before the truck down there returned to the city. All to do with throwing the cops off the scent in case the original truck was spotted and identified. They rendezvous with the second truck and transfer the package." Blancanales shrugged. "It's only a theory."

"Got me confused," Schwarz said.

"Smoke and mirrors," Lopaka said. "Get people to look in one direction, while the real deal is going down somewhere else."

Lyons nodded. "Maybe I should trade this pair in and take you on."

"I could be hurt from remarks like that," Blancanales said.

"Comer. Hartz. Circle to the rear. Lopaka with me. If that panel truck doesn't have the package, we need to find out where it is and fast. Give me a cell buzz when you're in position."

"See," Schwarz said. "He always gets the girl."

Blancanales patted Lopaka on the shoulder. "He'll watch your back. Stay safe."

The Able Team pair slid off into the shrubbery, leaving Lyons and Lopaka alone.

They crouched in the foliage and watched the frontage, the pair of armed guys below doing little except surveying their surroundings.

It took a good eight minutes before Lyons's cell buzzed. It was the signal he had been waiting for.

"We're up," he said.

Lopaka raised her shotgun. "Let's go."

They used as much cover as they could, working their way toward the house and the pair on watch.

"Just remember what these dirtbags did when they hit that convoy," Lyons said. "They get no favors."

He didn't need to elaborate. Lopaka understood his mood and was prepared herself for dealing with the strike team.

"You take the guy on the right," Lyons said quietly as they cleared the last of the shrubbery, exposing themselves as they moved across the driveway.

Lyons shouldered his SPAS. Beside him Lopaka raised her own weapon.

Movement alerted the watchers. The guy closest to Lyons and Lopaka swung around, his weapon lifting.

Lopaka, already on track, moved the barrel of her shotgun and fired. The target jerked to one side as the shotgun charge slammed into his left shoulder. He went to his knees, dropping his weapon and clutching a hand to the wound, blood oozing thickly from between his fingers.

Lyons saw his mark spin around and drop to a crouch, reducing his body mass. The guy brought his autorifle around as he moved, lining up for a shot. The SPAS slammed out its sound, the powerful 12-gauge shot catching the guy in the throat. The force of the burst ripped the guy's flesh wide open and his head flopped to one side, held now by torn stringy muscle and tissue.

"Keep moving," Lyons yelled.

Lopaka stayed at his heels as they closed on the house...

BLANCANALES AND SCHWARZ met no resistance as they circled the property and edged in to the rear of the house. The lush Hawaiian foliage had been left untouched and had encroached on the building. A wide patio area showed growing weeds.

"This is a temporary billet," Schwarz said to his partner.

"Maybe it's time to flush out the pack rats."

The distant crack of shotguns reached them.

"Sounds like our cue," Blancanales said.

They moved across the wide overgrown patio, heading for the closed French doors.

"Got your invitation?" Schwarz asked.

"Yeah," Blancanales said, raising a booted foot and slamming it against the lock mechanism set in the wooden surround. The frame splintered and glass shattered. Blancanales reached in and yanked open the doors.

Schwarz spotted movement on the far side of the shadowed room beyond the doors.

"Down," he yelled.

He and Blancanales dropped to crouches as a figure ran across the room in their direction, an SMG tracking ahead of him. He opened fire, his shots high, and glass blew out of the frames.

Schwarz made a decoy move and the shooter turned in his direction. The moment he was distracted, Blancanales opened up with his 9 mm Uzi, the Israeli weapon crackling loudly as it delivered a long burst. The advancing guy was caught in the upper body, jerking to one side as Blancanales's volley impacted against him. He toppled back, colliding with a cane chair, and thumped to the floor.

Blancanales had moved to the door, now pulling back as autofire directed a hail of slugs toward him that ripped out splinters from the frame. Schwarz heard him mutter as a sliver gashed his cheek.

"They don't want to invite us in," he said.

Schwarz crouched low on the other side of the door as a second burst hammered into the wood. He pushed his Uzi around the frame, low-down, and triggered a burst along the outer wall. Someone gave a pained yell. Blancanales

burst through the door, slamming against the wall on the
far side of the passage. He saw the shooter, still holding his
weapon with one hand as he clutched at the bloody wound
in his lower calf. Blancanales brought the Uzi into play and
hit the guy chest high, knocking him to the floor.

Schwarz joined him, and they moved quickly along the
passage toward the front of the house, hearing a sudden,
intense round of gunfire...

"WHAT THE HELL...?" Ralph Spelman yelled as he heard
the muffled sound of shotgun blasts coming from outside
the house.

He pushed up out of the deep chair and made a grab for
his Desert Eagle lying on the side table. "Gabe, check the
rear. Go with him, French."

As Spelman left the room, turning across the entrance
hall, he saw dark shapes through the glass panels of the
front entrance.

A moment later the double doors were kicked open. Two
armed figures showed: one male, one female. The woman
wore the black uniform of the HPD, and both intruders
carried shotguns.

Spelman triggered a hasty shot at the pair, more out of
respect for the lethal weapons they were wielding; he understood the concept of a shotgun and the deadly spread of
its load. His .357 Magnum slug went over the heads of the
targets. Spelman had turned aside by this time, desperate
to get fully clear before either of the shoguns fired.

Lyons and Lopaka triggered in the same moment, the
twin blasts of their weapons filling the hallway with sound.

Spelman took one shot in his left shoulder, flesh and
bone torn apart by the impact. The second shot, from Lopaka's weapon, caught him between his shoulders, burning
through to shatter his spine and dump him fully flat.

"Keep moving," Lyons yelled.

They swept the area, muzzles up and tracking every shadow, every corner.

A figure appeared at the top of the stairs, SMG angling down. The shooter fired, and his 9 mm burst hit Lopaka in the left side. Her body armor absorbed the punch, but the force kicked her backward, breath driven from her body. She stumbled but kept her feet, face twisted in pain.

Lyons had leaned forward, shotgun sweeping up and firing. The distance reduced the full impact of the shot. There was enough to pepper the shooter's torso and unbalance him. Before he made any kind of recovery, Lyons had replaced the SPAS with his Python, sending a pair of .357 slugs into the guy. He fell back against the stairs, slithering down until he was hit by Lyons's third shot. This one plowed in through his head and out the rear of his skull.

"Lopaka?"

"I'm okay," the cop said, sucking air back into her lungs.

She turned even as she spoke, the Benelli's muzzle following and blasting a shot at the shadowy figure emerging from a doorway. Splintered wood from the frame exploded as her shot caught the armed guy in the face and neck. He dropped to his knees, groaning from the pain, blood starting to well from the punctures in his flesh. His autopistol slipped from his fingers. Lopaka crossed over and kicked the weapon out of reach.

"Don't you move," she snapped at the guy.

He had his hands clasped to his face. Blood was seeping between his fingers.

Across the hall Lyons was scoping the stairs and the hall, his shotgun back in his grasp.

The sudden crackle of Uzi SMGs came from the rear of the house.

Schwarz and Blancanales were making their presence known.

There was no more sound following the shooting until the Able Team pair moved into view. They spotted Lyons and Lopaka.

"Clear at the rear," Blancanales announced.

"Check the upper floor," Lyons said.

Schwarz and Blancanales covered each other as they went up the stairs, then moved from room to room. Lyons followed through on the ground floor and cleared each room, making sure there were no hidden shooters.

It was only when they were satisfied that they rejoined in the hallway.

"We done?" Lyons asked.

"Clear," Schwarz said.

"I didn't see any package," Blancanales said.

"Not down here," Lyons said. "They've got it at another location."

Lopaka had her shotgun held on the guy she had wounded.

"Maybe this guy can tell us what we need to know," she said.

"I'm hurting," the wounded man said.

Lyons stood over him, his Python in his hand again.

"You want Officer Lopaka to call this in? Ask for medical aid?"

"I damn well don't need Smokey the Bear," the guy grumbled.

"Wounded *and* a comic," Schwarz said.

"I'd let him bleed all over the floor," Lyons snapped. "Save us a lot of trouble."

Lopaka leaned against the door frame, left hand pressed to her ribs. Her face had paled as the effect of the shot increased.

"Hey, you take a hit?" Blancanales asked.

"Over my ribs. Jacket took the worst."

Blancanales moved her from the door to check her out.

"*Hey!*" The wounded guy was trying to get attention. "You going to call?"

"Where's Macklin and the rest of your crew?" Lyons asked. "And the package?"

"Do I look as if I give a damn?"

"You look ready to pass out," Schwarz said. "Blood loss will do that for you."

The guy held his blood-dripping hands in front of his face.

"We should get Officer Lopaka out of here," Blancanales said. He had closed her shirt back over her exposed side. "I'd say she's got a couple cracked ribs. She needs treatment. Now."

Lyons nodded. "Clear any weapons away. Get her in a car, and we'll head for the hospital."

Schwarz checked the wounded man for a cell phone. He found one and took it off the guy. "I'll clear all the others," he said. "Don't want this guy calling his buddies."

"I can show you the way to the hospital," Lopaka said. "No need to call it in."

She had caught on to what the others were doing and fell in with the deception. As Blancanales helped her, she slid an arm across his shoulder for support.

"All clear here," Schwarz said.

"What about me?" the wounded guy said. He was slumped on the floor now, leaning against the door frame.

"I don't see you on our list," Lyons said.

"Leaving me to die? What about me?"

Jenny Lopaka said, "That hit you made on the convoy left six HPD officers dead. Six, you piece of trash. So *what* about you? Only one cop survived and he identified one of your crew. Jake Borgnine. We checked you all out. Macklin. Borgnine. All the others in your scumbag crew. We know who you are. We know what you did."

"Lady's right," Lyons said. "Your days will be numbered now by how many you have left to serve. And it will be a hell of a lot."

"You figure to leave me here? Christ, I'm leaking blood all over the damn floor."

"Tough," Schwarz said. "I thought you military types were hard. Sounds to me you could do with some help."

"*Yeah?* What will it cost?"

"Where's Macklin and the package?" Lyons said.

"Give up my buddies? Go screw yourself."

"Your choice," Lyons said. "Let's get out of here."

Outside they could still hear the guy ranting at them.

Lyons said, "Take one of their vehicles and go pick ours up. Lopaka can stay with me and call in the cavalry. Get the perp picked up."

SCHWARZ AND BLANCANALES had driven off in one of the cars parked outside the house.

Lopaka called up Kalikani on his cell and gave him a rundown on what had happened. He told her that he would send HPD and medical help to the house.

While Lopaka spoke to Kalikani, Lyons went inside and saw the wounded guy unconscious on the floor. He checked the man. His pulse was thready, but the man was still alive.

Making his way back outside, Lyons walked by the rented panel van. He stopped as he did, something clicking in his head.

"Hell, I'm an idiot."

Lopaka turned. "What?"

"We can track the second truck, if it has the equipment installed," Lyons said. "Let me speak to Oscar." He took the cell from Lopaka. "Oscar, check with the rental company. If they have the tracking system on their vehicles, we can pin down where it is."

"I'll get back to you," Kalikani said.

SCHWARZ AND BLANCANALES showed up just behind a convoy of HPD cruisers and a pair of ambulances. The local cops had been briefed by Kalikani, so Able Team got no hassle from them. Kalikani had informed the cops that the men who Able Team had taken down were from the group who had hijacked and killed their fellow officers.

Under protest Lopaka was made to climb into one of the ambulances and have her injury checked out.

Lyons told Schwarz and Blancanales about Kalikani checking out the tracking system.

"Good thinking. Could pan out," Schwarz said. "Most rental companies fit the systems as safeguards to their vehicles these days." He glanced at Blancanales. "Now you can see why he's the boss."

Straight-faced, Blancanales shook his head. "No," he said.

"I hate a bad loser," Lyons said.

Kalikani called back minutes later. "You were right," he said. "The truck has the tracking system installed."

"Do we know where it is?"

"Private airstrip off Kamehameha Highway. About five miles from your present location."

"Satnav coordinates?"

"Sending to your cell. You need any backup?" Kalikani laughed. "Silly question."

Lyons checked and saw the information download.

"Time we weren't here," he said. "We need to move fast before that package gets airborne."

He headed for the 4x4, Schwarz and Blancanales following.

As they piled into the vehicle, Blancanales taking the wheel, Lyons saw Lopaka exiting the ambulance. She started toward them, then saw they were in too much of a hurry. She stood by the ambulance and raised a hand as Blancanales swung the big vehicle around and out toward the road.

Lyons tapped in the coordinates and the inbuilt satnav sourced the route. Blancanales took a tire-squealing right onto the road.

While Blancanales drove, Lyons and Schwarz loaded and checked their weapons.

"She was handy to have along," Blancanales said.

"Hey," Schwarz said, "the Polster is smitten."

Blancanales ignored the gibe and slammed his foot down on the gas pedal.

"Just remember that, when we reach a bend, you go around it," Schwarz said.

"Trust me, I've done this before," his partner said.

They hit the Kamehameha Highway minutes later. If there were speed limits, Blancanales ignored them as he steered the 4x4 past any vehicles he encountered, ignoring the occasional angry blasts from punched car horns.

"This is good," Schwarz said. "If we get killed in an auto smash, I can have one of those traditional Hawaiian funerals with all the flowers and a nice big canoe taking me out to sea."

"If we crash at this speed," Lyons said, "there won't be enough of you to float."

"In a quarter mile, you will have reached your destination," the soothing voice of the satnav informed them. "Take the next right."

"Slow down, cowboy," Schwarz said.

"I prefer it when the satnav speaks," Blancanales said.

He took his foot off the gas and touched the brake. The heavy 4x4 dipped, and the tires left marks on the tarmac as Blancanales pulled on the wheel. He took the SUV in through the entrance to the airstrip, bouncing off the concrete and partway onto the grass, before he brought it under control.

Ahead of them was the long, low building and the small control tower that serviced the airstrip. As Blancanales followed the short service road, Lyons pointed through the windshield to where a Gulfstream Executive twin-engine jet had just touched down at the far end of the single runway.

"There's our rental truck," Blancanales said.

"It has company," Lyons said.

Blancanales swung the 4x4 around the end of the admin building.

"Hit the brakes," Lyons yelled.

He had seen the two cars parked close by the truck, and the figures standing beside them.

Figures that turned in their direction.

And who instantly produced guns lifting in Able Team's direction.

CHAPTER TWENTY-EIGHT

ABLE TEAM

As Blancanales hit the brakes hard, bringing the SUV to a stop, Able Team grabbed at their weapons and exited the vehicle. They used it as cover, hearing the thud of slugs ripping into the bodywork and windows.

"They keep us pinned down long enough," Schwarz said, "they might get that package on board."

"If that jet gets in range," Lyons said, "take out the tires."

"He makes it sound so easy," Blancanales muttered.

"Be easier to put an engine out of commission."

"Tires. Engine. I don't care as long as that plane doesn't get to lift off again."

"I think one of the reception crowd is heading this way," Blancanales said.

He eased around the bulk of the 4x4 and made out the ducking-and-weaving outline of a man in a dark suit approaching, firing as he moved. Blancanales pushed the muzzle of his Uzi around the wheel in front of him and dropped the guy with a steady burst. The man folded and slid on his face across the concrete. The autopistol he carried bounced from his hand, and the guy lay bleeding on the ground.

Seeing one of their men go down galvanized the other armed men, and they fanned out from the parked cars.

The airstrip echoed the sustained round of gunfire.

Slugs thudded against the 4x4.

"Don't let them go wide," Lyons yelled.

He had seen the way the opposition was starting to form a ragged line, moving away from the 4x4 to allow them wider access.

Schwarz, down on one knee, saw a darkly clad figure edging into view on his side of cover. He gave the guy a few more seconds before tracking him and hitting him with a short burst from his Uzi. As the guy slid to his knees, Schwarz took a moment to line him up and put a second burst through his skull, flipping the target onto his back.

His action drew a vicious round of shots that blew one of the headlights and raked the front fender over his head....

IT TOOK ROSARIO Blancanales only a few seconds to become aware of his own vulnerable position on the opposite side of the vehicle from Schwarz. He understood only too well that, once the enemy moved wider, they would be able to see him clearly and then target him.

Not a bright idea to sit and make yourself available, he decided.

He checked out the opposition and chose his targets, cradling the Uzi close as he aimed and fired, taking down one guy, hitting a second in the shoulder.

Blancanales saw his hits go down, angled his SMG and stroked the trigger again. He knew he had missed the moment he had fired. Saw his burst shatter the window on one of the parked cars.

He didn't hear the shot that found him but simply felt the hard blow to his hip and the abrupt pain that engulfed him. Blancanales rolled back along the side of the SUV, fighting off the hurt. There was no time to lie down and feel sorry for himself. The enemy shooters weren't about to allow him that luxury, so Blancanales braced himself against the bulk of the car and held his position.

The shooter rushed into view, his weapon seeking a target. Blancanales had a view of a slim black-haired Chinese gunner. His face held a bland expression as he rounded the front of the SUV.

The muzzle of the Uzi tilted, and Blancanales squeezed the trigger and held it there. The 9 mm SMG crackled with fire and the Chinese hardman halted in midstride as the slugs tore into his chest. He gave a stunned moan, stumbled back and slammed to the ground. His spine arched as he fought the pain, blood spreading across his torso and bubbling from his lips.

CARL LYONS HAD turned and moved to the rear of the SUV, his attention fixed on the jet rolling along the strip. The exchange had to be prevented, and while his partners concentrated on the shooters, Lyons targeted the aircraft.

His initial move took the group by surprise, though only for a short time. When they saw him angling across the concrete, it was obvious what he was doing, and they moved to intercept.

MACKLIN AND BORGNINE had delivered the panel truck to the airstrip, meeting Xian Chi and his Chinese escort. A pair of Macklin's team accompanied them in a backup vehicle.

The sudden appearance of the three Americans had been unexpected and, as far as Macklin was concerned, a pain in the butt. He had been hoping for a smooth, problem-free exchange, just passing the package to Chi and receiving the final payment for services rendered. Now it looked as if he and Borgnine were going to have to put in some extra work.

"Son of a bitch," Macklin said. "Stop that mother."

Both men slid their handguns from holsters and moved

to intercept the big blond man cutting across their path toward the strip.

The backup pair crossed to reinforce Borgnine.

Borgnine powered in the guy's direction, bringing his pistol up and firing. His slug chipped concrete yards from the fast-moving figure. The guy didn't even miss a step.

"Hard bastard, huh," Borgnine said.

He hauled himself to a stop and pulled his Glock back on line.

A sudden noise intruded, breaking his concentration.

The high scream of a vehicle motor and the screech of tires on the concrete.

Borgnine turned his head as the noise increased. He caught a glimpse of an HPD cruiser, lights flashing as it bore down on him.

Borgnine tried to jerk aside.

Too slow.

The front of the cruiser slammed into him. The impact lifted Borgnine clear off his feet. He spun into the air and slammed down across the hood of the cruiser, his head hitting the windshield before he was tossed aside. His body slammed facedown on the concrete, twisted and broken. He moved a couple times, before he became still.

Macklin's backup team launched a volley of fast shots at Lyons. The cruiser lurched forward, taking it between the shooters and the blond Able Team leader. Slugs slapped against the cruiser's side panels. Glass in one of the rear doors imploded.

Lyons didn't need to be told who was behind the wheel. He had already spotted the swinging dark hair and the black-clad female outline.

Jenny Lopaka.

The lady cop had made an unexpected but welcome appearance.

Lyons made good use of the distraction, ducking behind the HPD vehicle, making one of the fastest speed-loader changes he had ever done, then leveled his Colt Python at the moving shooters.

He triggered a couple shots, followed by the hard sound of Lopaka's shotgun as the HPD cop emerged from the cruiser, leaning over the roof. She laid down a burst of fire that threw 12-gauge blasts at the pair. Close-fired shots caught one guy in the upper chest, throwing him back in a bloody mist of red. Lyons's .357 Colt boomed, the muzzle flaring as the slug burst from the barrel. Never one to do anything halfway, Lyons fired twice more, his shots ripping bloody holes in the surviving shooter as he was turned around under the impact. The man dropped hard and lay still.

"That was a crazy stunt," Lyons growled, as Lopaka lowered her shotgun, one hand pressed to her strapped-up side.

"You're welcome. It worked, though," she said. "Now let's go stop that bastard Macklin."

Lyons needed no further offers. He joined her in the cruiser, slamming the passenger door as she jammed her foot down on the pedal.

MACKLIN HAD CUT and run, seeing the way things were going. His team had been put down, and Chi was in no position to help. The Chinese man had his own problems.

Macklin made it to the panel truck, swinging in behind the wheel, and fired up the engine. He had his gaze on the jet, rolling along the strip in his direction. At the moment he was thinking about one thing.

His escape.

Macklin had learned long ago that, when a mission went bad, there was no point standing around moaning about it and ending up dead yourself. Once you were dead, that was it. You were a piece of meat, ready to rot away until there were only the bones left. Macklin saw no profit in that.

If he got out alive, he could regroup, collect the money he had stashed away in various accounts. There were always plenty of other men ready to earn their money by signing up with a pay-as-you-earn outfit. The world was awash with conflicts needing experienced hands.

He would miss his dead guys. Especially Borgnine. They had outfitted for a number of years. But today had been Borgnine's time to cash in. It was the way of the business. A merc took on a contract, received his money and did the job. Dying was an accepted risk. No one wanted it to happen. When it did, there was nothing to gain by weeping over the dead.

Tires howled as Macklin hit the airstrip. He slammed his foot on the gas. He swung in behind the rolling Gulfstream and rode the blast from the engines. He needed to get alongside in an attempt to get on board.

The jet was his ride out of the mess around him. The aircraft was almost at walking pace now. It would need to turn about before making a takeoff run. So he still had a chance.

Or he might have had one, if the HPD cruiser hadn't come screaming into view, the rear end sliding as it bounced onto the airstrip. The Crown Vic had power under the hood and thrust the car past him.

Macklin could barely believe what he saw next, as the cruiser drew level with the coasting jet. The blond guy Macklin had seen earlier leaned out the passenger window, a shotgun in his hands. He angled the muzzle down and pumped a pair of 12-gauge shots into the jet's front wheel. The tire was shredded, rubber fragments filling the air. The nose of the Gulfstream dropped as the wheel deflated, the metal rim scoring the concrete. The aircraft veered to one side, jigging awkwardly. It rolled on for twenty feet before coming to a dead stop.

The HPD cruiser pulled away from the aircraft, slewing sideways.

"*Son of a bitch*," Macklin yelled, pounding a fist on the rim of the steering wheel.

He braked hard, stared out the windshield, pure frustration holding him immobile. Just as quickly he regained his composure.

Okay. No plane.

He wasn't going to get far in the panel truck. The damn thing had no speed. It was a lumbering box on wheels.

Even as the thoughts coursed through his mind, Macklin was feeding a fresh magazine into his handgun. He had a couple more in his pocket, so whatever happened, he was not going down without a fight. He realized his recent decision to simply get the hell away would most likely fly out the window if he didn't move quickly. He was going to have to fight for his freedom. Not the way he would have chosen, but what the hell, he would give it a try.

He shoved open the door and eased out of the cab, weapon at his side, ready if needed.

He found some humor in that.

If needed.

There would be no other option open to him. Macklin decided, if he moved fast, there might be a chance.

Hell, there had to be a chance.

A chance that meant the difference between staying alive or ending up on the pavement.

He glanced across the strip. On the far side of the runway, the open ground gave way to a mass of vegetation. Trees and lush shrubbery. If he could make it that far, he *might* find his way out.

For a few seconds Macklin imagined he just might. Self-preservation was a strong impulse. The desire for a man to survive. To stay alive. It drove William Macklin to push himself to the limit, to ignore the possibility he might not escape the inevitable. He was physically fit. Had always kept himself in shape, because, in his line of work, it was a foolish man who allowed himself to weaken. And right at that moment he was running for the most important prize ever.

His life.

He had cleared the concrete strip, legs pounding as he raced across the grass. Body coordinated, muscles working well, he hadn't even begun to sweat.

He might make it.

That was until he heard the beat of the police cruiser's engine coming up behind him. He didn't waste a second looking back. There was no need. The damn car was closing the gap, and there was no way he could outrun it.

"You want me to run him down?" Lopaka asked.

"Hell, no," Lyons said. "This one is mine."

"Sounds personal."

"He and his crew murdered six cops when they hijacked that package. He's not getting away with that."

Lyons slid his Python across the seat.

Lopaka eased the cruiser level with the running man.

She saw Lyons slip his door off the catch and slam his foot into the panel as the cruiser matched Macklin's pace. The door swung wide and caught the man, knocking him off his feet. As Lopaka stepped on the brake, Lyons was out of the car and bending over Macklin.

Lyons saw Macklin had lost his grip on his handgun. Lyons picked it up and threw it wide. He caught hold of Macklin by the back of his shirt and hauled the man upright, swung the man around and slammed his bunched right fist into Macklin's face. The blow was loud and hard. Macklin's lips were mashed back against his teeth. Blood spurted, thick and warm, running down his chin. Before Macklin had time to fully register, Lyons hit him again. And again. The third blow knocked Macklin off his feet, and he slammed down on the ground, gasping and spitting blood.

Lyons moved in, his face flushed with the rage that was driving him.

With a sudden response Macklin scissored his legs and swept Lyons off his feet. As the Able Team leader crashed to the grass, Macklin hammered his right heel into Lyons's stomach. Lyons had anticipated the move and held his muscles tight. Even so the blow hurt. The pain galvanized Lyons.

He rolled away from Macklin, coming to his feet, and met Macklin's rushing attack. They collided with a solid thump, hands seeking the best hold. Lyons felt the man's arms circle his torso, closing tightly. Macklin braced his feet apart to stabilize himself, squeezing his arms hard over Lyons's ribs.

Lyons sucked in a breath and reached for Macklin's head, pushing it back. The merc's bloody face came into view, eyes staring into Lyons's. Lyons pulled his own head back, then slammed it forward, butting Macklin with his forehead. Macklin's nose was crushed, reduced to a pulpy mass that streamed blood. Lyons repeated the head butt. He heard Macklin roar in pain, eyes glazing over. More blood poured from his nose.

The brief moment was enough for Lyons. He twisted his powerful body, breaking Macklin's weakened hold. For a moment they stood apart, then Lyons punched hard, left and right. Macklin's jaw crumpled under the brutal impact, and he fell to his knees. Lyons stepped around the man, leaned in and took hold of Macklin's head in a two-handed grip. There was no hesitation as he wrenched Macklin's head, hearing the soft crunch as the move severed the man's neck from his spine. Macklin became a dead weight. He fell face forward onto the grass.

Lopaka was out of the car, staring across at Lyons. For once she had nothing to say, as he walked back to the cruiser.

"We're done here," Lyons said.

The lady cop nodded. "I guess we are," she said.

WHEN HE SAW Macklin go down, Xian Chi began to understand the concept of defeat.

His own men were out of action, and the two Americans were cutting across to intercept him.

He saw his plan unraveling. The NNEMP unit, still sitting in the parked panel truck, would fall into American hands now.

All the scheming. The resistance and the effort. It was for nothing.

He glanced at the disabled jet. The package would not be leaving on the plane, and neither would he.

Chi thought back a few days, before the North Korean experimental strike. His life on Hawaii had been almost peaceful then. But the moment the Koreans had launched their trial, everything became tangled, and control was quickly lost.

He could have blamed it all on Soon Il Tak, and the way he had acted. Yet Chi was not blameless. His own way of handling things had not been as subtle as it might have been.

He stared around him. His team was down. So was Macklin's.

Chi put his cell to his ear as he pressed a speed-dial number. It was answered within seconds. It was Kai Yeung.

"Just listen. It is over," Chi said. "The Americans are here. We have lost the package. Our men are down, and I am going to be arrested. Save yourself, Yeung, and perhaps you can help me later."

Chi threw the cell onto the ground at his feet.

The American team and the female police officer were in control, their weapons turned in his direction.

In the distance, Chi heard the wail of sirens. More police on their way.

He sighed in resignation, raising his hands and clasping them on top of his head. There was nothing else he could do. He would be arrested and placed in an American prison. At least, with luck, Kai Yeung could avoid capture.

If he got back to Beijing, there was always a chance. Then Chi realized he was beyond help from home. When he thought about it, perhaps he would be safer here, than if he did go back to China. Returning to Beijing as a failure, he would not have been treated so well. His management of the affair in Hawaii had not been a success, and with all that had happened, his masters in China would be less than pleased.

At Chi's level of command, there were no excuses. His actions had wasted a great deal of money for no return. He had lost face, and such matters were taken extremely seriously in Beijing. Repercussions could reach a high level, leaving much to be explained by his government.

Although China had not been the actual culprits, the connection with North Korea could be used by the Americans to assess blame. Political embarrassment was something Beijing could do to avoid. Chi knew that the Americans would leap at the chance to point the finger and make China squirm under the spotlight.

Whatever else happened, Xian Chi would become the scapegoat. For his sins, if he returned to China, he would undoubtedly suffer. If the authorities had it in their minds, he could be quickly shot and forgotten about. Or, worse still, he might be confined in one of the remote prison camps where he would be alive but left in isolation.

Better then that Kai Yeung simply looked after himself. The younger man was smart. He had a low profile that would allow him to move on, and with the generous amount of money in safe accounts, he could live comfortably. Chi wished him well.

As he watched the armed Americans approaching, Chi knew he would be marginally better off in their custody. With his knowledge he might be able to bargain for his life. He carried information in his head that would be of much use to the Americans. If nothing else Xian Chi was a survivor. In his current position his continued existence depended on being able to convince the Americans he could offer them information they could benefit from.

He watched as the female put away her gun and produced a pair of handcuffs. She held them out, and Chi lowered his arms and extended his wrists.

"Turn around," Lopaka said.

Chi did as ordered. He felt the cold bracelets snap on his wrists. As they did, he experienced a moment of relief. His former responsibilities no longer existed. From this moment on, a new phase of his life began. A phase that might yet offer him salvation.

He met the gaze of the blond-haired American.

"I wish to make a deal," Xian Chi said, thinking about his future.

CHAPTER TWENTY-NINE

OSCAR KALIKANI

The niggling thoughts in Oscar Kalikani's mind persisted. Like a teasing itch just out of reach, they refused to go away.

He sat at his desk, recent events playing over and over in his mind. Replaying in his thoughts, there but just out of reach. He wanted answers to things that had happened. Which shouldn't have happened. Too many matters to be simply ignored, or simply accepted without question.

The attacks launched against the three agents from the mainland. All so neatly directed at them when barely anyone knew of their presence. Then the attempt on his own life, only averted because he had brought in Jenny Lopaka to cover his back.

Someone knew in advance.

Had to have known.

And the logical next step for Kalikani forced him to confirm the possibility there was a leak within the department. Someone had to be passing out information that was enabling those responsible to be ahead of the game.

Kalikani found his suspicions distasteful, but he had to take the consideration on board. He wished it was otherwise. Unfortunately he saw no viable alternative.

The leaks came from within the department. His own department.

One of the cops he worked with was passing operational

information, giving details to—what did he call them—
the enemy?

How else would the schedule regarding the police convoy moving the package get to the people who had staged
the attack? The attack that resulted in six dead cops and
the loss of the package. Timing and route had been kept
inside the department. Nowhere else, and no civilians had
been given that information.

The bitter truth came back to Kalikani like a slap in
the face.

The son of a bitch worked alongside him in the department. It had to be someone close....

Too damn close.

It took an effort for Kalikani to remain still. His initial
urge had been to lunge from his seat and...*and do what?* He
had to stay calm, show no outward sign that he suspected
a problem. So Kalikani stayed seated, his body taut with
the contained anger he felt. Tensing his muscles had only
agitated his wounds, set them to aching with a vengeance.
He felt a sheen of sweat break out across his face.

Don't give yourself away, Oscar. Keep it under control. Whoever might be the one could be watching you.
Checking to see if you had any suspicions. Let it out and
the guilty one will back away. You need to stay relaxed—
on the outside. Use your eyes. Your ears. Watch and listen. That way he might make a mistake and that would be
when you take him....

There was too much at stake to screw this up. Kalikani
realized he had to alert Lopaka and Matthews's team. He
couldn't risk them walking into another setup. He also knew
he daren't use any department phones in case there was a
tap on them. Whoever was behind the leaks would have
covered that avenue. Kalikani knew he had to make contact from an outside source away from the department.

He took his S&W from his desk drawer and slipped it into the belt holster on his hip. He turned off his police-issue cell. Then dropped his personal cell into his pocket and slid his chair away from his desk.

"You okay to go out, Oscar? You don't look too good."

Kalikani turned and saw Tasker watching him. Kalikani raised his good hand. "Pain's kicking in again," he said. "I need to take a walk. Swallow some more painkillers."

"You should take some time off," one of the other cops said. "Like the doc said."

"Too much happening," Kalikani said. "I just need some time out. I'll be back to take the strain off you guys soon enough."

The good-natured banter followed him out of the office.

Kalikani made his way outside. He paused on the sidewalk, checking his position and recalled there was a pay phone halfway along the block. He tugged his shirt over his holstered pistol and walked in the direction of the phone, hoping it hadn't been vandalized. Back in the day, before cell phones sprouted like mushrooms in a dark cellar, there were pay phones everywhere. Not anymore. The phone companies, adding up the cost of keeping pay phones working, had reduced the numbers.

He saw the phone just ahead and made for it. It was in working order, and he felt in his pocket for coins. He dialed the number of the cell Matthews had given him by checking it on his cell's caller display. He listened as the number rang out, then recognized the blond ex-cop's brusque voice.

"Kalikani. I'm calling from an outside line. Call me paranoid but I think there's a bad cop in my department. I've been sitting at my desk for the last couple hours working this over. It's the only way this could be happening. Insider information is being passed to the opposition from the inside. We haven't broadcast our details outside the office.

Leaves one conclusion. Bad cop betraying his buddies." Kalikani paused, then said, "And getting them killed."

"Lopaka told us what you suspected. What are you going to do?"

"Try to find him."

"Then what?"

Kalikani's laugh was harsh. "Ideally I'd like to shoot him. Then set him on fire and watch him burn. But I can't do that, because I'm a cop myself."

"Shooting and burning is too good for a cop who turns on his own. If that was how you wanted to deal with it, I'll light the match myself."

"You get your result?"

"Done and dusted. The package is safe, and the bad guys handled. One prisoner on the way to your department."

"Good to hear," Kalikani said.

"Stay safe," Lyons said and ended the call.

Kalikani took out the plastic vial holding his painkillers and swallowed a couple dry. Then he retraced his steps to the station house and made his way back to the office.

The main office was quiet. Only a couple cops were at their desks, hunched indifferently over piles of paperwork.

Kalikani slumped in his seat behind his desk. He could smell freshly brewed coffee from the refreshment station across the room.

"That coffee fresh? If it is, I could use a cup."

The cop, Larch, laughed. "Only because I feel sorry for you," he said.

He crossed to the coffeepot and filled a mug for Kalikani, then took it over.

"Thanks, Phil."

Kalikani swallowed some of the coffee. As he scanned the communal office, he cast his eyes across Tasker's sectioned space. There was no one behind the glass panels.

"Tasker out?" he asked.

"Yeah," Larch said. "Funny thing, he took a call before you got back and busted out of here like his house was on fire. Not like Tasker to scoot like that. These days he's stuck to that office chair like he has Super Glue on his butt."

Kalikani swallowed more coffee. "He say where he was going?"

"Uh-uh. That was weird, too. Usually never goes out without telling where he's going. You know that." Larch shrugged. "Hell, things have been weird around here the last few days. Ever since that thing out at the Coast Guard station."

"Tell me about it," Kalikani said.

He hung his head over his coffee mug, eyes focusing on Captain Rudy Tasker's office.

Kalikani became aware of what he was thinking.

Rudy Tasker?

The head of the department?

Kalikani slipped the vial of painkillers from his pocket and placed it on the desk. Maybe he was taking too many. They were muddling his brain.

Not Tasker.

Long serving.

A man the department trusted.

The father to the team.

Oscar, you are delusional, brother.

Rudy Tasker couldn't be the one.

He sat back, staring at the wall. Only a short time ago he had convinced himself there was a traitor in the department. If he was thinking that way, then he had to suspect the whole team.

Including Tasker.

But why Tasker?

Hell, because Tasker was no different from any of the

others, when it came down to it. He had the same strengths and weaknesses as they all did.

And Tasker had access to more information than anyone else within the team.

Bigger men, men with far more power and responsibility than Tasker, had succumbed to temptation.

Kalikani couldn't rid himself of the image of the attack at the market.

Or the setup at the Wiseman apartment complex.

Tasker had sent him there to meet Mojo, when there was no Mojo to meet.

Kalikani sat upright, angry with himself. He was practically accusing Tasker of being the one based on nothing more than vague suspicion.

Okay, the guy had left the office in a rush. Walking out without a moment's notice. That didn't prove anything.

Get a grip, he told himself. Think it through before you lose it altogether.

Kalikani's reason slowly gathered itself. He needed to work this through calmly. If he still felt Tasker was involved, the only way to deal with it was by sense and reason. Take it step by step.

Be a cop.

Watch and listen.

Observe.

A partial answer eased its way into his consciousness. Kalikani tried to dismiss it, but the thought remained and refused to disappear.

He couldn't wipe the doubt in his mind. It *had* been Tasker who had sent him to the meet with Mojo. The captain had practically insisted Kalikani go alone.

A meet that had proved to be a deliberate setup. Men had been waiting for him. Ready to cripple him. To persuade him to drop his nosing around.

The question was, had Tasker's call to go meet Mojo simply been a passing along of genuine information?

Or had Rudy Tasker been making sure Kalikani ended up in the right place, so that a pair of hired thugs could beat him to death?

Kalikani hated what he was thinking. But the thought was lodged in his brain now. It would stay there, until he resolved it, one way or another.

Now Tasker had received a call and had exited his office in a rush. Had that call been to let him know the game was over? Warning him to get out, before his deal was exposed?

Kalikani reached for the phone on his desk. He had realized there was at least a way he could pin down the authenticity of Tasker's call from Mojo. For the next few minutes he made calls, spoke to whoever picked up, then moved to the next.

He was on his sixth call, when he received the answer he was looking for.

"Yeah, he's here. Been sittin' on that stool for the last couple hours."

"Bring him to the phone, Andy, that's all."

The bartender mumbled, then laid the receiver down and yelled.

"Hey, Mojo, move your skinny ass and get over here. Call for you."

In the background Kalikani could hear someone making noise. That would be Mojo. The guy was always noisy. Always questioning. *Why* was his favorite word. The bartender, Andy, yelled back at him. Finally Mojo made his way to the phone and picked it up.

"*What?*" he snapped.

"That the way your mother taught you to speak over the phone, Mojo?" Kalikani asked.

"Who the hell is this and why you callin' for me?"

Mojo's words were slow, slightly slurred. Kalikani could hear his uneven breathing and was surprised the alcohol fumes didn't come down the wires.

"This is Kalikani. Think slow, Mojo. I just want to ask you something."

"Hey, brother, I'm supposed to call *you* when I got the word. Why you callin' me?"

"So you don't have anything for me?"

"Didn't I just say how it be? What you doin' playin' with my head?"

"You haven't called the station? Didn't leave a message you wanted to meet me over at Wiseman's?"

There was a long pause as Mojo digested the questions. It was plain he had been drinking heavily, and his functions had slowed down.

"You messin' with my head, Kalikani? I ain't called you in weeks. And you damn well know I don't go near that place. Wiseman's is only for crackheads and low-life asswipes. You go there, those strung-out dopers will cut you open just for breathin' the same air they do." Mojo paused. "What is this all about, Kalikani?"

"Nothing, Mojo. You've just cleared something up for me. You can go back to your stool now. Hey, put Andy back on."

Mojo, obviously not clear on what had just happened, handed the phone to the bartender.

Kalikani heard his last words as Mojo wandered to his bar stool.

"Why'd he call me? He doesn't call me."

"Give Mojo a twenty-dollar tab, Andy. I'll settle up next time I'm passing by. Do that for me, huh?"

"Sure thing, Kalikani. Just don't forget to drop by."

Kalikani laughed. "Would I mess you about, Andy?"

After he had put the phone down, Kalikani sat in silence.

He had received the answer he needed, but it did nothing to make him feel better.

Tasker had openly lied about the supposed call from Mojo.

Tasker had taken his most recent call and, whatever he had been told, had forced him to leave the office quickly.

Kalikani had the feeling Rudy Tasker was getting ready to run.

CHAPTER THIRTY

ABLE TEAM

With Chi secure in the rear of Lopaka's police cruiser, Able Team was able to wind up the incident.

As HPD cars arrived, Lopaka marshaled a couple to block off the jet. Someone had added a med unit to follow the HPD convoy. Lopaka sent the medics to attend to Blancanales and take over from Schwarz, who was kneeling beside his partner. Blancanales had a deep flesh wound, the bullet still embedded in his hip. He had lost a great deal of blood. They did what they could before loading him into the ambulance, and despite his protests, hit the sirens as they sped back to the city.

With Lopaka at his side Lyons opened up the panel truck, and they took their first look at the piece of equipment that had been the prime cause of all the problems.

The unit of metal, a configuration neither of them could fully understand, was strapped down to the bed of the truck. It was heat seared from the power discharge and looked almost like some sculpture designed by a hyped-up artist.

"What are all the gizmos for?" Lopaka asked, hands on her hips as she studied the unit.

"How the hell would I know?" Lyons said. "I'm just a simple grunt. I leave the science to the smart guys."

"This thing... It caused all that damage at the Coast Guard station? Shut off all the electric power?"

"Yes."

"Now that is scary. What happens if a larger one goes off?"

Lyons watched a U.S. Air Force vehicle roll across the concrete and stop behind them. Armed figures exited the vehicle and came up to Lyons and Lopaka.

"You can step aside now," a uniformed captain snapped. "We'll take it from here."

"They teach you that in training?" Lopaka asked.

The captain stared at her. "What?"

"The bad manners and lack of respect."

"I don't have to explain myself to you..."

"Try me, flyboy," Lyons said, planting himself in front of the man. "You're a little late in the game. Where were you when all this was going down?"

The captain reddened. "This matter comes under my jurisdiction. My orders come from Air Force Command."

Lyons actually grinned. "Mine come from way above that, so call your boss and check if you don't believe me."

Lopaka gripped his arm. "Hey, Matthews, let the Boy Scout play soldiers. Just take me away before I shoot him."

They walked away to join Schwarz.

"What was that all about?"

"Now we've pulled their chestnuts out of the fire, we're out of the loop," Lyons said.

"Let's get out of here before they realize we have Chi sitting in the back of Lopaka's cruiser," Schwarz said. "We can turn him over to HPD, then go check on our wounded hero."

Lopaka commandeered one of the HPD 4x4s for the trip back to the city. Schwarz drove, while Lyons sat in the rear with Lopaka. A silent Xian Chi sat between them. Lopaka had her Benelli shotgun in her hands, the muzzle never far from Chi.

Lyons called Stony Man and had a conversation with Brognola.

"Mission accomplished," he said. "We recovered the package. The Air Force took control and made it clear we were no longer needed."

"Any casualties?"

"Comer took a shot in the hip. We're on our way to check him out at the hospital after we hand over our other prize. Chinese guy called Xian Chi. He was the one running interference for the North Koreans. He doesn't want to go home because he already asked for a deal. He could be useful."

"Nice bonus," Brognola said. "Our people will want a long chat with him. The way this all worked out, everyone is going to want a piece of this guy. A lot of questions will need answering."

"I don't envy anyone that job," Lyons said. "And I'm guessing there are going to be red faces in Pyongyang and Beijing, as well."

"We can debrief when you guys get back. But no rush. Hawaii should be nice this time of year. Take some R & R."

"*Yeah?* On your dime, of course."

Brognola chuckled. "I don't suppose I can make too much fuss about that, can I?"

"Not really," Lyons agreed and shut off his cell.

"That was a pretty smart backup play you made back there, Jenny," Schwarz said. "HPD always respond so fast?"

"No mystery," Lopaka said. "I called Kalikani, and he gave me the same coordinates you had. So I borrowed a cruiser and took off after you."

"A good move." Schwarz glanced at Lyons. "Right, boss?"

After a moment Lyons nodded. "Not bad."

"He always so generous with his praise?" Lopaka asked.

"Only on a good day."

When they arrived at the precinct, Xian Chi was escorted inside. While Lyons and Schwarz stayed with Chi during booking him, Lopaka climbed the stairs to the next floor to speak to Kalikani.

She was back in a couple minutes, a frown on her face.

"Something wrong?" Schwarz asked.

"O isn't here. I spoke to one of his detectives. O left some time ago. Didn't tell anyone where he was going, and that isn't like O. I tried his cell but he isn't answering."

"You learn anything else?"

"Just one thing. You might find it odd."

"After everything that has happened since we stepped off our plane, nothing on this island would surprise me," Schwarz said.

"Detective Larch mentioned that Rudy Tasker, the head detective, upped and left the department some time before O did. One minute Tasker was in his office, the next he simply left. No word to anyone."

"Anything happen that could have made him leave?"

"There was a bank heist going down in the city. Local cops were handling the scene, including detectives from Tasker's department."

"Maybe Tasker decided to check it out, as well," Schwarz said.

The expression on Lopaka's face told Lyons and Schwarz there was more behind the reason for Kalikani leaving the office.

"O was convinced the department had a leak," she said. "The way things have been happening, it was just a suspicion. He didn't have any proof. Just a cop thing."

"But now he's taken it further," Schwarz said. "He thinks this Tasker might be involved?"

"Maybe I'm seeing something that isn't there," Lopaka said.

"And maybe not," Lyons said.

"So what do we do?"

"We drop Hartz at the hospital," Lyons said. "He can stay with Comer. Let us know how he's doing." Lyons stared hard at Schwarz as he spoke.

"Okay," Schwarz said. "No problem."

"If Kalikani calls in, tell Larch to find out where he is," Lyons said to Lopaka. "He knows how to contact us."

They made their way outside. Lyons took the wheel, Schwarz beside him. Lopaka guided them across town to the hospital. It took no more than ten minutes. Lyons swung into the grounds and dropped Schwarz near the main entrance. He stepped out of the 4x4 and joined Schwarz for a quick word, before getting back in and driving off.

"Where do we go from here?" Lyons asked.

"What did you say to Hartz?" Lopaka asked. "Something you didn't want me to hear? I worked that out for myself."

"Our people back home have the best computer technology available. They can check into Tasker's profile. We might come up with something useful."

Lopaka folded her arms and stared out the windshield. Lyons could see the set of her jaw and understood she was not too happy at being sidelined.

"Should I just drive around in circles, or do you have somewhere in mind?" he asked.

"You can be a bastard, Matthews."

"At last a compliment. So while you're in a friendly mood, tell me you know where Tasker lives."

CHAPTER THIRTY-ONE

KALIKANI AND TASKER

Kalikani gave thanks to whoever came up with the idea for automatic transmissions. If his unmarked Crown Vic had been cursed with a manual transmission, he would not have been able to check out his theory. In case he was mistaken, this particular HPD cop did not want any witnesses. So being able to drive solo meant he could follow up on his, admittedly, unproven idea without having anyone with him embarrassed. He could accept that for himself; it wouldn't be the first time Kalikani had laid himself open to ending up with a red face, so that part didn't faze him.

He heard his cell vibrate in his shirt pocket. He was pretty certain it would be Lopaka again. She had been calling every twenty minutes. Kalikani grinned. That girl's persistence was off the charts. Get something fixed in her mind and she hung on like a stray dog with a juicy bone. As he had done before, Kalikani ignored the call. He had something to do and refused to be diverted.

He had a fleeting thought it might even be Tasker himself. Trying to get through to Kalikani with police business. Somehow Kalikani decided that wasn't it. He focused on the road ahead, hoping that whoever was calling would get tired eventually.

Traffic thinned as Kalikani drove out of the city and picked up the highway that rose into the wooded hills above Honolulu. He cruised steadily, working on the theory Tasker might have driven to his home. If someone had questioned him as to why he was following up on his suspicions, Oscar Kalikani would have been hard put to give a clear explanation. He was still having a difficult time convincing himself fully.

Experienced cops developed an instinct. It came through years of dealing with lawbreakers, with duplicitous individuals who spent their lives lying and cheating, and in the extreme, using violence to get what they wanted. Contact with these people gave a cop the ability to sense when matters were less than genuine.

It was Kalikani's ingrained cop sense that keyed on Tasker's attempt to conceal his nervousness during that call about the Mojo meet. And now his sudden departure from the office. His eagerness to get out of the department, according to Larch. It was so unlike Rudy Tasker's usual demeanor. It had prompted Kalikani's need to look further into the man's behavior. And the more he allowed his suspicion to grow, the stronger became his desire to bring the matter to a head.

When Kalikani took the curve and saw Tasker's home standing back from the road, the next thing he saw was a second vehicle standing alongside the detective's. Kalikani turned the cruiser off the road, into the shadow of trees and foliage. He reached into the glove box and pulled out a compact monocular. He zeroed in on the car and checked the rear plate.

For the first time since leaving the department, Kalikani took out his cell and hit the speed-dial number for the station. He identified himself when his call was answered and asked to be put through to the vehicle division. The man who answered recognized Kalikani's voice.

"I need a quick check on a plate," Kalikani said, giving the registration number.

He heard the soft tap of keys as the number was fed into the system.

"It's a rental," the cop said. "A city company."

"We have a make on the renter?"

"Let me check."

A name came up in Kalikani's mind, and he was not surprised when it matched the one he was given over the phone.

The same name as the one the invoices went to for the panel van and truck used by the hijackers who hit the police convoy. A Chinese-owned company was being used as a front for car rentals to cover the real hirer.

"Thanks, Eddie. You just made my day."

"Clint Eastwood. *Dirty Harry.* 1971," Eddie quoted.

"You never cease to impress me," Kalikani said as he ended the call.

His cell rang instantly. Kalikani looked at the screen.

Lopaka calling again. He checked previous calls, and saw she had dialed him over a dozen times during the past hour.

"Don't you ever give up?" Kalikani said as he answered and heard Lopaka's voice.

"Not when it's important, O. You should realize that by now. So what the hell is going on, and where are you? Larch told me you took off in a hurry. Something bugging you, O?"

"Right now I'm sitting at the side of the road near Rudy Tasker's home."

"*Tasker?* You think Tasker is involved? He's the department leak?"

"You catch on fast, Jenny Lopaka. Answer this. I just identified a rented car, sitting alongside Tasker's. Came from the same rental company who provided the vehicles involved in the recent hijack. And the rental agreement was billed to the same company as the one that footed the bill for the trucks."

"Matthews and I are minutes out. O, don't you go doing anything crazy until we get there."

RUDY TASKER HAD thought his life was mapped out for him the day he had joined the police force. He was young, and he was eager for advancement. It all seemed to go well. He sailed through the early years, passing promotion exams with ease. He persevered through the years when he wore the HPD uniform. Did his street time. Made sergeant. As soon as the opportunity came, he applied for a detective's badge.

No one was more surprised than Tasker himself when he was accepted. He moved into plainclothes and started to make his way through the ranks. His career was steady but not spectacular. Tasker applied himself, watched and listened to the senior officers, and played the waiting game. He made lieutenant in a reasonable time, took his share of knocks. He survived three shooting incidents, and took down two armed perps in separate incidents that earned him credits and a step up the promotion ladder.

Life, though, had a few nasty surprises in store for Rudy Tasker. The woman he loved—beautiful and full of life— who he was going to marry, went behind his back and found herself another lover. To her credit she faced him with the facts and told him their relationship was over.

It knocked Tasker back.

Another man might have hit the bottle and taken the slide down to obscurity. Rudy Tasker did not. He grieved for his loss but kept it inside. The experience soured his attitude toward women. He found he was happy enough with his solo life. He had his work, and he plunged into it.

He became obsessed with his career. The problem now was, no matter the heights he might rise to, it was little more than a way to get through the days. He saw the years stretching ahead, with only a lonely retirement at the end, and even when he became a captain, the rise in salary wasn't going to keep him in a style he desired.

So he had looked around, had used his contacts and found ways to supplement his income. Call it what you want. Bribes. Payoffs. His retirement fund. Tasker began to build his future. He was smart enough to salt away his side money, as he called it, in a number of accounts, under false identities scattered throughout the islands. As a high-ranking cop he understood the ways to do this without raising suspicions. And he *was* clever. Never showing any outward signs of his accumulating wealth. Never letting loose talk reveal what he was doing.

Five years later as his side money grew, Tasker began to lose interest in his work. Maybe it was because he had seen too many years of the underside of life. The criminals. The violence. The bureaucracy that was slowly strangling police work. He spent days out of each week behind his desk, simply filling out paperwork. Tasker had begun to hate it. He wanted out. All he needed was the final big score that would bring his retirement fund to the top level.

And it was around that time he was approached by Kai Yeung. The quiet, soft-spoken Chinese had come recommended by one of Tasker's longtime clients, another Chinese man who he had done business with in the past.

In a private club Yeung had introduced Tasker to his principal, the urbane Chinese man called Xian Chi. By the time they parted company that evening, Rudy Tasker had

his future sewn up. The money he would earn by assisting
Chi was far beyond anything he had been offered before.

In reality the services were easily achieved. Chi needed
to be informed of police activities regarding certain matters. Tasker had his own informants within the force, people
in a position to offer the kind of information Tasker needed
and could pass to Yeung on Chi's behalf. As well as his
own fee, Tasker was given substantial cash amounts to satisfy his in-house informers, enough money to ensure they
would not be tempted to talk about their clandestine efforts.

It all seemed to be going smoothly.

Until events become increasingly awkward.

The arrival of the three Americans from the mainland
made Tasker realize his deal might not continue as he would
have liked.

And Oscar Kalikani, assigned to liaise with the newcomers, made life uncertain.

Kalikani was a damn good cop and had been assigned
to the HPD Task Force. He was street smart, and Tasker
knew there was no way the man could be swerved from his
duty. Tasker had informed Chi, through Yeung, about the
new team. Almost before Tasker knew it, the Americans
were digging, along with Kalikani, into the very incident
Tasker was keeping Chi informed about.

When Kalikani and his new buddies were attacked at the
Maunakea Market by one of Yeung's hit squads, they had
shown how good they were. At the docks, following their
investigation into the sinking of the *King Kamehameha,*
they again had overcome the opposition. Though one of
them was snatched and taken for interrogation by Yeung,
the man had broken free, killing his Korean watcher and
escaping.

Yeung had had a lucky break that day. The phone call he
had received—Chi raising a query—had taken him away

from the warehouse. He had then called Yun to inform him and, as an afterthought, ordered him to dispose of the American. That had proved unfortunate for Yun.

In desperation, urged on by Chi's displeasure at the way things were going, Tasker had concocted the bogus meeting that sent Oscar Kalikani to the Wiseman apartments. The intention was to have the Hawaiian cop crippled and put out of action. It didn't work. Not only did Kalikani survive, but he and the female cop Tasker had been forced to send along had taken down both of the hit men.

The writing started to show on the wall. Tasker had the sense to realize he was stepping close to the edge. Kalikani was putting the pieces together. Despite being injured and away from the actual field of work, Kalikani was making the jumble of facts clearer. Tasker knew he had made a bad mistake by drawing Kalikani to a fake meet. His agile mind would bring him to an inevitable conclusion.

When he heard what had gone down at the airfield, Rudy Tasker made his decision to get out before it became too late. He had left the job behind, driven home and packed what he needed to leave the island.

"THIS IS NOT GOOD," Rudy Tasker said.

He was pacing his living room, his agitation showing. His tie was askew, hair mussed where he had been running his hands through it. He turned to face the lean, silent Chinese man watching him pace.

Kai Yeung.

"I have already explained, Tasker, that the exercise is over. The Hawaiian police and the American security team were responsible for ending the matter. Macklin and his team are dead. So are my comrades. Only Xian Chi survived, and he is now in custody."

"Exactly," Tasker said. "Chi is alive, and if I know anything about human nature, that son of a bitch is going to do everything he can to save his ass. Including naming names. He will talk, Yeung. The cops, the FBI, Homeland Security will all be getting a list of names. And you know what? I'm afraid my name will be right there at the top. And most likely yours."

"You understood all of these possible setbacks when you became a willing assistant. The chance of discovery was always there. But you chose to join us and risk that when you took the money we offered." The man stared at Tasker. "I believe you are wrong about Chi. He will not betray us. I will do my best to help to have him released when I reach home."

Yeung spoke quietly. No agitation. Simply telling Tasker how it was. He could see the fear in the eyes of the *gweilo*. His greed for the money Xian Chi had offered had overcome any future risk—but now that the risk had become reality, Tasker was showing another side to his character. It was a trait Yeung despised. The American had no strength of character. Now the inevitable had happened, and knowing the possibility of discovery, the man had panicked. Had walked away from his position and was preparing to run, believing that putting distance between himself and his misdeeds would protect him.

TASKER HAD CALLED Kai Yeung, demanding they meet at his home, telling Chi's negotiator he wanted his final payment so he could leave.

Rudy Tasker saw little ahead except a long jail sentence, and he knew, if that happened, his life behind bars would be one long term in Hell. There were certain crimes that were openly hated by convicted felons. At the top of the list were any involving children; child molesters were despised and the perpetrators could expect the worst kind of

treatment. A close second were crooked cops; a cop behind bars became a target the minute he walked in. Life
expectancy became short, and it took a special kind of cop
to survive in prison.

Tasker knew his limits. He knew he wouldn't last long
on the inside. He made the instant decision to pack his
bags, take his money and vacate Hawaii. It was a decision
born out of pure fear. He didn't think it through, because
his terrified mind couldn't think that far ahead.

Once he walked from his job, he would mark himself
as guilty. He would in effect become a fugitive. Wherever
he went, his face and description would be passed out. A
BOLO would be issued. He would be a wanted man, and
cops wherever he went would know he had been involved
in a crime that resulted in the slaughter of fellow officers.
That would be his epitaph.

Rudy Tasker—*cop killer.*

"I need to get off the islands. As far away as possible,"
Tasker said. "You have to help me, Yeung. I did good work
for you. Provided information. Helped you get what you
wanted."

"But we did not actually get what we had expected."

"Yeah, I know, but that wasn't down to me exactly. Am
I to blame for all that?"

Tasker knew he was starting to babble. Sounded
alarmist.

Okay, so the plan fell through.

He couldn't be blamed for that. His dealings with Xian
Chi and the rest had been good. His information had always been sound. He had consistently given Chi and the
North Korean, Tak, what they had requested. Their own
internal squabbles had not been because of Tasker. That
had been *their* business.

Why should he have to be blamed because they screwed each other over?

That was the trouble with the Asians. They were all too ready to double cross each other. Always looking to do the dirty. ChiComs. Koreans. They were all the same. Not to be fully trusted. So very polite. Respectful on the surface while they waited quietly to cut your throat.

Well, this time the whole bunch had ended up the losers.

No big surprise. Just a goddamn mess all around. As far as Tasker was concerned, they had deserved it.

His regret was his own part in it. The man in the middle. He should have seen it coming and got out before the foul-up. Now it was too late. So all he could do was try to save his own skin.

Unfortunately he was going to have to depend on Yeung. It wasn't as if he actually trusted the guy. Yeung was Chinese himself, and Tasker was wary of having to be dependent on him. A poor choice, but the only one available.

"Yeung, you have the contacts to get me out of the country. I need to get away. Those agency guys and HPD will come looking for me. I don't have a lot of time. Look, you'll be leaving yourself now. *Yes?* Let me go with you. Away from Hawaii."

"Tasker, you are starting to sweat," Yeung said. His voice still calm. Controlled. "Are you hot?"

"No. But I *am* bloody scared. There. Isn't that what you want me to say? Right now HPD will be painting a target on my back. If I don't jump pretty quick, I'll be behind bars. Or dead in the street with a bullet in my skull."

"Then it seems you have a problem, Mr. Tasker."

Tasker didn't like the *Mister* part. It moved the relationship to a different level. One he wasn't too happy about.

"We starting to be a little formal, aren't we, Yeung? We not friends anymore?"

"Were we ever *friends?* I think not. More employee and employer, and within that criteria, there should always be distance. Not familiarity."

"Yeah, okay, so we won't ever be best buddies and share a beer while we watch baseball on TV. That doesn't mean not helping out in an emergency."

No response. Yeung's focus remained on the American, his stare hard. He had maintained his motionless pose for some time.

"If this whole mess has gone down the drain, Yeung, why did you take my call and come visit me? Chi is out of the picture. We're *both* out in the cold. So you must want something from me. What is it?"

"I considered walking away and forgetting you exist," Yeung said. "Then I realized that you have influence. As a senior police officer you could help me through official channels. Like custom checks.

"I would like to leave Hawaii this evening. My association with Xian Chi was always, as we say, under the radar. But with his arrest the authorities may have tightened up checks and such. So I need insurance.

'The plane Chi had arranged will have been impounded by the HPD. But there is a backup aircraft at Honolulu International Airport they do not know about. A flight plan for one of the other islands. As a police officer you could get us both on board, away from here. There is a hire craft waiting to sail from a marina. A fishing trip.

"Out at sea we will rendezvous with a larger boat to take us out of reach. Help me through any difficulties, and I am sure I could find a place for you on that vessel. We will be gone before anyone becomes aware.

"When we land in Hong Kong, I will turn you loose. Then you will be on your own to go where you wish." Yeung indicated the attaché case he had brought with him.

"In there is the completion of your fee. Plus a much larger amount. Enough to give you an extremely comfortable life in a place of your choosing."

Tasker nodded. He wasn't sure how grateful he should feel. Yeung's manner was cold. Indifferent. Tasker decided not to stretch his luck. Right at that moment he knew that leaving was his only chance. Before his deceptions were exposed. There were no guarantees—except the one that would ensure he went to prison if he was caught.

"I can be ready in a few minutes. Won't be taking much with me."

Yeung said, "That is what I expect." He turned to look out the window. "We will take only my vehicle. Leave your car here. Do not forget your passport."

He stepped toward the window, then paused as he stared outside and reached under his jacket for the autopistol he carried on his hip. Tasker heard him mutter something as he exposed the weapon.

"What is it?"

"That policeman we tried to have killed. Kalikani? He is approaching the house on foot. And he is armed."

"Where?"

Tasker stepped forward and saw Oscar Kalikani moving up behind the parked cars. He had his service pistol in his right hand.

"What does he want?" Yeung said, his voice angry for the first time.

"Son of a bitch hasn't come looking for donations to the HPD orphan's fund," Tasker said, a heavy lump forming in his stomach.

"Then he is looking for you."

"No shit," Tasker said. "Yeung, I can tell he's looking for trouble, because Oscar Kalikani only draws his weapon when he's about to use it."

CHAPTER THIRTY-TWO

CLOSURE

Kalikani spotted movement behind the picture window at the front of the house.

Two men.

One Chinese.

And he recognized Tasker standing beside the guy.

The bad cop held his position for a few seconds, then turned and said something to the Chinese.

Kalikani was covered by the parked vehicles but still in the open, and once he cleared the cars, there was nothing between him and the house. Thin choices. Make a run for the protection of the building, or stay where he was and hope Tasker and the Chinese came to him. They would want to get to the cars to make their escape. The cars were their way out.

A slow smile edged across Kalikani's face. He raised his S&W and fired into the closest front tire on each vehicle. The 9 mm slugs punctured the rubber, raising small puffs of dust as they ripped through. Kalikani saw the pair of vehicles sink onto their respective rims as air escaped.

"Let's see how far you get now," Kalikani said.

TASKER LET OUT an angry yell as he realized what Kalikani had done. "Shit, what do we do now?"

"We deal with your impetuous friend," Yeung said. "Then replace the wheel on one of the vehicles and leave."

"Easily said. Don't think for a minute Kalikani has come alone. HPD will be on its way. If we don't clear up this mess, Yeung, we are screwed."

"Not until we are dead." Yeung pointed toward the rear of the house. "We can go out through the back way and circle. One from each side, then engage your irritating friend."

"Don't you have any backup you can call in?"

"There is no one else. Xian Chi's defeat, along with his team, means there are no additional reinforcements ready to come to our aid."

"Where are all those millions of Chinese we're always hearing about?"

Yeung allowed a thin smile to show. "In China, Tasker. Not here."

Tasker checked his weapon. "Let's get this done."

They backed up through the house and exited by the kitchen door. Tasker moved left, Yeung to the right. They skirted the rear and moved the length of the building. Tasker had the attached garage at his side. He reached the front corner and edged forward, peering out across the open area. He could see the parked cars, but no sign of Kalikani.

Where the hell are you, Oscar?

Tasker crouched and looked for any sign of Kalikani under the body of Yeung's rental. At first nothing. Then he saw a flicker of movement.

Yes.

Kalikani was there. Concealed by the bulk of the parked cars.

Tasker aimed his pistol at a low angle. If he could get a shot beneath the car… He gripped the pistol in both hands, surprised to find they were shaking. He drew a breath to calm his nerves and aimed again. When he eased back on the trigger and the 9 mm fired, Tasker was surprised at the loud sound it made. The muzzle rose. He heard the metallic ring as the ejected shell casing hit the paving stone at his feet.

The slug hit one of the stone slabs under the chassis. It made a sharp sound as it bounced off the slab and struck the underside of the car.

Damn.

Tasker made to fire again, but Kalikani's shape had moved, putting the rear wheel of the car between himself and the shooter.

Now what?

If Kalikani stayed under cover, it was going to take better than one abortive shot to flush him clear.

And where was Yeung?

This strategy was getting them nowhere. Tasker was reminded of his own words inside the house.

HPD will be on its way. We are screwed.

He still believed the fact was true. Oscar Kalikani may have been prone to impulsive action, but he was also a smart cop. Backup would be on its way. HPD cruisers could show at any time. Once that happened, Tasker and his new partner would be surrounded.

If Kalikani got off a clear shot in the meantime…

Tasker leaned against the side of the garage. This was a colossal mess. He had been an idiot to allow himself to be drawn into the affair. Looking back, he realized the large amount of money he had been handed meant nothing. What good was the money once he was locked up?

Or even dead?

No damn use at all. His disenchantment with his career, which had been going nowhere, had allowed him to be seduced into believing money would enhance his life, enable him to live high. All it had done was bring him here, to a situation that had no golden light at the end of the tunnel. As far as Tasker could see, it would all be black if it wasn't done right. There was no good way out. Even if he tossed his gun and walked out with his hands held high, there was no Rewind. No wishing himself back in his office, juggling crime statistics and drinking stale coffee; Tasker had plowed his own road, and now he found himself unable to climb out of the ruts.

Gunfire came from the far side of the house.

Yeung had made his move.

It was time to end this, Tasker decided, and brought up his own weapon....

"THERE," LOPAKA SAID. "HPD cruiser."

She swept up her arm as the distinctive vehicle came into view. Lyons coasted up behind the car. He and Lopaka exited the 4x4, drew their pistols and moved to the opposite side of the road as they closed in on Tasker's property.

They were a hundred yards from the driveway when they heard shots.

"*Go*," Lyons said.

They moved together, angling in toward the house. Saw two parked vehicles. And Oscar Kalikani crouching between them. He had got himself in a bind.

A Chinese guy leaned around the corner of the house, then made a dash for the front of the SUV parked nearby.

YEUNG HAD TIRED of waiting. Tasker was not able to get a clear shot at the hidden policeman. If they delayed much longer, it was possible other police cars would arrive. Once they were confronted by stronger odds, escape would be blocked. Yeung had no desire to be captured and locked away in an American prison. He had heard stories about the way prisoners in the USA were treated and wanted no part of that.

He checked the position of the parked cars. From where he stood, he should be able to move around the big SUV and be hidden until he reached the gap between the cars. All he needed was a clear shot. He would place himself in danger. That did not worry him. He was young and moved quickly. If he closed in on the hidden Kalikani, he had a good chance of firing before the Hawaiian cop could react. It was a chance. A calculated gamble, with his own life at stake. Yet it was a risk he needed to take.

Yeung took a steady breath, bent low and ran for the parked cars. He reached the front of the SUV and pressed close. His heart pounded in his chest. There was almost a flush of excitement as he braced himself again and moved across the front of the big utility vehicle.

As he stepped into the gap between the cars, his eyes fixed on Kalikani's crouching figure. The cop, with his left arm encased in plaster and bandaged, sensed Yeung's presence. He turned his handgun in Yeung's direction.

Yeung fired without thought, pulling the trigger rapidly.

Only one of his shots found a target—Kalikani's right shoulder, turning the cop half around.

As Lopaka moved forward, pistol gripped in both hands, she saw a second shooter peering around the edge of the garage.

It was Rudy Tasker.

Kalikani had not been wrong about the man.

The image of six dead cops rose in her mind, unbidden but strong. They had died because of the hijack, and Tasker was involved. She kept moving.

She wanted Tasker. There was no way he could be allowed to get away with what he had done.

As she moved around the parked cars, she caught a

glimpse of Kalikani. Down on one knee, his right shoulder bloody. He had taken a bullet.

"GET TASKER," LYONS CALLED.

Lopaka slid around the rear of the closest car, tracking in on Tasker as the rogue cop stepped from cover. There was a wild look on his face, as if he had chosen to make a final stand.

Well, okay, she thought, I'll help you see that come true.

Lopaka moved into the open, her S&W tracking Tasker's moving shape.

"Tasker," she called out. "Put the gun down. Do it now."

She knew in that instant he was not going to take any notice. He turned his head, looking at her as if he couldn't believe she was there.

"Gun down now."

"No way," he screamed.

Lopaka saw Tasker's pistol arcing around in her direction.

No, you won't make it.

She put two fast shots into his chest. Saw them punch him back. He leaned against the garage door. His weapon kept coming toward her. Lopaka fired again, pulling the trigger as fast as she was able, and saw the multiple shots hit. Blood flew from the wounds. Tasker's face crumpled. His arms flew wide, his weapon slipping from his fingers. He twisted sideways, toppling along the garage door, leaving a wet smear where emerging slugs had spattered blood. He struck the ground, body arching in a spasm....

CARL LYONS HAD moved to the right, around the cars, his Colt Python lining up on the Chinese guy as the man opened fire.

Lyons saw the need for a fast result. Kalikani, hampered

by his injuries, had himself boxed in between a pair of shooters. The HPD cop's slowed responses were not going to help his situation.

Lyons was under no such disability.

The Chinese shooter was so intent on his current target that he hadn't even seen Lyons. Which worked for the ex-cop. He centered the Python's muzzle on the Chinese and put all six rounds into the guy.

Kai Yeung felt the solid slam of the first .357 Magnum slug as it ripped through his left shoulder and blew out in a bloody gush. The impact of the high-velocity round scrambled Yeung's nerves, and he was unable to stop himself from gasping. His arm dropped loosely at his side. Before Yeung had time to respond, Lyons's follow-up shots hit him with enough force to kick him off his feet. The powerful slugs dug into his body, tearing apart muscle and bone, reducing internal organs to mush. Yeung went down in a loose, ungainly heap, blood spreading across his body and the paving stones beneath him. The blood continued until his heart stopped beating and internal pressure dwindled.

Lyons recognized the Chinese man as the guy who had been asking all the questions when they had had him bound at the warehouse. The one who had walked away and left Lyons with the North Korean, Yun.

What goes around, comes around, Lyons thought. It was all tying up nicely.

As Lyons moved between the cars to go to Kalikani's aid, he automatically ejected spent cartridges and took a speed-loader from his jacket, inserting the fresh bullets into the Python. He holstered the pistol and bent over Kalikani. One of the bullets from Yeung had hit him in the right shoulder. It hadn't gone through, and despite the blood loss, Kalikani was still able to respond.

"Any more in the house?" Lyons asked.

"I'm pretty sure there are no more."

"That must be a disappointment," Lopaka said as she joined them. "You could go ahead and take them on, as well."

The tone of her voice showed she was not pleased with Kalikani.

"The guy is hurt," Lyons said.

"What part of *wait until we show up* did you not understand, O?"

"Yeah, okay, I guess I was a little hasty."

"*Really?*" Lopaka's face registered her feelings. She walked away, her back to Lyons and Kalikani.

"Oscar, I think she likes you," Lyons said. "That girl really does."

Kalikani glanced up. "You think so?"

The distant wail of sirens sounded, coming their way.

"HPD to the rescue," Lyons said.

"A little late, but still welcome," Kalikani said. He leaned against the side of one of the cars. "Brother, it has been a busy couple of days since you guys showed up. You always bring it to the party?"

Lyons said, "One way or another, I guess we do."

CHAPTER THIRTY-THREE

NORTH KOREA

Major Choi heard the rasp of sound from his comm set. He adjusted the microphone and spoke.

"Have you seen them?"

"No, Major. The foreigners have not returned to where they landed."

"They must have changed to another destination, once they saw you had discovered their equipment."

"Wait," the speaker said. He conversed with someone close by. "Major, they have been seen heading in the direction of the harbor. Perhaps going for one of the patrol boats there."

"Listen to me. Go after them. If they gain a boat, they will be heading out to sea. I will call for the roving patrol boat to meet me at the rendezvous point where they came ashore. The bigger boat can outrun our smaller craft."

"Yes, Major."

Choi used his comm set to raise area command and asked to be put into contact with the closest patrol boat. When he made contact, he asked for the captain's help in apprehending the infiltrators.

"Where will you be?" the patrol boat commander asked.

Choi knew his area well and told the patrol boat captain the exact beach location.

"I can be there in twenty minutes. I will send in a dinghy to pick you up."

Choi beckoned to one of his soldiers. "Go and commandeer a useable vehicle. I need you to drive me."

The man nodded and hurried away.

Choi turned and looked at his wrecked research site. Smoke still escaped through shattered windows and where the roof had collapsed. More smoke rose from behind the building where the wrecked helicopters and the fuel bunker still blazed. The anger inside threatened to overwhelm him as he realized just how quickly everything had changed. The infiltrators had destroyed his facility and the electronic equipment housed there. They had taken away the traitor Li Kam and were, even now, attempting to escape.

If he did little else before his failure reached Pyongyang, he had to locate and capture the people who had done this to him. He knew his own reputation was in tatters. There was nothing he could do about that. But at least he could make some kind of gesture toward Pyongyang by recapturing the invaders. A faint glimmer of hope began to burn inside. If he succeeded in making the infiltrators his prisoners, they could be used as propaganda. To show the world that it was North Korea that had been attacked by these illegal warmongers.

He picked up movement close by. Someone stumbling through smoke and over scattered debris. He recognized the lean figure in the white lab coat. That coat was streaked and dirty now, one sleeve torn. It was Emanuel Absalom. The physicist had a lost expression in his eyes as he stared around the demolished site. He saw Choi.

For once Choi knew he too looked less than smartly dressed. His uniform was streaked and torn in a few places, the result of the grenade blast he had survived with nothing more than his pride damaged.

"Now what do we do?" Absalom asked. "It is gone. All of it. All that research. Destroyed."

"So much for your ambitious plans, *Dr.* Absalom. Look what you have brought down upon us. And me."

Absalom rubbed at his streaked face with an equally grubby hand. "I do not understand. You seem to be putting the blame for this on me."

"If I do not succeed in catching the people who have done this, *my* career will be destroyed as this site has been."

"But how is this my fault?"

"I will explain, Doctor of Physics," Choi said. "We were sabotaged by someone who planted a code in the system. The Hawaiian trial backfired and sank our ship. A team was sent here to destroy our work. They have succeeded."

"I still do not understand."

"Simple. The saboteur was Li Kam. Your protégée. The woman you recommended we bring in to assist you."

"No. I do not believe it."

"Whether you believe it or not is irrelevant. But the fact cannot be denied. Li Kam is the saboteur. You were instrumental in bringing her here."

Choi's voice rose, his calm swept aside as fury clouded his thinking. "The mistake Pyongyang made was bringing in a foreigner, an incompetent who has brought down my research site."

Without hesitation he snatched his pistol from the holster at his waist and thrust out his arm.

"*No...*" Absalom said.

Choi stepped forward. He aimed and fired, placing two bullets in Absalom's head. The expanding slugs took the scientist's head apart. He dropped without a sound, his shattered skull leaking blood and brain matter onto the ground.

As he holstered his pistol, Choi heard the throaty rumble of a vehicle as it approached. He climbed in beside the driver and gave him directions to the beach.

"Take me there quickly."

"Yes, Major."

The small vehicle turned away from the wrecked building, weaving its way through the mud and out through the gate.

It picked up a faint trail that led through the trees and vegetation.

The driver, sensing Choi's mood, stayed silent, concentrating on driving the vehicle. He knew enough not to make any comments on what had happened, considering himself lucky not to have been a casualty of the unexpected attack by the infiltrators. Or a victim of Choi's anger, having been witness to the execution of Absalom.

The driver concentrated on who the strike force might have been. Enemies, true, but there was no doubt in his mind that they were skilled soldiers. The attack had been speedy, the objectives clear and the attack force had gone directly for the research center. He had picked up from his fellow soldiers how the infiltrators had destroyed not only the helicopters but had blown up the fuel reserves. And they had breached the technical lab and planted explosives that demolished the equipment and brought the building down.

The soldier wondered who the infiltrators were. One of the men had said they looked like Americans. One of them was black. He imagined they could have been one of the American Special Forces groups.

U.S. Marines maybe.

Or Delta Force.

Navy SEALS.

They had been told about these groups, used by the America government to carry out clandestine operations. Their NK instructors had always told them the Americans only used badly educated criminal types in these groups, men who had little intelligence and were trained to kill women and children, target the weak and destroy the North Korean homeland.

If there was truth there, he thought, something must have been missed, because the small team that had hit the research facility was far from that image. They had infiltrated well, had faced the North Korean force and taken down any who stood in their way. Their objective had been reached and dealt with. And now the enemy had escaped with the young woman identified as the saboteur.

Not the actions of a poorly trained and badly motivated team.

But those were his private thoughts, and he held his tongue. He understood Major Choi's anger. His need was to catch the infiltrators before they were out of reach. The soldier realized his own personal position was safer than that of his commanding officer. Choi would have to answer for what had happened. Pyongyang had little sympathy for failure. It would not matter about Choi's past record of high achievements. It only took one incident to incur the wrath and displeasure of the hierarchy in Pyongyang. If Choi did not bring back the infiltrators, he might be better off *not* coming back himself.

They reached the beach area, and the soldier rolled the vehicle to a halt. Major Choi climbed out, ignoring the rain, and stared out to where the patrol boat sat waiting for him. A small dinghy with two soldiers moved toward the shore.

"Major?" the soldier asked.

"Return to base," Choi ordered. "I will call if I need you. I will have the patrol boat circle around and approach the harbor. If these infiltrators manage to commandeer one of the small boats, we will intercept them."

The soldier watched as Choi waded out and stepped into

the dinghy. It swung around and began its return to the waiting patrol boat. Reversing the truck, the soldier set off.

For some reason he suddenly had the feeling he was not going to see Major Choi again.

Alive *or* dead.

CHAPTER THIRTY-FOUR

PHOENIX FORCE

It was Li Kam who had called for McCarter's attention when she heard what had happened at the beach.

"The harbor where the boats dock is our best escape route," she said. "There is a pair of small patrol boats Choi uses to check the shoreline and keep away any civilian boats."

"That's interesting," the Briton said. "Patrol boats. You hear that?"

Manning was quick to respond. "What are we going to do, steal one?"

McCarter said, "I never would have thought of that."

"We go back that way, we'll still have Choi's best on our trail," Manning said. "We knew this might happen. So why don't we just go for it and hope for the best?"

"Said like a true optimist," McCarter added.

"Surely we have little choice otherwise," Li observed. "If we stay here, Choi's men will surround us and close in."

"Can't argue with that," McCarter said, repeating what she had said over his comm set.

"Rest of you head out," Encizo said. "We'll provide covering fire, if it's needed. Important thing is getting Li and Kayo out safely."

"Let's do it," McCarter said, aware that it would be a waste of time arguing the point. The sooner they moved, the quicker they would reach their new rendezvous. "Li, you stay close by me."

The Korean nodded, eyes wide, her expression revealing she hated the thought of having to run some kind of gauntlet. In the same moment she realized there was no other choice. Major Choi would have put out a shoot-on-sight order on them all. In reality it came down to run and risk being shot, or staying and definitely being shot—or worse.

"We should go," she said. "Choi's soldiers will follow his orders to the last man. They will not give up."

"Let's stay sharp," McCarter said over his comm set. "The lady here says Choi's bunch are shoot-first-don't-worry types. So watch your backs and move fast."

McCarter grabbed Li's arm and moved her on. The young Korean needed no extra encouragement. She broke into a steady trot, with the tall Briton close on her heels as they pushed through the tangled undergrowth. Manning and Kayo Pak were only a few steps behind.

Li guided McCarter, her path through the trees sure and direct. She knew her way and that would save them time.

Behind them McCarter heard autofire. He recognized the hard rattle of the Type 68. More weapons fire came from another direction. Again it was from the Korean copy of the AKM.

McCarter brushed off the urge to go and check his partners. Instead he called them up through his comm set and breathed a sigh of relief when his team responded, each man reporting in as they pushed their way through the undergrowth.

"Those jokers are trigger-happy," Hawkins called breathlessly. "Full-auto on the run. No damn accuracy among any of them."

"Don't get too cocky, Rankin," James yelled. "Only takes one lucky shot."

McCarter heard the full-on sound of a now-unsuppressed P90 returning fire through his comm set. Then more as another Phoenix Force member engaged. He heard the distant crack of a fragmentation grenade. A distorted yell of someone in pain. The lack of knowledge over who was doing the yelling grated on McCarter's nerves. He forced himself to push away the thoughts, concentrating on the moving figure of Li Kam ahead of him.

Something made the Briton turn and check behind. He saw a lean uniformed figured bearing down on him, face beaded with sweat. Where he had come from was a mystery. McCarter didn't waste time on worrying about it. The North Korean soldier was racing ahead fast, the only one in sight. He was closing the distance quickly, openly pulling at the SMG slung from his shoulder.

McCarter turned about, the P90 coming into his hands as he tracked in on the Korean. Both men fired in the same split second. McCarter felt the 7.62 mm slugs burn the air over his left shoulder, then his finger was easing back on the trigger of his own weapon. The P90's full-auto function threw a short burst of 5.7 mm slugs that struck the Korean in the chest. He ran on for a few more steps, before his body absorbed the impact, and he lost coordination. He went into a stumbling fall, dropping facedown, his loose-limbed tumble dragging his body along the wet ground.

By the time McCarter turned, Li was yards in front, her slim form racing ahead, with Manning not far behind now, Pak following on hard. McCarter dug in his heels and headed to catch up.

Figures flitted through the shadows to one side. Rain glistened on rain capes. Bounced off steel helmets.

"*Incoming*," Li yelled.

She turned and raised her Type 68 autorifle, loosing short bursts that caught the North Korean soldiers as they broke cover. She hit the closest man in the chest, sending him to the sodden ground, then crouched and fired again. The second soldier took the burst in the stomach, screaming once as he stumbled and dropped to his knees, clutching his body. Li fired a finishing burst that took away half his skull and the punctured helmet.

"You okay?" McCarter asked as he urged her on.

The young woman simply nodded, unable to speak in the aftermath of the sudden encounter. She stayed by McCarter's side as they kept moving.

The rainfall became heavier and even the overhead canopy of leafy branches couldn't halt the fall.

The only good thing McCarter saw in the rain was the fact it might hinder the pursuing North Koreans a little. On the negative side, the fact was, it would also slow Phoenix Force.

A moving figure caught McCarter's eye.

Then a voice came over his comm set.

"I see you, boss."

It was Hawkins. Seconds later he emerged from the gloom of the trees and fell in step beside McCarter.

"You okay?" he asked the younger man.

"Hell, yes," Hawkins said. "I think I lost the bunch chasin' me. They ain't so fit."

"That you firing at them?"

"Yeah, but I laid an egg on them, as well. Scattered them real fast."

Up ahead Li had stopped, waiting for them to catch up. She was indicating something ahead, cradling her weapon to her chest.

"Where the trees end," she said. "Beyond that is an open slope down to the harbor. A wooden jetty where the patrol boats moor."

She led them forward. While McCarter stayed with her,

Hawkins took up a rear position, watching for the other Phoenix Force members and the North Koreans.

As McCarter, Manning, Li and Pak edged clear of the trees and took in the scene overlooking the harbor, Hawkins picked up the sound of someone approaching through the undergrowth to his right. He drifted into the foliage and watched as uniformed figures eased from cover.

He made out the features of the newcomers and saw immediately they were not his teammates. Hawkins didn't hesitate. He swung his P90 into position and laid down a concentrated autoburst, catching the North Koreans before they were able to make their own target acquisitions. Despite the urgency of the confrontation, Hawkins held his ground, tracking in his weapon with almost deceptive calm.

The suppressed weapon jacked out a killing stream of 5.7 mm slugs that found their targets and sent the Koreans stumbling back. Three went down while a fourth struggled to stay on his feet in spite of his wounds. A second burst from Hawkins hit high, punching in through the man's throat and lower jaw. He fell screaming, hugging his bloody throat, the lower part of his face a disfigured mass.

Off to the left Encizo and James rushed into view, weapons up.

"Best not to hang around here," Hawkins said. "Choi's best and brightest are coming up fast."

McCarter waved an arm downslope. "The harbor," he said. "We move fast we might pick ourselves a ride."

"There will be soldiers down there," Li said.

"You reckon they hire out the boats by the hour?" James asked.

"Let's check it out," McCarter said. "We'll be in trouble if they don't take Visa."

Encizo neared the group. "Give me a couple extra grenades," Encizo said.

Each Phoenix warrior passed over one of their grenades. Encizo followed them over the lip of the slope, then crouched, laying out the frag grenades in a line. He placed his P90 on the ground.

"Go," he said. "Just remember to reserve a seat for me."

Movement in the trees behind their position alerted the Cuban, and he picked up his first grenade.

"Don't hang about," Hawkins said, moving to join the others.

As the team headed down the slope, Encizo pulled the pin and lobbed the grenade with a powerful throw. It blew with a harsh sound and a flash of light. As the explosion faded, Encizo heard a man scream. He quickly followed with a second grenade, the hard crack of sound throwing a geyser of muddy soil and splintered timber into the air.

An autoweapon opened up to Encizo's far right. A ragged line of bullet hits traversed the area just short of his place of concealment.

"Fine by me, *cabron*," Encizo said and hurled a third grenade at the spot where the autofire came from.

As the grenade detonated, he caught a glimpse of a shrieking figure spinning through the air.

Over his shoulder Encizo saw his partners had reached the base of the slope and were engaged in a firefight as the harbor sentries resisted their appearance. He pushed his remaining grenades into his pockets, snatched up his P90 and headed downslope to join them.

CHAPTER THIRTY-FIVE

PHOENIX AT SEA

The jetty comprised a timbered section that jutted out into the deep water. It was here two old wooden patrol boats were tethered. There was a fuel dump on the landward end of the jetty. A stack of steel and plastic fuel drums. A little way from the fuel was a large sprawling wooden hut. A sagging tin chimney stack issued smoke that was instantly whipped away by the rain and wind.

The rainfall obscured vision down to a couple hundred yards. Beyond the jetty the water rose and fell in choppy waves that swung the patrol boats back and forth on their mooring lines.

A pair of armed guards, glistening capes over their uniforms, had been alerted by the gunfire from beyond their area. They were turned in the direction of the long slope, weapons up and firing as they made eye contact with Phoenix Force. Muddy geysers sprouted as slugs struck the slope.

Hawkins plucked a grenade from his harness and tossed it in the direction of the guards. It fell short, but the blast radius was wide enough to inflict minor damage. The aggressive fire faltered as the pair of guards stepped back, giving the Stony Man commandos the opportunity to return fire. The combination of rapid fire from their weapons put the Koreans down hard.

"Watch that hut," McCarter said, waving a hand in the building's direction.

Almost on cue a door opened and uniformed figures spilled out, weapons in their hands. The crackle of auto-fire sounded.

Phoenix Force split apart, offering single targets, and firing as they reached the base of the slope.

Kayo Pak went down on one knee, his SMG braced against his shoulder as he aimed and fired, aimed and fired. He put one man down with his first burst.

Calvin James yelled, "Cover me," as he skirted the base of the slope. His P90 dangled by its strap as he pulled a pair of grenades from his harness. He ran full tilt, weaving an erratic pattern, until he reached the end of the hut. Pulling the pins, he jabbed an elbow through the end wall's window glass and tossed both grenades inside the hut, then turned and pressed his back against the exterior wall. The grenades exploded with a solid sound, blowing out every pane of glass at the front of the hut. Any Koreans still inside would stay there, bodies bloodied and shredded by the concentrated grenade bursts.

The shock of the blast and the flying glass fragments caught the Koreans who had exited the hut off guard for a few seconds, and those seconds cost them dearly as McCarter and the rest of his team unleashed their full ordnance. More autofire peppered the air, slugs cleaving flesh and bone, and the five North Koreans, alive when they had emerged from the hut, were driven to the ground in lifeless sprawls.

The torrential rain was the only sound for a few seconds as everyone wound down.

Thick smoke began curling from the windows of the hut, and as James moved to rejoin the rest of the team, he caught a glimpse of rising flames through the window.

McCarter scanned the top of the slope. "No hanging about," he said. "Choi isn't done with us yet. Pick the best boat and check the fuel. If we need any, get one of those barrels off the stack. Rankin, Fredo, you stand watch over that slope. Anything shows up there, shoot it."

Kayo Pak made his way along the jetty, checking out the patrol boats. He picked the one that looked marginally sounder than its sister boat and raised an arm. Then he jumped on board and went to the aft section where the diesel tank was situated. He unscrewed the cap and assessed the fuel level.

"Full," he shouted.

McCarter acknowledged the call.

"Okay, let's get aboard the *Jolly Roger* and steam out of here, before Major Choi catches up."

He told Encizo and Hawkins to fall in line. As Manning went to join the others, McCarter caught his sleeve and flicked a thumb at the stacked fuel drums.

"Anything left in your backpack?"

"Always keep something in reserve," the Canadian said.

He produced a couple of Thermite canisters and showed them to McCarter.

"Nice," the Briton said.

"Go and get that tub fired up," Manning said. "I'll plant one here and one on that other boat. Be ready to shove off, because when this fuel goes up, they'll see it in Pyongyang."

McCarter took Manning's backpack and P90 and headed along the jetty. As he jumped the gap and landed on the deck, he heard the patrol boat's diesel engine rumble into life.

"Get ready to cast off those lines," he said. "It could get hot round here any minute."

Hawkins and James stood ready to free the lines fore and

aft. Li stood at the stern, her autorifle steady and aimed at the hill, should any enemy soldiers show.

Manning moved away from the fuel dump, running down the jetty. As he passed the second patrol boat, moored on the opposite side of the jetty, he paused briefly to drop the remaining Thermite canister onto the wooden deck. He sprinted forward and jumped on board as McCarter gave the command to free the lines. As soon as they fell free, Pak, at the helm of the boat, gunned the power and the forty-foot vessel pulled away from the jetty.

They had cleared the end of the jetty when the first Thermite canister blew, the tremendous heat from the burning chemical mix flaring quickly. The high temperature of the Thermite reaction, reaching around 4000 degrees Fahrenheit, easily melted plastic and metal. It took all of twenty seconds before the fuel ignited, bursting apart the stacked containers and sending a massive fireball skyward. Flaming fuel spilled out along the wooden jetty. The canister Manning had dropped into the second boat was burning by this time, the intense heat igniting the timber and spreading rapidly.

Having no need of the bulky suppressors attached to their P90 barrels, the Phoenix pros removed them and secured them inside their backpacks. The team took time to check and reload all their weapons.

McCarter stepped inside the covered wheelhouse to where Li Kam was unrolling charts on the navigation table. He held one side down as she indicated their current position.

"If Major Choi makes contact, he can call for help from the North Korean navy. There may be a coastal patrol vessel that could respond. If that happens, we could really be in trouble."

James, standing close by, said, "As opposed to what?"

The young woman glanced at him, seeing the faint smile on his lips.

"The navy patrol boats are better vessels than the one we are on. They are of steel construction and will be much faster."

"Let's hope we can raise that Navy sub first, then," McCarter said.

He fished out the signal unit from his backpack and activated the send transmission. The compact device sat silent in his hand for many long seconds. McCarter willed it to go active. When it did, the feeling of relief from everyone was palpable.

"That was scary," Hawkins said. "Thought for a minute you'd forgotten to put the battery in."

"Do we need to be on a specific course?" Pak asked.

"As long as it's away from North Korea and due east, I'm not about to be too fussy," McCarter said.

Encizo, who had stayed on deck checking out a canvas-covered shape at the stern, called out. "Hey, this might come in handy."

He had stripped off the canvas to expose a deck-mounted .50-caliber heavy-duty cannon. It was fed from a large side-mounted box. The weapon looked powerful. Encizo gripped the twin handles at the breech end, swiveling and arcing the weapon. They all knew the tremendous power and impact such a weapon had. With an approximate length of five inches, the .50-caliber shell was a formidable piece of ordnance.

Hawkins walked around the weapon, nodding to himself.

"Hell, I really feel much safer now, knowing we have that around. You think we could sink a Korean destroyer with it?"

Encizo grinned. "We could give it a good scare at least."

As they moved farther away from the coast the water became rougher. The comparatively small patrol boat was pitched heavily by the swell. And the unceasing rain added to the discomfort.

"How long before your submarine picks us up?" Li asked.

"Hard to say," McCarter said. "Sooner they get a fix on us the better. You feeling uncomfortable?"

"I never was a good sailor," Li said. "I prefer to be on land looking out to sea, not the other way round."

"We don't have much choice in our mode of travel." He patted her shoulder. "Miss Li, you already proved yourself back there. You handled that gun pretty well."

Li smiled briefly. "I was conscripted into the army in my early twenties. Figures for the much vaunted military numbers needed a boost, so more young women were admitted. In three years I went through the normal training every recruit does. That included combat and weapons training. I learned martial arts and became proficient in those. So, yes, I can use a gun and defend myself, as well."

"So how did you end up in the physics game?"

"Female recruits could transfer to a noncombat unit after a period of time. I had shown interest in physics, and it seemed I had a natural aptitude for the science. I was eventually removed from my military service and sent to a science college where I was placed in the program. Anyone who showed a degree of talent was pushed forward. I was a lucky one. Physics held no mysteries for me, so I moved up in qualifications. I gravitated toward the weapons division, and it was from there I was offered a working position here under Absalom. He had asked for me personally after he had read a paper I wrote on pulse technology."

"But things had changed for you by then?"

"Yes. My parents had been singled out as traitors to the

state and imprisoned in a camp. It was all fabrication. They never came out of the camp alive. I was lucky that I did not become tainted by their arrest. But I was forced to stand in front of a committee and denounce them."

Li paused, memories of that time still strong enough to affect her. "I must have convinced the committee of my loyalty. I was allowed to carry on with my studies as a way of proving my loyalty to the state. I was lucky that my work skills in physics were of a high standard. I had always been at the top of my classes, and my experience with pulse technology made me valuable.

"During free time in the city, I had been involved in small discussion groups and had met an undercover agent for the South. He knew what had happened to my parents and encouraged me to consider becoming an undercover agent.

"I found I wanted to do it. To hit back at the government who had taken my family from me. After I wrote the paper on Absalom, it raised my status. Next thing I knew, Absalom had recommended that I be attached to his team at the research site.

"The man I met in the city told me I would meet Kayo Pak. He was already established in the local village, observing what was happening in the research lab. When I was sent there, it was an opportunity for us to learn more.

"The lab workers were allowed visits to the nearby village, where we could buy fresh food to bring back to the site. It was a small reward given to us by Major Choi. A tiny acknowledgment of our work, and a break from the extremely long hours we spent inside the lab. Each time I visited the village and bought fish from his stall, I would pass over the handwritten data I had gathered to Pak."

"A bloody risky business," McCarter said. "If you had been caught…"

"I was prepared to take the risk. Any loyalty to the state had been destroyed by what it had done to my father and mother—innocent people who wanted little more than to live their lives as best they could. They were betrayed by a corrupt official and killed because of it. Kayo Pak offered me a chance to strike back, and I was only too ready for that."

McCarter's admiration for the young woman went up a few more points.

Li reached inside her coat and drew out two computer data sticks. She handed them to McCarter.

"I managed to download these. More data. Look after these," she said. "In case anything happens to me...."

"Nothing is going to happen, love," McCarter said. He took the sticks and secured them in a zip pocket of his combat jacket.

"I hope not, too. But I'm being realistic. Things do happen." She smiled at McCarter. "All the data on the NNEMP development is on those drives. I have more in my memory, so we have two chances of success."

The patrol boat yawed to one side as heavy waves rolled against it, and they all had to cling onto something for support. Cold seawater surged over the side and washed across the deck. Even though McCarter and Li were under the open wheelhouse, they were soaked.

"Why is it men get all the fun jobs?" Li asked.

McCarter smiled. "Is this really your definition of *fun?*"

"After working for Major Choi," Li said, "this is much better."

ON BOARD THE North Korean patrol boat, Major Choi was on the radio, speaking to the pilot of his remaining helicopter. The aircraft was returning from a wide-ranging patrol it carried out every couple days, and Choi had realized he could use the machine.

He spoke to the pilot and explained the situation.

"We saw the smoke, Major," the pilot said. "I turned about, and we are already very close."

"Make for the harbor. I believe the strike force is attempting to commandeer one of our patrol boats to make their escape. We must prevent that. I am on board another vessel. We will make our way to intercept. If you spot these invaders, they must not be allowed to get away. Do you understand?"

"Yes, Major."

THE HELICOPTER PILOT glanced at his partner. The man had heard the conversation on his own headset. Now he moved to the rear of the helicopter and slid open the side hatch, swinging out the chopper's machine gun on its gimbal. He checked the ammunition belt and racked the weapon. Then he attached himself to the safety harness.

He felt the helicopter slide as the pilot laid on the power and took the aircraft in a wide curve toward their new destination. Cold rain blasted in through the open hatch, soaking the Korean gunner. Below them the water was gray and choppy, visibility reduced by the constant rain that had settled in for the duration.

"Ahead," the pilot said. "There is smoke rising from the harbor."

The gunner leaned out his hatch, squinting against the rain. It took him a moment before he spotted the smoke. As the pilot swung the helicopter in a wide sweep, the extent of the smoke and now flame could be seen. The harbor hut was burning and so was the fuel supply. There were normally two boats based at the harbor. One was burning at its moorings.

The gunner cast around and spotted the second boat, well clear of the harbor, moving out from the coast.

"They have already taken one of the boats. I can see the second boat," he called over his headset.

The pilot confirmed the sighting. He made contact with Major Choi on the incoming patrol boat, reporting what they had seen.

"Do not allow them to escape," Choi said. His voice was taut with anger. "These criminals must not be allowed to evade us." His final words were screamed out. "*Stop them.*"

ENCIZO CALLED, "HEADS UP. I hear a chopper."

The Phoenix Force commandos moved to the main deck and scanned the gray sky in all directions. They could hear the low sound. It seemed to be coming from more directions than one. Rising, then falling. Buffeted by the wind. Distorted by the constant rainstorm.

"West...coming in from the west," Manning said. He thrust out an arm. "There."

They all picked it up. A dark shape rapidly becoming larger as it swept down from its height and hurtled at them, low to the sea swell. It was an MD-500 Defender, the same model as the ones Phoenix Force had destroyed back at the site.

"Bloody good pilot," McCarter murmured in admiration. "Pity he's not come to pick us up. And where the hell did he spring from? Did we miss it back at the base?"

"Choi must have called it in," Pak said. "Maybe diverted it from a regular patrol flight."

"Looks like he's about to deliver something for us," Hawkins suggested.

Encizo swiveled the .50-caliber cannon around and started to track in on the helicopter as it came directly at them. The machine gun mounted in its side hatch opened fire, the slugs marching through the water as it closed in. A number of slugs chewed at the patrol boat's transom, splintering wood in passing.

Leading the thundering shape, Encizo waited for his chance and then triggered the cannon. As the helicopter flew over, Encizo turned the cannon on its swivel and followed the retreating aircraft. The thundering roar of the powerful weapon was deafening, even in the open. The tail end of his long burst clipped the chopper's landing gear and the craft wobbled slightly before the pilot corrected.

Kayo Pak ramped up the engine, pushing it faster through the water, though even he realized there was no way they could outrun the much faster helicopter.

"Let him come around again and I'll take him down," Encizo vowed. "No way he's going to outgun me."

"Hey, I think you're going to get your chance," Manning said.

"Do you think Choi is on board?" Li asked.

"We couldn't be that lucky," McCarter said.

They saw the helicopter make a wide banking turn, then drop and sweep in across the waves for another pass. The machine gun opened up again, this time far earlier and the side gunner rode the line of slugs as it chopped through the water. The shooter had his range now and was prepared to use a great deal of ammunition to maintain his line of fire.

"I HAVE HIM," the gunner yelled into his headset. "Hold your course."

The pilot maintained the line of flight, seeing the small patrol boat grow larger as the helicopter swept in. As the target expanded, the pilot saw the deck-mounted .50-caliber cannon locking in on his aircraft. He wanted to pull away, but he remained on course.

"*Quickly,*" he yelled to his gunner. "*Quickly now...*"

RAFAEL ENCIZO WATCHED the helicopter, steady on his own trigger. The Cuban refused to be fazed by the stream of slugs slamming the water and marching closer. His eyes were fixed on the aircraft, the muzzle of the cannon barely moving.

The wooden side rail of the boat exploded in a cloud of mashed timber, the slugs cutting across the deck directly in line with the waiting cannon.

It seemed the helicopter was going to pass over again; it was coming in so close...

And then Encizo's finger stroked back on the trigger and the machine gun began to hammer out .50-caliber shells, the large brass casings pouring from the ejection port to bounce off the splintered deck planks.

Encizo was enveloped in a haze of shredded wood and swirling smoke. The insane roar of the helicopter drowned out every other sound as it shot over the boat. The howl of its engine and the powerful downdraft from the beating rotors engulfed them all.

McCarter had pushed Li to the deck, stepping out to add autofire from his P90 as the helicopter filled his eye line. The FN hammered out streams of 5.7 mm slugs at the underside of the aircraft; McCarter had no idea whether his shots had any effect on the chopper, or those coming from the rest of Phoenix Force.

In the seconds the helicopter was over the boat, Encizo had swung his big .50-caliber cannon in a 360-degree turn and continued hammering away at it. The deck at his feet was littered with more hot shell casings.

The helicopter took a hard turn away, then appeared to hover for seconds as the nose came up—it might backslide and fall across the boat. Smoke began to issue from the engine compartment and the smooth roar became irregular.

The hard beat was broken by ragged coughs. Flame showed from the engine cowling.

The mounted cannon fired up again, Encizo taking advantage of the close target. He raked the helicopter until the cannon ran out of ammunition and fell silent.

Ragged holes peppered the fuselage. The side gunner had fallen back inside the helicopter, his weapon drooping and silent.

More flame erupted, then thick black smoke. The engine stuttered, coughed and fell silent. The chopper dropped slowly, turning on its side before slamming hard into the choppy water. One of the long rotor blades snapped, the broken section spinning across the water. The stricken helicopter settled and began to sink, displaced water bubbling around it. Leaking fuel created multicolored rings on the surface.

"If Choi doesn't have insurance, he's going to be getting a big bill," Hawkins murmured.

"*Hey,*" James called out and ran across the deck.

Encizo was on his knees, hands still gripping the big cannon's firing handles. His head was down on his chest, and the gleam of blood showed across the side of his head and down one side of his body. As James neared him, Encizo let go of the gun and sprawled across the deck.

McCarter joined him, calling for Manning and Hawkins to stand watch.

"Get us out of here," McCarter yelled to Pak and the Korean pushed the throttle levers to maximum, bringing the boat around the downed chopper as it slid out of sight, leaving trails of smoke and oil rings on the surface.

James was on his knees beside Encizo, turning the Cuban on his back. As the team medic began to check Encizo for wounds, McCarter stood over them, reloading his P90.

"You want to move him under cover?" he asked.

"Let me see how bad he's hurt first," James said.

"Can I do anything?" Li asked, standing at McCarter's side, her face taut with concern.

"Landis is a trained medic," McCarter told her. "He can handle it."

Li shook her head and moved forward, kneeling by Encizo. She raised his head and laid it across her lap, stroking hair away from his face. Encizo, half-conscious, stared up at her and managed a smile.

"Okay, I never thought of that," McCarter conceded.

James had seen the ragged tears in Encizo's camou jacket. Down the left side from shoulder to waist. He peeled the jacket open and cut Encizo's clothing away with his combat knife.

"Looks like he caught some flak," James said as he inspected Encizo's flesh. "We can move him under cover now," he said.

With help Encizo was carried beneath the wheelhouse and laid out on the deck so James could tend to his patient. The Cuban had lost blood before James was able to seal the wounds, using his limited medical supplies.

Hawkins had been checking out the equipment lockers fixed to the deck and found additional ammunition boxes for the .50-caliber cannon. He tossed the empty magazine overboard and loaded a fresh one, feeding the loaded heavy belt into place and then racking back the lever to prime the big machine gun.

"You think we're in the clear?" Kayo Pak asked from his position at the wheel.

McCarter had been looking out beyond the boat, watching and waiting for any sign of the U.S. Navy sub. At that moment all he could see was water and the rain that showed no sign of slacking off. Behind them the North Korean land mass had receded into the gray light.

"Kayo, mate, I have no bloody idea."

Manning had moved to the stern to check the damage. He called from his position. "Something on the port bow."

"Hold our course until we identify," McCarter said to Pak, slapping him on the shoulder as he moved to join Manning.

Li glanced up from where she had resumed her position with Encizo. James didn't even raise his head from tending to Encizo's wounds.

"I see it," McCarter acknowledged as he stood beside Manning.

"I'm no sailor," Manning said, "but that's not a submarine."

"No, it bloody isn't," McCarter said. "It's another North Korean patrol boat. A big one and it's heading right for us."

CHOI HAD WITNESSED the helicopter go down, had heard the frantic voice of the pilot and the solid sound of gunfire. He had seen the incident and shook his head in disbelief.

How many more disasters could be heaped on his head?

The North Korean military was supposed to be the best. Without equal. Constant training. Obedience to the state. All these things placed them above any other military force. Yet these invaders, small in number, seemed to best his people at every turn.

How could that be?

He wished he could stand face-to-face with this invasive team and find out who they were.

Despite himself he found he held a grudging respect for their fighting skills.

They had proved superior with the unexpected strike

against the research facility, resulting in so many deaths and the total destruction of the lab.

If he had been a religious man, he might have accepted the gods were conspiring against him.

He turned to the patrol boat captain. "Now it is up to us," he said.

The captain agreed, shouting orders to his crew. The patrol boat surged forward, the powerful motor winding up as the helmsman pushed the throttle to the limit.

"Man the gun," the captain screamed. "Sink that boat."

No prisoners, Choi thought. We will bury them all at sea.

CHAPTER THIRTY-SIX

SURRENDER OR DIE

"This could be embarrassing," Manning said.

"We're all loaded up here," Hawkins called. "What is it they say in these situations? Put a shot across the bows?"

"Pretty big bows compared to ours," McCarter pointed out.

"Below the waterline, then," Hawkins persisted.

McCarter wiped rain from his face, watching the approaching patrol boat.

"Those patrol craft move faster than we can," Pak called from the wheelhouse. "Steel construction. Pretty heavy. That's why they sit low in the water. Not a clever design but they are powerful boats."

"So we use that…" McCarter muttered, more to himself than anyone else.

Manning glanced at the Briton as McCarter leaned against the side rail, staring at the oncoming patrol boat.

"Kayo, what drives her?" McCarter asked. "Propulsion wise—single or twin screw?"

"Just the one," Pak said.

"What about ordnance?"

"Same specification we have. But fixed on the bow deck. Difference is it can only traverse left and right, or straight ahead. Wheelhouse gets in the way and won't let it fire over the stern."

"That's what I was hoping," McCarter said.

"I can hear the gear wheels turning," Manning said. "Tell me, great leader."

"If that bugger gets in range, he can hit us hard with that .50-caliber. We're sitting on a big wooden packing case. Look how that chopper chewed us up, and he was only using a small-caliber gun."

"Yeah, and that boat over there is made of steel. No way we can do much harm."

"Maybe not. But if we could stall that thing and leave it floating while we sail away…"

"How?"

"You might think this is a wild idea."

Manning turned his face to the falling rain for a moment. "Damn," he said, "not a flying pig in sight."

"Kayo swings us around the rear of that tin can. Brings her up close."

"You're starting to interest me. But only vaguely."

McCarter pointed at the big .50 Hawkins was manning.

"Look at the size of those .50-caliber shells. They are big, ugly and capable of tearing things apart. We burn off the full magazine against the propeller. Hit it with nonstop .50-cals. Enough hits could either distort the blades or maybe even blow holes in them. We keep up the pace. Have a second ammo box ready. Keep hitting that prop until it gives."

Manning thought about it for a few seconds. He turned to check out the big .50.

"We'd have to come close to the stern in a turn. Give Rankin his shot before we move away."

"This baby can deliver about 650 rounds a minute," Hawkins said. "I can open fire once we swing in close and keep the hammer down. All I need is for you guys to keep those North Korean heads down while we pass."

"Any good me pointing out this might be a bad idea?" James said.

"The alternative is no better," Li said. "I don't want to give myself up. Or give that boat the chance to shoot at *us*."

"You hear all this, Kayo?" McCarter asked.

"Every scary word," Pak said. "But Li's thoughts persuade me, it's a choice worth making."

"Bring us around," McCarter said. "Keep us at a distance until we can put them ahead of us, then swing in to their stern. Close as you can."

The patrol boat began to circle, staying clear of the other vessel's course. Pak had a steady hand and he persuaded the smaller craft to maintain a deceptive run.

"WHAT ARE THEY doing?" Choi asked. "They cannot outrun us."

The patrol boat captain said, "Trying to maneuver out of our path. Staying away from our weapon."

"Do they believe they can keep that up?"

The captain smiled. "Let them try," he said. "We will keep them in our sights until the right moment."

Choi watched the smaller craft as it veered around the patrol boat. His thoughts were at odds with the captain's. Whoever was piloting the other vessel seemed to be making deliberate moves.

What, he wondered, were they trying to achieve?

His thoughts were disturbed when the patrol boat's machine gun opened up, sending a stream of .50-caliber shells at the smaller craft.

"LI, STAY WITH FREDO," James directed. "He's stable now. Nothing else I can do, until we get him on board the sub. He just needs to be kept still."

Encizo opened his eyes and said, "The patient can hear what you're saying."

"Don't argue with the doctor," James said. "Stay still. No liquor or greasy food, and no flirting with the nurse."

"See what I have to put up with? He's such a party pooper," Encizo protested weakly. "This goes on all the time. Day in, day out."

"He doesn't mean it." James grinned. "It's just the meds talking."

"Don't go and get yourself shot, amigo," Encizo said. "I might need more loving care and attention."

"Any problems just yell," James told Li.

The young woman nodded and watched James join his teammates at the side of the boat.

The staccato rattle of the opposing big .50 reached them. The shots fell short, splashing harmlessly in the water yards away. Even through the rain mist, they were able to see the weapon's barrel rising as the North Koreans wound it up. The next burst of fire came even closer, water spouting up and dropping across the smaller boat's bow.

"Kayo," McCarter yelled.

The Korean didn't bother to reply. Instead he spun the wheel and took the boat in beneath the rising arc of the enemy gun. It was a sharp, smart move. When the next salvo came from the North Korean gun, the shells cleared the wooden boat and splashed into the water on the far side.

"Nice one," James breathed.

They were all aware they wouldn't be able to keep up such tactics forever. The enemy vessel would eventually range in and start to unload its magazine of .50-caliber shells. If that happened, the less sturdy timber construction was not going to be able to withstand a heavy attack.

Pak brought the boat around, coming in line with the North Korean vessel. The big .50 traversed until the wheelhouse prevented further action. Instead uniformed NK soldiers lined the rail and opened fire with SMGs, peppering the smaller boat with 7.62 mm slugs. Every window in the wheelhouse was shattered, showering Encizo and Li, who were on the deck. Pak ducked, holding the wheel with one hand as glass shards struck his back. He felt the sharp bite as one sliced his cheek.

"We can all play that game," McCarter said.

With James and Manning at his side, the Phoenix Force commander opened up with his P90. The NK shooters had been concentrating their fire on the wheelhouse. They were still bringing their weapons around to challenge Phoenix Force when the Stony Man team hit them with shots, seeking human targets rather than wood and glass. Two of the Koreans, exposed, were hit hard, bloodied forms dropping to the deck. Calvin James took a steady aim and triggered a short burst that caught a third man high in the chest. He fell back against the wheelhouse, blood already spouting from a throat wound. He rebounded from the wheelhouse and toppled forward, against, then over, the side rail. The surging water enveloped him quickly, and he vanished.

"Coming around," Pak yelled, spinning the wheel so the smaller craft made a tight turn, the stern of the larger vessel being presented to them. He cut back on the power, giving Hawkins and his .50-caliber gun a clear target.

REALIZATION DAWNED TOO LATE.

The smaller boat had swung in behind the patrol craft. It took it out of range because their machine gun was unable to make a full turn.

"They cannot remain in that position long," the captain said.

"Long enough," Choi said.

He had seen the barrel of the smaller craft's weapon

lower, the muzzle locking on to the patrol boat's stern. Choi realized exactly what was about to happen.

"The propeller," he shouted. *"They are going to try and disable the propeller."*

HAWKINS WAS READY, the barrel of his big .50 arcing down and lining up on the water directly behind the target. Hawkins tripped the trigger and laid in his full-on volley, the large shells cleaving the water and kicking up silver spouts. Even as the boat drew away Hawkins traversed to keep up his line of fire. As the boat cleared the stern of the other vessel, Pak pushed hard on the wheel and brought it around in a tight full circle for a second run. Hawkins spun the big .50 to the opposite side, and as Pak made his approach behind the larger vessel again, Hawkins was ready and repeated his concentrated fire.

The thunderous blast of the .50-caliber rocked the boat. Hawkins moved the muzzle to keep on target. The deck at his feet was littered with shell casings and the barrel of the heavy machine gun began to smoke.

"GET US CLEAR," the captain screamed.

His warning came too late. A fresh heavy burst from the opposing boat hammered into the churned water. There were harsh metallic sounds as the .50-caliber shells ripped into the blades of the prop, splitting apart the metal. Fragments erupted out of the water. The shaft continued to rotate, but the shattered blades no longer offered any forward motion and the patrol boat slowed and floundered.

"I THINK YOU got the son of a bitch," James yelled.

He had seen fragments of metal fly up out of the white foam at the rear of the other vessel. The North Korean patrol boat began to slow as the churning screw lost its thrust. It settled back into the water, as forward movement lessened, and wallowed helplessly. The strong surge of the ocean took over and the patrol boat started to drift away.

Hawkins let go of the trigger and the big .50 fell silent.

"If I hadn't been watching that, I wouldn't have believed it," Manning said.

He stepped up to the machine gun and helped Hawkins ditch the empty ammunition box and replace it with a fresh one. They wanted to be ready in case more firing action was called for.

MAJOR CHOI, AWARE of what had happened, slammed his fist against the bulkhead.

"*No,*" he shouted. "This cannot happen. Get your crew on deck and use your weapons."

"They will be killed by that damn cannon," the captain protested.

"I order you to obey."

"On this boat *I* am in command, Major Choi. Not you."

Choi cast around the cabin, searching for something he had seen earlier. His gaze settled on the RPG-7, clamped on the cabin bulkhead. He reached for the launcher, snatched up a rocket and slid it into place, and took the weapon in his hands.

"Then I will stop them myself," he said. "These enemies of the state must not be allowed to go free."

The captain stepped aside when he recognized the unreasoning expression in Choi's staring eyes. There was little he could do to stop the man holding a loaded rocket launcher in his trembling hands. Choi's finger was already curled around the RPG-7's trigger mechanism. The captain waved his men back, giving a shake of his head, as Choi pushed open the door and moved out along the deck, raising the launcher to one shoulder.

"Hey," James said.

He had seen a figure emerge from the drifting patrol boat's wheelhouse. Dressed in full uniform, the man was carrying a long tubelike object that was instantly recognizable.

"RPG-7," Manning said.

He was referring to the old Russian handheld rocket launcher. A weapon that had been in existence for a long time, and while it might be old, the piece still packed a wallop.

Li had pushed to her feet, curious to see what was happening. She stared out through the shattered window of the wheelhouse as the uniformed man moved along the length of the patrol boat, raising the launcher to one shoulder.

"It's Choi," she called out. "Major Choi."

Kayo Pak followed her pointing finger, nodding as he recognized the man. "He doesn't give up," he said. "Refuses to stop."

"You reckon," Hawkins said and swung the armed machine gun on line.

His finger stroked the trigger and the machine gun hammered out its powerful sound again. Hawkins tracked the impact of the shells as they slammed into the wheelhouse, tearing ragged holes through the metal. Then his moving volley caught Major Choi before he was able to bring the rocket launcher fully on target. The large-caliber shells impacted him, shearing off his left leg at midthigh and moving up to shred Choi in a bloody burst. He was literally torn apart and dumped in a grisly heap on the deck plates, the side of the wheelhouse bloodily spattered with flesh, spilled entrails and fragmented bone. The RPG's muzzle drooped to the deck and Choi's finger tripped the trigger in a final spasm. The launcher belched flame and smoke, the rocket impacting against the deck. It detonated with a roar, the full charge burning its way through the deck. The explosion blossomed below the deck, blowing out through the hull and the patrol boat began to list as water rushed in through the ruptured plates.

"Now he's stopped," Hawkins said.

He raised the barrel of the .50-caliber and raked the superstructure of the North Korean boat, hammering at the wheelhouse and anything he saw moving. The .50-caliber shells punched holes in the thinner steel of the wheelhouse, tearing flesh from the bodies of the captain and crewmen as they ripped through, literally blowing them apart. The relentless power of the .50-caliber was totally unforgiving. The further disabled patrol boat was drifting now, helpless without power and taking on water. Any of the surviving crew were staying out of sight.

"Get us clear," McCarter ordered Pak. "They've had enough."

The Korean turned the patrol craft and headed away from the coast.

McCarter glanced at the transponder in his hand. The light was still pulsing as it sent out its signal to the submerged Navy sub.

He moved across the deck, slapping a hand on Hawkins's shoulder as he passed him.

"Nice shooting, T.J."

"We aim to please, boss."

When McCarter reached the wheelhouse, he crossed to where Encizo lay. Li had located blankets in a locker and had covered the Cuban. A second blanket, rolled into a pillow, supported Encizo's head.

"Some people will do anything to stay out of the action," the Briton said.

"I decided taking down a helicopter entitled me to a break," Enciso said, his words slurring as the meds James had given him took over.

"Just this once, then," McCarter said. "Don't get too used to it."

THREE-QUARTERS OF AN hour later the massive bulk of the U.S. Navy sub surfaced. It came up within a hundred yards of the tiny wooden patrol boat, heavy rain bouncing off its steel hull. Armed crew members emerged from the aft hatch, and McCarter identified himself. Ropes were handed down so that the boat could be hauled in close. It took no longer than ten minutes for Phoenix Force, Li Kam and Kayo Pak to make the transfer. Enciso was helped on board by Navy medics who dropped down onto the boat and was then taken to the sub's infirmary, with James following to advise on his injuries.

The sub captain gave the order to submerge and depart the area. When he decided they were well clear, he made his way to the galley where his passengers, changed into dry clothes supplied by the Navy, were having hot food and much needed coffee.

McCarter offered his hand to the captain.

"Best sight I've seen in days when you showed up," the Brit said.

"You get it done?"

McCarter nodded, introducing Li and Kayo. "These are the stars of the show," he said. "They made it all possible."

"If you hadn't walked in to pull us out," Li said, "things might have been different. Thank you."

"We liable to have any interference from the North Korean navy?" Hawkins asked.

The captain smiled. "If we do, they'll go home with a

bloody nose." He glanced at his watch. "In ten minutes we'll be out of NK waters and diving deep. If they want to follow, I can assure you that they won't like what they find."

"Captain," Manning said, "that sounds like fighting talk."

"Damn right it is. Is there anything else you need?"

"Secure communication with our base," McCarter said.

"No problem."

"HOW ARE YOU guys doing?" Brognola asked over the Zero link.

"Better than the residents of camp Choi," McCarter said. "We blew the research facility, brought out Li Kam and Kayo Pak. Li brought a couple memory sticks with data on the NNEMP device."

"Anyone hurt?"

"Few bumps and bruises, and Fredo caught some flak. He's going to be laid up for a while, but he'll survive intact."

"The insertion go as planned?"

"The Navy did us proud," McCarter said. "Brought us in and picked us up when we called."

"How about the North Koreans?"

"Suitably pissed. We had a tricky getaway but managed to drop one of their choppers and a patrol boat on the way out."

"So nothing for Pyongyang to get too upset about, then?"

McCarter laughed. "If they do, that's up to the diplomats to sort out. Let's face it. North Korea started this mess with the attack on Hawaii. Nothing about that is going to make the President happy."

"He's already made that clear. Pyongyang starts getting uppity, he'll have a few choice words for them. He's still smarting over what happened on Hawaii. If North Korea makes a fuss, he might go hard on them. Act-of-war type thing and do they want to take it further." Brognola paused. "So what can we do for you guys?"

"Have a flight organized for us, Hal. Bring us home, and we can debrief later. We have Li Kam and Kayo Pak with us. They're ready for a time-out. Li has information referencing the NNEMP device, so she'll have a lot of talking to do. And she managed to download data onto memory sticks, clever girl, so the mad scientists will be busy, once they get their sweaty little hands on it."

"Your flight will be standing by once you get back to South Korea," Barbara Price said over the comm link.

"You been listening in to my conversations again?" McCarter said. "That's a bad habit, young lady."

"So sue me, tough guy. If you don't talk nice, I'll make sure you get seated in the cargo section during your flight home."

"Bloody hell, love, it's an Air Force plane. They only have cargo seating."

"Oops, so they do."

"Any update on Able?" McCarter asked.

"Confusing," Brognola said. "Turns out they had more than one party interested in that piece of North Korean hardware. But they've wound everything up and prevented the NK package from leaving Hawaii. So a nice result there."

"I guess our lab techs wouldn't say no if that box of tricks turned up Stateside."

"Not wrong there. Now go and enjoy your ride. We'll talk when you get back. I'm going to bring the President up to speed. I think he'll be pleased by your results. Tell the rest of the team thanks."

TEN DAYS LATER, STONY MAN FARM

"ENCIZO IS BEING given his medical discharge tomorrow," Price said. "Pol is going to be out of action for a week or two more. His hip has responded well."

Brognola nodded. "With everything that happened, I guess we got off lightly. What about Carl?"

McCarter, the only team member at the War Room table, said, "A bang on the Ironman's head isn't going to put him down for long. Hard as nails, that bloke."

"David, be a little more sensitive," Price said.

"I was being supportive," the Brit said. "Carl would be the first to complain if he thought we were being soft on him."

Brognola opened the mission file on the table in front of him. He flicked through the first few pages, then closed the cover and sat back.

"I don't need to read through this damn thing again," he grumbled, "I know it by heart."

"Okay," McCarter said. "We've been back for ten days World War III hasn't started yet, so...?"

"Kayo Pak returned to South Korea yesterday. He has a lot of work to do updating his own people on what occurred."

"Good bloke," McCarter said.

"The data Li Kam managed to download is being analyzed by our people. The information is giving us a lot to think about. Absalom's NNEMP work was sound. Red faces all around because we were slow in recruiting him."

"Any sign of him since we left?" McCarter asked.

"No," Brognola admitted. "If the North Koreans still have him, they're keeping very quiet about it. We have no proof one way or the other whether he's alive or dead."

McCarter drummed his fingers on the surface of the

conference table. "If we didn't get him, it would be better if he *was* dead. Then at least North Korea won't be able to pick him up and start over."

"We are being very cynical today," Price said.

"I won't apologize for that. Absalom represented the worst side of his business. It was obvious he didn't give a damn who he worked for, so as he's not one of the good guys, we're better with him out of the picture."

Brognola cleared his throat. "North Korea is staying silent over the whole affair. The fact they were caught employing their pulse weapon on American soil doesn't give them much to make noise about. We have it. They know we have it, but both sides are pretending it doesn't exist. They start making a fuss, and we could produce evidence of its existence and make them choke on it."

"Our Chinese friend, Xian Chi, is making deals faster than they can be written down. He's been hidden away because his ex-employers are going to be very upset with him," Price added. "From what we've been hearing, the guy is very smart. He doesn't fully admit to aiding North Korea in its attempted pulse strike. Or to the Chinese government funding their research."

"I'll bet my next month's salary he doesn't think going back home would be a wise move," McCarter said.

"Returning to Beijing or staying in the West," Brognola said, "either way, he's got to be looking over his shoulder. The Chinese have long memories. And they can be extremely patient."

"Xian Chi is going to have some sleepless nights," Price said. "He's about to pay the price." She picked up a printed sheet. "The Chinese guy who ran the food distribution company in Honolulu—responsible for being the cover for hiring the vehicles used by Macklin's merc crew and transport in general has been arrested by HPD. They have linked him to Chi. Guy is another sleeper. Been in Hawaii for over six years. Crazy thing is, the business he ran was pulling in a damn good profit. He should have read one of his own fortune cookies. Might have told him to quit while the going was good."

"And how has the big man taken all this?" McCarter asked.

Brognola smiled. "With an extremely satisfied look on his face. I think he's a little disappointed at the lack of response from North Korea. He was getting himself ready to have a slap-down fight with the Koreans. I think he likes being able to hold all the cards."

"North Korea lost big this time around," McCarter said. "They are not going to be happy about that. Somewhere along the line, they'll try again. If it isn't with a pulse weapon, it'll be something else."

"We have to be sharper from here on in," Brognola said. "Make sure we back up allies like South Korea. They're on the knife edge."

"Like Kayo Pak. A bloody good bloke. I'd hate to have to hear if he got taken down."

Price said, "Talking of good guys, I checked on Oscar Kalikani. He's still on sick leave. Making a slow recovery."

"Pol was telling me about him," McCarter said. "Sounds like the kind of guy you want on your team."

"Did he tell you about Kalikani's partner?" Price said, a mischievous smile on her lips. "Pol is very enthusiastic when he talks about her."

"Officer Lopaka? Now there's a lady I wouldn't want to upset."

Brognola said, "I get the feeling Hawaii might be on Pol's vacation list sometime soon. And not just for the sunshine."

"Can't keep a good man down," McCarter said.

"I could say that about the Stony Man teams," Brognola added.

Price pushed back her seat and stood. "While you two indulge in some well-earned backslapping, I have work to do." She turned as she went for the door. "Any thoughts about revisiting North Korea, David?" she asked, a sparkle in her eyes.

"If things get slack around here, I might take you up on that," the Briton said, "but only if I'm *really* bored."

* * * * *

GDL115